DIMITRI

The Italian Cartel #1

SHANDI BOYES

Copyright

Copyright © 2020 by Shandi Boyes

Model: Jonny James
Photographer: Wander Aguiar
Cover: SSB Covers and Design
Editing: Nicky @ Swish Editing and Design
Beta: Carolyn Wallace
Proof Reading: Kaylene @ Swish Editing and Design
Writing: Shandi Boyes

Created with Vellum

There's a moment in fighting when strength of muscle ain't everything because the enemy has already given you enough energy to gain the victory.

— Toba Beta

Want to stay in touch?

Facebook: facebook.com/authorshandi

Instagram: instagram.com/authorshandi

Email: authorshandi@gmail.com

Reader's Group: bit.ly/ShandiBookBabes

Website: authorshandi.com

Newsletter: https://www.subscribepage.com/AuthorShandi

Also by Shandi Boyes

Denotes Standalone Books

Perception Series

Saving Noah *

Fighting Jacob *

Taming Nick *

Redeeming Slater *

Saving Emily

Wrapped Up with Rise Up

Protecting Nicole *

Enigma

Enigma

Unraveling an Enigma

Enigma The Mystery Unmasked

Enigma: The Final Chapter

Beneath The Secrets

Beneath The Sheets

Spy Thy Neighbor *

The Opposite Effect *

I Married a Mob Boss *

Second Shot *

The Way We Are

The Way We Were

Sugar and Spice *

Lady In Waiting

Man in Queue

Couple on Hold

Enigma: The Wedding

Silent Vigilante

Hushed Guardian

Quiet Protector

Enigma: An Isaac Retelling

Twisted Lies *

Bound Series

Chains

Links

Bound

Restrain

The Misfits *

Nanny Dispute *

Russian Mob Chronicles

Nikolai: A Mafia Prince Romance

Nikolai: Taking Back What's Mine

Nikolai: What's Left of Me

Nikolai: Mine to Protect

Prologue

Dimitri

While cracking my knuckles, I peer out a window spanning one wall of my suite. Cabs honk, commuters pepper the sidewalks clouded by ominous skyscrapers blocking out the sun, and pompous pricks in Tom Ford suits weave in and out of buildings similar to the one I'm stationed in, unaware their existence doesn't depend on the digits in their bank accounts or the nine-to-five investment banking job their daddies secured them straight out of college. It's wholly dependent on the men who built this city from the ground up.

I don't care what you say, New York was built by the Cartel. The Italians, the Greeks, hell, even the Albanians had a hand in making this what it is. Blood, sweat, and tears went into every skyscraper—literally. More bodies are buried under the buildings surrounding my hotel than my hotel caters for guests each night.

Before the assassination of the boss of all bosses in 1973,

every inch of this godforsaken town was the territory of the Italian Cartel. If you worked here, we ran your union. If you lived here, you were living in an apartment built by my ancestors.

If you ran drugs here without permission, you were a dead man.

Nothing happened here without the Lucianos, Gambinos, and Petrettis knowing about it. They were the governors of this realm and feared more than they were respected. It was the golden era to be a member of a criminal association, a time I'd give anything to go back to.

Alas, all good things must come to an end.

If that ending had been because of criminal prosecution, I would have a different viewpoint of my family's demise. Regretfully, that isn't close to the truth. The three families mentioned above operated as one unit. The Lucianos controlled Queens, Staten Island, Brooklyn, and Long Island. The Gambinos influenced the Bronx, New Jersey, and Connecticut regions, and the Petrettis had a stronghold on Manhattan, New York City, Westchester County, and parts of Florida.

Between 1889 and 1953, these sanctions were untouchable. Law couldn't catch them, rivals couldn't compete with them, and money, drugs, and guns were in abundance.

It all went downhill when Bria Petretti and Eleonora Gambino birthed sons only a month apart.

If they had followed in their fathers' footsteps by forging a mutually respected relationship, my grandfather, Giulio Petretti, III, and his best mate, Benito Gambino, were set to become the next boss of all bosses. They worked hard for their greater families, and the Lucianos didn't have a suitable candidate, so originating a dual-leadership was the fairest option.

However, as I said earlier, all good things must come to an end.

My father, Col, and Benito's son, Matteo, didn't have the comradery their fathers had. They hated each other. Women, wayward drug shipments, even the sizes of their cocks were constantly bickered about. They didn't want to be the boss of the bosses. They wanted to be *the* boss—point-blank. And that's precisely what happened when one of my father's coked-up friends decided he needed some extra coin he wasn't willing to work for.

Theft never ends well in this industry. If you cross the Cartel, you die. Can't explain it any simpler than that. Regardless, your family, friends, and children are supposed to go unharmed.

My father couldn't let bygones be bygones. He was only sixteen when Leone was taken out to The Hole, a grisly dumping ground regularly used back in the day, but he massacred the people he believed responsible for his death like the repercussions of his actions wouldn't have blow on effects for decades to come.

He should have been dead. The penalty for killing a son of a prominent family member always results in the death of both the person responsible and the hierarchy of his realm. However, my grandfather fell on the knife on the agreement his son would be spared.

His negotiations were unheard of at the time. I doubt they would have been considered if it weren't for the friendship he had with Giulio. My father forgot centuries-long relations in an instant. Giulio couldn't. He didn't want to kill his best friend, but he had no choice. He had lost a son. His death needed to be avenged.

The story of my family's demise grows weary from that point. Some say my father was removed from all Cartel activities and left to fend for himself. Others say he was gifted the Florida chapter with the hopes he'd eventually straighten his life out and resurrect our family name from the grave.

I say they should have killed him instead of my grandfather. That would mean I wouldn't be here, but then I also wouldn't be twiddling my thumbs in a hotel room, waiting for word on if the ransom I paid for my pregnant wife has been received. My family name is tainted with so much disrespect, my rivals think I'm a schmuck to be messed with.

That is also far from the truth.

Rimi Castro, leader of a subsidiary criminal entity that branched off the Gambinos two decades ago, was smart when he requested a third-party drop off the 3.8 million-dollar ransom he demanded for the safe return of Audrey. I would have tortured him until he told me where she is, then I would have killed every member of his crew to show him I'm nothing like my father.

You don't mess with me and expect to live. I have all the markings of my father. I'm a merciless, heartless motherfucker who kills before thinking. Audrey chipped away some of the decay the past ten months, but it will never be entirely gone. You can untwist the ugliest wreck, however no amount of straightening will smother scars hidden deep within. They're more hideous than the ones our bodies wear and take longer than a lifetime to fix.

I learned that the hard way almost a decade ago.

Rimi will learn it tonight.

I still can't understand how he got the upper hand on me. I'm cautious about everything I do, untrusting of anyone, most notably those who share my lineage. My marriage is unknown, the baby growing in my wife's stomach hasn't been publicly acknowledged even with our daughter being due in a little over four weeks. I don't even live in the same state as my wife for fuck's sake, yet, she still got snared by a life someone as pure as her should have never been invited into.

I'll be sure to fix the injustice once she and our daughter are returned safely. It won't be just the Castros feeling the sting of my wrath, though. It'll be the industry as a whole. An unspoken rule was broken earlier this week.

Famiglia prima di tutto. Family first of all.

Audrey may be excluded from that motto, but our daughter most certainly isn't. She's mafia royalty and will be protected accordingly.

When the beep of an electronic lock sounds through my ears, I spin to face the entryway of my room. The knot in my gut takes on a new meaning when Clover enters the opulent space with the ransom bag he left with. It's noticeably slimmer, but still, why wouldn't Rimi's men take it with them?

I scoff when Clover pushes out, "They checked the bundles for bugs." His voice is rough with an Arabian accent. He isn't called Clover because he shines luck down on anyone who locates him in a patch of weeds, it's because you'll be wishing for a lucky charm when he enters your life. The chances of escaping him are similar odds to finding a four-leaf clover in a patch of an overworked field. Basically nonexistent. If he doesn't kill you before you spot the clover tattoo on his cheek, you'll beg for a weapon to kill yourself.

Mercy isn't something Clover often gives. It's why I sent him to do the drop. If I couldn't do it, he was the next best choice. Clover is a hired hitman. He has worked for my family on many occasions, and usually gets the job done without the slightest bow to his brow.

He isn't giving me that vibe today. He looks a little undone, like his wish to kill isn't as strong as mine. I get he's a killer in every sense of the word, but we have to play the game as Rimi is requesting.

Once Audrey is returned, all bets will be off.

My decision has nothing to do with money. Despite my father's many fuck-ups, I have plenty of it. The wholesale price in the industry is ten percent of its street value. There's money to be made if you're willing to get your hands dirty, but that isn't what this is about. It's the principle. If I let Rimi play me for a fool, I'll take it up the ass from my competitors even more than my father has the past fifty-plus years.

My family name might not be what it once was, but it will take more than a weasel of a man like Rimi Castro to have me cowering from a fight. The older generation started the war, but it's the younger generation fighting their battles.

I don't mind. I was born to fight, and fight I will.

I battle to keep my anger on the down-low but fail when Clover places the ransom bag onto the entryway table. It's brimming with the bundles of cash I withdrew at multiple locations earlier this week. I know federal agents are watching every deposit and withdrawal from my account, so I kept the transactions below ten thousand to ward off suspicion.

"Where's Audrey?" Nothing but desperation is heard in my voice. Clover follows orders. He's paid to do precisely that, so why the fuck did he go off script today? His facial expression reveals he drew blood, his itch to kill has been satisfied. That can only mean one thing—he went against direct orders. "You were to hand over the money, get Audrey out, *then* we were to make our move."

"Plans changed when they handed me this." He tosses a USB stick onto the round table housing a vase of Audrey's favorite flowers. India, Audrey's neighbor/best friend, thought they'd lessen Audrey's anxiety once she was freed from captivity. She's been at the mercy of a rogue crew for five days. If a hundred-dollar bunch of flowers would weaken the clutch they had on her, I was open to the suggestion.

"It was supposed to tell me Audrey's location." Clover locks his eyes with mine. They're deadlier than ever. "It was nothing but a snuff film. Those fuckers are playing games, so I played back."

I'm not surprised to spot a number of dismembered fingers when he yanks open the ransom bag. Clover's proof of deaths always arrives with some sort of body part. "I got a majority of your money back, but a few bundles fell through the cracks."

Falling through the cracks means he used the money to find marks. It isn't a negotiation tactic he often uses, so the fact he needed it tonight exposes how dire things are.

After finding the object he's seeking in the bag, Clover hands it to me. He doesn't speak any words, he doesn't need to. I recognize the ring on the mutilated index finger in my hand. It's the same one in the bottom right-hand corner of the photo couriered to my office last week. That's how we unearthed Audrey's kidnappers' identity. All Castro 'family' members wear the same trademark.

"Was there any indication Audrey was there?" I know Clover didn't find her. If he had, we wouldn't be having this conversation. Clover would be holed up with some hookers and the best cocaine money can't buy, celebrating his victory, and I'd be at the hospital with my wife, having her and our daughter checked over.

My jaw works through a hard grind when Clover shakes his head. "She *had* been there, though. The room the ransom photo was taken in was at the back of the compound, and I got DNA proof by the bucketloads."

"What type of DNA?" I'm shocked I can talk. I'm so fucking angry, I am five seconds from blowing my top. If Clover's switch-up of the rules has fucked me over, *he* will be fucked over. No fear.

"Blood," Clover answers nonchalantly like his life isn't in danger. "Lots of it."

My blood boils over when he digs his cell phone out of his pocket to show me the photographs he took at the scene. Bodies litter almost every inch of the floor space, but my focus is on one thing and one thing only—the dingy, dirty mattress they had Audrey sit on when they snapped her picture for the ransom request.

Although she's missing from Clover's images, I can still see her ashen face and cracked lips with precise clearness. She has always been the quiet one. Softly spoken and happy for everyone else to steal the attention.

The last image I have of her isn't close to any of those things. It's one of pure fret. Like she didn't believe I could get her out of this in one piece.

If the horrifying thoughts bombarding me now are anything to go by, she had reason to fret. The mattress is covered in blood. It isn't formed how you'd expect from someone being fatally wounded by a knife or gun. There's an outline of a body—a slim, you-wouldn't-know-she's-eight-months-along-if-you-were-looking-at-her-from-behind outline.

I snap my eyes shut, hopeful it will suffocate my wish to kill Clover when he announces, "Preacher did a quick swab of the mattress. Amniotic fluid was present."

Confident I'm hearing him wrong, I shake my head before reopening my eyes. "She isn't due for another four weeks. It's too early—"

"Scalpel was also found..." He scrubs at his jaw before he pushes out, "And fetal matter."

"Fetal matter? What the fuck do you mean fetal matter?" As my eyes bounce between his, horrifying notion after horrifying notion smack into me. "My daughter..." The rest of my question lodges in my throat when despair darts through Clover's eyes. He doesn't show emotion, not ever, but there's no denying the sympathy in his eyes now.

Those fuckers didn't just kidnap my wife.

They've taken my daughter.

Before he knows what's hit him, I pin Clover to the entryway door of my suite, then press my gun against his temple. He's almost three inches taller than me and nearly double my width, but that doesn't mean shit since my fury is fueled by blackened hate.

"You killed her. You fucking killed her!" The spit off my roar sizzles on his cheeks. "If you had followed the plan, they would have let Audrey go, and my daughter would be safe."

Some of my anger turns to vengeance when Clover shakes his head. "The fluid was almost dry to touch. This shit ain't on me. Rimi has you played."

The confidence in his tone should lower my agitation.

It doesn't.

I'm seconds from ending his life as he had tried to do mine years earlier.

Arabian oil tycoons weren't happy when they didn't get what they paid for from my father. I've been making it up to them ever since.

Don't feel sorry for me. They're the reason *all* my bank accounts are in the eight-figure range. Whores, crack, guns, and unlimited entertainment are readily available in Bahrain, but you don't enjoy it as much with your family breathing down your neck.

Rich dignitaries from the twenty-two Arab nations are invited into my home to discuss oil exchanges, money laundering, and weaponry distribution all 'families' are associated with. The above-mentioned is the icing on the cake, and the only reason I'm not fish food.

Only a fool would turn down a proposal worth eighty-three million dollars a year.

Clover isn't one of them.

With that in mind, I suck in a big breath before lowering my gun. Killing Clover won't get my wife and daughter back. If anything, it will delay their return.

"What was on the USB drive?" Rimi's men wouldn't have given this to Clover for no reason. His family's legacy is as bad as my mine, but instead of rising it above the ashes, he's tainting it with more controversy.

My lips purse when Clover mutters, "Sick, twisted shit." He has an ironclad stomach, nothing ruffles him, so for him to say the video is fucked up, it most certainly is. "I wouldn't recommend watching—"

I cut off his words with a slice of my hand. My relationship with Audrey isn't close to traditional. She fell pregnant within weeks of us hooking up, we got married to ensure she could stay in the country to birth my child, and we have more things out of common than agreed upon, but she's my wife and the mother of my child.

Our daughter makes her my family, and family comes first of all.

My heart thumps against my ribs when I crack open my laptop. Details of the ransom drop are still displayed on the screen. A team of cyber specialists have been working on it since it was received. They've yet to find a single snip of evidence to identify where it was sent from. For all we know, Audrey may not even be in the country.

"*Cazzo...*" I push out with a growl when the video commences playing on a woman being held down on the stained mattress. I can only see the lower half of her body, but her strength is undeniable. Even with four goons pinning her to the filthy bedding, she thrashes and kicks, her will to live seen without a single word being spoken.

Her stomach is gleaming from how far it's extended, but its redness tapers when a scalpel is dragged across a section of skin usually hidden by a panty line. Although the video has no sound, I can imagine how blood-curdling her screams are. They're removing her child from her stomach without anesthetics, acting like ruthless barbarians with callous rules.

My skyrocketing blood pressure gets a boost when one of the goons moves to the right of the frame, exposing the tiniest birthmark on the lower left side of the victim's stomach. It's the shape of a mulberry leaf and unearths the victim's identity in an instant.

"It's Audrey," I mutter out while dragging a hand over my almost black hair. "It's my fucking wife."

While Clover commences putting actions into place to respond to Rimi's break of the rules, I continue watching the video. The footage is horrifying, but I have no choice but to watch every sickening second. The simplest thing in the background could be the *only* clue to Audrey's whereabouts. I can't miss seeing it because my stomach is twisted up in knots.

On instinct, my thumb caresses the screen of my laptop when a bloody and white film-coated baby is pulled from Audrey's stomach. Aware I'm most likely watching, a man concealing his face with a balaclava holds my daughter by her feet like he's showcasing a prize-winning catch before he shifts to face the camera.

I freeze the image when the cuff of his sleeve rises half an inch. His tattoo is the typical flame design most bottom-dwellers have. I stare at it until it's burned into my retina before hitting the play button. He just signed his death certificate, and I'm the Grim Reaper coming to collect his soul.

When the body of my child is dangled an inch from the

camera, my eyes whizz over every inch of her upside-down face and grubby body, seeking any signs that she's breathing. Her chest is as flat as mine, her nostrils un-flaring. She's as still as a statue, her legs as frozen as her mother's in the background.

"Come on, Fien," I beg under my breath after taking in an identical mulberry leaf birthmark on her stomach. "Fight like your mother did when choosing your name." I didn't hate the name Audrey had picked, but I wasn't a fan of it either. I wanted our daughter to have a traditional Italian name. Fien is of Dutch heritage, just like her mother. It's short for Jozefien which is Audrey's mother's name. Fien's grandmother.

My eyes shoot to the left of the screen when a pair of tiny hands enter the frame. This person's wrists are slimmer than the man's clutching my daughter's feet and nowhere near as hairy, making me confident she's female.

Just as the unseen woman removes Fien from the goon's clutch, a white sheet is draped over Aubrey's lifeless form, then the video ends. As I struggle to keep a rational head, I wring the screen of my laptop as if it's Rimi Castro's neck. I would wholly destroy it if the USB stick would come out of the carnage unharmed.

That horrifying video is the only proof I have that I have a daughter. No one knew she existed. No one *knows* she exists, but if I have it my way, those who now know will die to ensure my revenge lives.

Famiglia prima di tutto.

Vengeance is a very close second.

Chapter One

Dimitri

Nine long months later...

Ignoring India's concerning glance, I scream for the driver to stop. It's pissing down rain, and we're running late to a function with a mafioso seeking a new realm in a town he isn't wanted, but the redhead standing under the awning of a Publix supermarket has too many similarities with Audrey to ignore. Same svelte frame, fiery red hair, and enticing curves I'm certain won't alter no matter how many kids she rears.

"Dimitri… it isn't her—" I lodge the remainder of India's words into the back of her throat with a stern glare. She may very well be Audrey's neighbor/friend, but she has no right to speak to me in such a manner.

Until Audrey and Fien are found, my search won't end. I thought India understood this. If she doesn't, she should leave now, because my belief that she understood my quest is the sole reason I've kept her around this long. She has a face that encourages visitors to our side of the pond, but her beauty is a dime a dozen—easily replaceable.

It will do her best to remember that.

While raking a shaky hand through my hair, I growl out, "I'll never stop looking for her."

"I know that."

India scoots closer to my side of the bench seat. We've put bells and whistles on tonight's festivities. A stretch limousine, whores by the bucketloads, and a woman who will never eye him as she forever eyes me. In a way, India should consider herself lucky Audrey classed her as a friend, or her unwanted sideways glances the past nine months would have caused her demise. She's trying to profit from her friend's downfall, or worse, use me as part of her grief process.

If I were to believe rumors, India's husband has been presumed dead as long as Audrey has been missing. Although I feel sorry for India, I will *not* tolerate her suggestion that two broken hearts can meld into one.

Alas, I have to keep my cards close to my chest until it's my turn to show my hand.

"But I also know the redhead isn't her, Dimitri. Audrey only cut her hair the week she…" my tightened jaw slackens when tears well in India's eyes, "… went missing."

Just like me, she refuses to say Audrey is dead. Her legs were as still as Fien's when she was torn from her stomach, but that doesn't mean anything. I'm granted confirmation on the third of every month that my daughter is alive, so who's to say Audrey didn't find the same strength?

Despite having the weaponry and capital for a century-long war, and a crew of blood-thirsty men, Rimi has yet to man up. Although it frustrates me to no end, I can't say I don't under-stand his tactic. Why risk a net profit of 1.8 million dollars annually when all they have to do is provide proof my daughter is alive?

My grandfather would roll in his grave if he knew how cartels were being run these days. In his era, it was about infrastructure, drugs, and weapons. Now nothing but profit is on the mind, and innocents like my daughter get caught up in the bullshit.

Although pissed, I'll find Fien, and when I do, there will be hell to pay.

The old saying, 'Before you embark on revenge, you should dig two graves.' I'll need more than two. At last count, the Castros were sitting at eighty-nine men. That will take my quota to over ninety because despite what my father says, the Castros aren't acting alone. Rimi isn't smart enough to pull off a stunt like this without help. His family has only been in this industry for the past twenty years. Exploits like this require decades of experience. If it were simple, my father would have dabbled in it years ago.

He learned nothing from our family's downfall and is forever looking for a way to make a quick profit. I could challenge his leadership, however my bend of the rules wouldn't have the same outcome my father achieved. He didn't kill the leader of the allied crew. If he had, he would have been dead no matter what.

After laboring my jaw side to side, I get back to the task at hand. "I'm not saying she's Audrey, but there's no harm in checking."

Before India can issue a single worry I see in her eyes, I snatch up an umbrella from the storage in the door, then slide out the back seat of the limousine. With rain making it seem as if winter arrived early, I tug up the collar of my coat, hiding both my neck tattoos and goosebumps that have nothing to do with the winds whipping in from the east.

Nothing says gangbanger like a set of neck tattoos.

"Audrey…" I won't lie, my heart stops beating when the redhead commences pivoting my way. India is right, her hair is a little longer than Audrey's, and more an orange-red than a sapphire coloring, but their similarities are uncanny.

"Dimitri, hi," greets a woman I swear I've seen before.

It takes me a few seconds to click on to who she is, but when I do, I am shocked. I'm not just chasing ghosts of my past anymore. I've caught up to them. "Justine." She appears stunned I remember who she is. I don't know why. We were born in the same hospital and attended the same school. I've just had my head up my ass too long for immediate recognition. "What are you doing out this way? I didn't think the Walsh's would ever leave Ravenshoe."

When she smiles, I discover how well she grew into her buck teeth. She's always been beautiful, but her legs were miles too long for her body, and her front teeth seemed to have a mind of their own. I can't say I fared much better during the awkward preteen years, but my family name stopped it from being mentioned—as did my fists.

I stop smirking about times bygone when Justine discloses, "They still live in Ravenshoe. I'm heading home for Thanksgiving weekend. Thought I better grab some supplies first. As my mother always says, an empty hand is an unwelcoming one."

"Do you live around here?" Shock echoes in my tone. Justine has four brothers. That's the equivalent of living in a convent when you're both the youngest *and* the only girl in your family. Why do you think it took me so long to realize she's grown into her rabbit teeth? I wasn't sure getting through her brothers would be worth the effort. Despite the heavy knot in my stomach advising me differently, I'm slapping myself up the back of the head right now.

Locks of red lava fall onto Justine's shoulders when she notches her chin to our right. "I'm a sophomore at Eastwood State. It's—"

"An easy hour drive to Ravenshoe," I interrupt, unsurprised. Her brothers would never let her lead get too long.

Justine smiles again like she heard my inner monologue. "Yeah." After a nervy swallow, she asks, "How about you? Last I heard, you were in New York."

Is she keeping tabs on me? If so, I don't mind. Our unexpected reunion has the first rays of sunshine breaking through the murky cloud that's been hanging above my head the past nine months. I even feel capable of sucking in an entire breath. It's been a long time since I've felt this way.

When Justine coughs, prompting me that I've failed to answer her question, I say, "I've been floating in and out of states. I'm about to head home for a couple of days this weekend as well." Her unique aquamarine-colored eyes widen when I unexpectedly add, "We should catch up?"

"Umm… sure. That's sounds good."

She doesn't sound eager, but I pretend not to notice. "Do you have your phone on you?" Nodding, she pulls her cell out of her clutch purse before handing it to me. I'm not surprised to discover she doesn't have a lock code. She's lived a sheltered, naïve life.

When she drinks in my tattooed hand as I punch my details in her contacts, I gabble out, "My nonna warned me to keep my body art to an area only the privileged get to see." With a hidden smirk, I mutter, "It's the *only* region on my body not inked." The way I say 'it's' leaves no doubt about what I'm referencing. Excluding my cock, I have tattoos from my ankles to my jawline.

Like all teens craving a rebellion, I did the opposite of what I was told. I didn't keep my mutiny to a tiny bicep tattoo on my eighteenth, I had my entire back done. My artwork has grown substantially since then.

I wait for Justine's cheeks to flame to their full potential before muttering, "Do they bother you?" I'm not surprised when she shakes her head. Even hundreds of miles from my hometown, I heard rumors she was getting around with a tattoo artist during summer break. "Do you have any?"

Her nod switches to a shake. "I've not yet built the courage. I'm not a fan of needles." Her cheeks whiten as a tiny shudder racks through her body. "Or blood. Brax tells me I have nothing to worry about, but how can I be sure he isn't giving me the line he gives all his clients?"

That's the name I've heard thrown around with the rumor —Brax.

"Is Brax your boyfriend?" That came out way more possessive than intended, and I'm not the only one noticing.

While accepting her phone, Justine does a nervous twist on the spot. "No. It's not like that." She sounds like she's trying to convince herself more than me. "We're... *friends.*"

My lips furl at the way she stammers out friends. With how low her tone dipped, she should have said fuck buddies.

Although I have no intention of calling her out on her 'arrangement' with Brax, I can't help but move forward with a plan that suddenly popped into my head. Knowing she isn't as innocent as her brothers make out will progress things along nicely.

After popping open the umbrella I grabbed to act chivalrous, I commence guiding Justine to the car I'm certain is hers. It's the only decent one in a lot full of shit boxes, and even then, it would be an effort to fetch a few thousand for it at auction.

My intuition is proven spot on when Justine stuffs a wonky key into an outdated lock a few seconds later. Once the latch pops up, I open her door for her. She's surprised by my chivalry but also pleased about it.

I wait for her to place her bag of groceries onto the passenger side seat before saying, "We should do dinner."

"Dinner?" She swallows her spit before she chokes on it, then wrings her sweater with her hands, torn on if she should act excited or play hard to get. We're doing dinner either way, so she can act however she likes. "Umm…"

"Come on, J. A girl has got to eat." Her brother's infamous nickname will get me over the line long before my wolfish grin. Maddox is the only one who calls her J, and he's the apple of her eye. Reminding her that we are 'friends' will do me more good than harm. "I heard the Petrettis signature dish is still to die for."

"It is. Maddox and I were there only last month," she replies, her smile matching mine. After sliding into the driver's seat of her bomb, she raises her eyes to mine. "Maddox and Demi have a casual thing going on. We could always do a double date with them?"

"That might be a bit awkward." When confusion blasts through her eyes, I mutter, "Trust me, Maddox won't enjoy his meal if he's forced to watch his sister exchange spit with his *friend*." I air quote my last word like a pompous, no-dick prick. My dealings with Maddox extend further than friendship, but its best to keep that between us for now. "I never did when riding shotgun with Ophelia's dates."

The lust firing through Justine's eyes shifts to sorrow. "I heard about her accident. I'm sorry for your loss."

"Prove it. Share a meal with me *without* a tagalong." Using my dead sister to get a date is wrong, but if it gives me a chance to get back my daughter sooner rather than later, I'm willing to go there.

Although shocked about my eagerness, Justine falls for my ruse. "I only have Thursday and Monday free."

"Thursday works. I'll arrange for a car to collect you at seven." As domineering as I am cocky, I close her car's door, spin on my heels, then walk away, stealing her chance to reply.

I can't have her driving to our date in her car. Not only will it weaken the authenticity of my ruse, but her shoddy engine gives her an excuse to back out of our date. I've heard all the lines before—*I have to wash my hair, my car broke down, I'm engaged to another man*—and every one of them came from Audrey.

Chapter Two

Roxanne

As I drag my mouth away from my boyfriend's kiss-swollen lips, goosebumps break across my skin. It's cooler today than usual for this time of the year, but the drizzly weather isn't to blame for the icy chill shuddering through me. Not even Eddie's hand tracing the seam of my panties can be held accountable. There's a weird sensation in the air, like more than an inappropriate hook-up location is set to cause trouble.

Eddie and I have been dating for two months. Even being in my second year of college won't see my nanna bending the rules when it comes to boyfriends. Until we're in a 'solid' relationship for six months straight, I can't bring boys home. Hence the reason Eddie and I are getting frisky in the alleyway between the movie complex and our local grocer. It isn't the ideal location, and a mattress would be more comfortable than a brick wall, but beggars can't be choosers.

When the prickling of the hairs on my arms grows to a

point I can't ignore, I shift my head to the side. Since it's late in the day and stormy, I can't see out of the alleyway as clearly as normal, but there's enough light to unearth the reason for my body's odd response.

A man is making his way to a stretch limousine idling in the lower section of the parking lot. Despite the fact he's clutching an umbrella, his trench coat is the only protection his pricy suit has from the downpour. He has an arrogant walk, similar to the one a quarterback does when running onto the field during State Championship weekend. It's more teasingly paced, though, and mesmerizing.

I'm paying more attention to his cocky strut than the sneaky slip of Eddie's hand. Instead of caressing the lace edging of my panties, his hand is now burrowed deep inside the inexpensive material.

Although this is the furthest we've gone, and we could be busted at any moment, for the life of me, I can't get the word 'stop' to fall out of my mouth. My jaw is hanging too low from my eyes briefly colliding with the stranger's to follow the prompts of my brain.

He's spotted my gawk, but instead of calling for security, he slants his head to the side and rakes his eyes down my body. He drinks it all in—my black mid-thigh boots, my miniskirt and skin-tight shirt, and my bleached to within-an-inch-of-death hair.

He even takes in Eddie's fumbling hand as he strives to find my clit.

The last part he finds more amusing than arousing. His smirk tells me this, much less the humor blazing through his expressive eyes when he returns them to my face. I expect him to wink, then walk away, too cultured to watch two teens fumble their way to third base, but he surprises me for the second time this afternoon by sticking around to watch the show.

His scrutiny should have me clamping around Eddie's fingers in disgust, but it seems to have the opposite effect. Instead of announcing to Eddie that we have an audience, I adjust the span of my thighs to ensure he can notch the rest of his finger inside of me before breathing heavily into his neck, encouraging his pursuit.

The stranger's dark, rain-flopped hair hides most of his face, only the tiniest snippet of blue pops out of the flattened mess, but I'm confident in saying he's gorgeous. You don't have the suffocating aura he does with a cat's bunghole for a face. His whole persona screams of wealth and superiority, albeit a little blackened by haunted memories.

I guarantee he's brutally beautiful, and the thought of unearthing his dark side has me acting wildly reckless.

A grunted moan leaves Eddie's lips when he finally locates my clit. He thinks I'm giving myself to him, when in reality, that's far from the truth. I'm not imagining his thumb circling the bundle of nerves between my legs. My focus isn't on him in the slightest. I have nothing but the piercing blue eyes of a stranger on my mind, and they have me even wetter than the downpour that's drenching the handsome stranger.

"You're so responsive to my touch," Eddie mutters into my ear a short time later while flicking my clit like he knows what he's doing. He doesn't, but my body is wired so tight from the dark-haired man's watch, it's happy to pretend he does. "I knew you'd be explosive. All blondes are——"

I clamp my hand over Eddie's mouth, shutting him up. "Shh, you'll get us busted." I'm not really worried, his words are barely whispers, but I can't hear him and the stranger's shallow breaths at the same time.

Even the way the dark-haired man breathes is sexy, all

rugged and unhinged. I imagine his heated breaths fanning my skin when he places feather-like kisses from my ankle to my inner thigh. Just the thought of his mouth floating over my aching pussy has zaps sparking through me. I bet he gives good head, and he'd smell divine while doing it—like expensive cologne and over-priced whiskey. He wouldn't wear shop-bought deodorant just like he wouldn't drink bottom-shelf whiskey. He's too refined for that, too sophisticated, so wickedly evil he'll watch a woman be brought to ecstasy on a lazy Friday afternoon like it's the most natural thing in the world to do.

"Yes, Roxie," Eddie moans on a growl when the sinfulness of what I'm doing unexpectedly slams into me.

He's barely touching me, but I swan dive over a cliff, shuddering, moaning, and coming wholly undone. I've always been a little edgier than my friends. I don't shy away when challenged and am willing to give anything a try once, but this, this is new even for someone with as little morals as me.

"Give me the sweet nectar of your loins."

I cringe through the remainder of my climax instead of relishing it.

Sweet nectar of my loins? Who says that?

I'm not the only one shocked by Eddie's lack of class. I can't hear the stranger's laughter, but I most certainly can see it. His chest is rising and falling as rapidly as mine. He isn't sucking in much-needed breaths like me, though. He's struggling to hold in the laughter rumbling in his chest—laughter he loses the ability to harness when a security guard arrives out of nowhere.

"Hey, you, you can't do *that* there!"

When the guard sprints down the alleyway, Eddie dumps me onto my feet so quickly, my backside is subjected to a nasty graze compliments to the brickwork he had me hoisted against. I'm horrified for the second time in under three seconds when he pivots on his heels and darts in the direction opposite the one the guard is coming from, leaving me defenseless to the angry, weapon-wielding man.

I just climaxed. I can't run, and I'm not going to mention how my legs can't pump in the stupid boots I bought specifically to woo him. Furthermore, the security officer isn't a standard old overweight, balding man. He's so fit-looking, he'd be able to chase me down even if I hadn't orgasmed.

"Eddie, come back!"

When he continues hightailing it, I realize it's me against the world—*as it always is.* My wit is the only currency I have, and its rarity doesn't make it priceless.

After flashing a quick glance to the stranger, I dash in the direction Eddie went. I'm on a scholarship to college. If I get arrested, my plans will go up in smoke like this godforsaken shithole did a decade ago. The community was supposed to rebuild. Instead, half the townsfolks packed up and left, leaving nothing but a wasteland of desecration.

I'm partway down the alleyway when the bang of a gun booms into my ears. While freezing like a statue, I survey the area. The guard's boots no longer thud against the road surface. I can't even hear his frantic breaths. If I didn't know any better, I'd swear I was the only person in the alleyway.

With my heart in my throat, I crank my neck back to add images to the theories running through my hazy head. The euphoria pumping through me seconds ago shifts to despair when I spot the security officer slumped on the ground. Blood is seeping through the back of his uniform, and his arms are pinned beneath him like he was struck down midstride.

When I stray my eyes to the end of the alleyway, my heart thumps out a jazzy melody. My wide-with-terror eyes make the dark-haired stranger hard to see, but I don't need 20/20 vision to recognize the black object in his hand. He has a gun, and its barrel is pointed my way.

I blink several times in a row when the bang of a gun being fired for the second time ricochets down the alleyway. While my stomach braces for impact, my pathetically-short life flashes before my eyes. The video montage is over in less than two seconds, but disappointed is the only pain I'm experiencing. Even with the cruel sound of a bullet shredding through a hard surface echoing in my ears, I somehow remain uninjured.

Certain my mind is playing tricks on me, I pivot around to investigate where the crunching sound originated from. I grow untrusting of my legs to keep me upright when I take in remnants of a security camera hanging messily from the corner of a Publix supermarket chain. Its exposed wires reveal it's a hardwired device, however it won't be recording anything but brickwork right now.

Although lost on what the hell is happening, I can't help but shift my focus back to the unnamed man at the end of the alley. I should be in fear for my life, but for some reason, I'm not. He gunned down a guard for me, I'm certain of it.

My lungs take stock of their oxygen levels when he winks at me as I anticipated earlier before he spins on his heels and enters an idling stretch limousine, leaving me alone with a dead man and no alibi.

Crap.

Chapter Three

Dimitri

Smith's dark eyes lift to mine when I slide into the back seat of our shared limousine. "Remove all footage from before the guard commenced undoing his belt."

Smith is my tech guy. If I want something permanently deleted from the World Wide Web, he gets it done within minutes. I want this deleted. I don't give a fuck someone may view the footage and think I'm a perverted bastard who gets his rocks off watching a teen get fingered in an alleyway. I'm more worried I showed weakness by gunning down a man because he liked what he saw as much as me.

The security officer wasn't approaching the blonde to make a citizen's arrest for performing a lewd act in a public place. He wanted in on the action, and from the way he grabbed at his belt while sprinting after her, he was going to join in even if she said no.

I hate fuckers like that.

The Petrettis have been meddling in the prostitution

conglomerate for as long as I've been born, so you can trust me when I say not all hookers cater for high-end johns. Some are willing to break a twenty depending on what you're seeking. You don't need to force a girl to do a sex act on you if you're down on your luck. Go see my father, he'll negotiate with a homeless man if it benefits him in some way.

Smith jerks up his chin, understanding where I'm going before he pulls his laptop out of his bag. He's never without a bunch of equipment. It's as vital to him as the blood in his veins. "And the girl?"

I drag the towel Rocco, my number two, handed me over my wet head before replying, "Listen for chatter. If they don't rule this as self-defense, I'll put other measures in play."

Rocco twists his lips, shocked. Usually, I don't give a fuck about anyone but myself. This time around is different. Not only am I forging ahead with plans to get my daughter back sooner rather than later, but I'm also the hardest I've ever been. It wasn't watching what the punk-faced weasel did to the blonde that caused my cock to press against the zipper in my trousers, it was the way she stared at me while he touched her.

It takes a lot of gall to get off when the person you're fantasizing about isn't touching you. Imagine how quick she'll explode if I were to touch her? The thought should disgust me. I was only in the rain chasing the ghost of my wife, but for some reason, it doesn't. What can I say? I was raised by a mongrel of a man. Mental stability isn't my favorable trait, and neither is chivalry—*usually*.

"And you?" Smith asks, shocked I left myself out of the equation. That's as rare as my father doing something ethical because it would do more good than harm.

"I doubt the footage of me is more than a blur of black." I know this as I strained my eyes while striving to take in the blonde's features. "If it's more, let them have it. The Feds haven't done me any favors the past nine months, so I'm not inclined to cooperate with them either."

Against my better judgment, I sort help from a contact my family had many years ago when Audrey's ransom note arrived at my office. Although he doesn't follow the book to the letter of the law like his pompous counterparts, he still has too many rules and protocols for me to follow. He wants to get Fien back without bloodshed.

I'd rather endure a bloodbath than endure another long nine months pass without seeing my daughter in the flesh. Our opposing opinions don't meld well, and they often find us placed on different teams. I guess that's expected when one side of the duo works in law enforcement, and the other is well-known for his criminal ties.

"Call Joshua." India hands a business card to Smith like he's her personal assistant. "He'll have the slug removed from the guard's body before the coroner and will keep an eye on proceedings." With her jaw as set as mine, she slumps low into her seat before twisting her torso to face me. "What was that about?"

I arch a brow, wordlessly suggesting she check her tone. I don't know who the fuck she thinks she is, but she's neither my wife nor my mother, so she has no right to badger me. If I want to watch a truckload of women being pleasured by men incapable of the task on a rainy Friday afternoon, so be it.

I can do whatever the fuck I like.

That's the joy of being me.

Either stupid or hoping to die, India disregards my stern glare. "You can't replace Audrey and Fien. It isn't possible."

"I know that." I lean so close to her, her hot breaths take care of the droplets of rain on my face the towel missed. She isn't worried. She's excited she forced a response out of me. I rarely give her the time of day. This afternoon won't be any different. "But that doesn't mean Rimi Castro won't believe that. Look at you, all rattled and upset thinking I'm moving on. Who's to say he won't reach the same conclusion?"

Because she's fighting to keep a calm head, India's accent comes out more pronounced than normal. I'm not exactly sure of her ancestry. I just know she's foreign like Audrey. "I'm upset for Audrey, Dimi." Calling me Dimi puts her in my shit book, only my friends are allowed to call me that, much less what she says next, "She doesn't deserve to be replaced with a cheap, knock-off version of herself."

"Shh." I push her platinum blonde hair out of her eye before tucking it behind her ear. "No more lies. We both know you're praying Audrey is never found." When a flare of deceit fires through her eyes, I speak faster, "Just like you'll forever wish we didn't bump into her when we fumbled into your apartment after our date." I track my thumb over her ruby-painted lips and across her jaw before stopping it at the throb in her throat. "It must have stung having her steal my attention the way she did."

"She wasn't supposed to be there," India mutters before she can stop herself.

"But she was, and you were discarded... *again.*"

I take a second to suck in the fear slicking her skin before inching back with a smirk. India plays the role of a widower well, however her husband is only 'presumed dead' by her. From what Smith unearthed earlier this month, India's husband is a foreign aristocrat with a fascination for little blonde playthings. Rumors are he tossed his wife aside with the hope his favorite whore will become the queen of his realm.

"Is that why Audrey was taken, India? Because you once again had your crown stolen?"

"Not at all," she immediately fires back. She's a damn good actor. Even someone trained to seek deceit would have trouble spotting hers. "I attended your wedding. I'm the one who encouraged you to get married so Audrey wouldn't be deported—"

"And you were the last person to see her alive!" I'm back up in her face in an instant, my hand around her throat, my lips an inch from hers. "You told her to meet you at the restaurant."

"Because I was hosting a surprise baby shower for her. I had no clue there were men there waiting for her. You didn't even see them when you walked her to the door." Her words are breathy and weak, strangled by the fierce clutch I have on her neck. I'm not just furious at her, I'm angry at myself. I glanced away for barely a second, and *poof*, Audrey was gone. "I would have never hurt her, Dimitri. She was my best friend… my *only* friend."

I don't want to believe her. I want to hang her out to dry as I've desired many times over the past nine months, but there's too much truth in her eyes for me to ignore. Women like India and Audrey don't make friends. They're ridiculed for their beauty like they should be punished God gifted them with enticing features, and we won't mention the fact they're foreigners living in a country known for its disrespect of women. In my motherland, women are treated like goddesses. It's one of the reasons my father rarely visits Italy.

After a few big breaths, I weaken my grip on India's throat. Once I've worked my anger down a few notches, I sink back to my side of the bench seat before straightening the disheveled collar of my trench coat.

My clothes are drenched through, but you wouldn't know it from the fiery heat teeming out of me. It's so blistering hot, I'm confident I'll be bone-dry in seconds.

Certain I've got everything in order, I stray my eyes to Smith's side of the cabin. "Once you cleared the footage, commence implementing the ruse we discussed last week. Any chatter regarding me moving on is to come directly through me."

"Understood." Smith gets straight to work like he's already cleared away the footage of the unknown blonde getting fingered in the alleyway and was dying for another task. He likes to keep busy. "Do you want the compound included in the catchment zone?"

India doesn't move her head, but I can feel her eyes on me when I dip my chin. "Word got out about my marriage. It was a guarded secret, so either someone in this car is a snitch, or we have eyes and ears in unknown locations." It sucks to admit you can't trust your own blood, but this isn't the first time I've felt this way. Why do you think I kept my relationship with Audrey a secret?

"And tonight's plans?" India asks, jumping back into the conversation like she wasn't almost choked to within an inch of her life.

I don't look at her. I can't. If I do, I'll want to finish what I started. "Will continue as planned." While tapping out a quick message to my father, telling him we'll be delayed a couple of minutes since I stopped for some lighthearted entertainment, I add, "While you convince Miceli your husband's claims about you disliking oral sex are fraudulent, Clover, Smith, Rocco, and I will convince his crew they'd rather settle anywhere but Hopeton."

By convince, I mean we'll get heavy. New York was run by three separate entities of the Italian Cartel, however Hopeton most certainly isn't.

Famiglia prima di tutto... until it isn't.

Chapter Four

Dimitri

Ignoring my cracked and bleeding knuckles, I raise a recently printed photograph of my daughter off a dust-coated desk. Unlike last month's shotty and blurred image, this one shows every inch of Fien's chubby cheeks, toothy grin, and birthmark-blemished stomach with precise clearness.

The figure attached to her picture speaks a thousand words. My ruse is working. I've been requested to deposit one hundred fifty thousand dollars into a foreign account on the third of each month without fail the past nine months. This month's demand only cites one hundred thousand dollars.

Her kidnappers didn't lessen the amount of her ransom because her upkeep this month is less than the previous nine. They've lowered it because they're worried I'm weeks from forgetting her. Why pay out of the eye to keep someone safe when you can replace them within months? It seems demoralizing and cruel to even consider, but it's exactly the way men in my industry operate. They wouldn't pay to keep their blood safe, especially if that blood has female hormones running through it.

My father loved my mother, yet, he profited from her death instead of mourning it. If he'd known how beneficial her death would have been, he would have put plans into play years earlier. Guaranteed.

My mother was killed during a joint FBI and CIA sting many years ago. Her death sparked controversy across the globe. The outrage ensured my father would never be prosecuted for his crimes. The uproar about the loss of an innocent was louder than the calls for my father to serve time. If he were put away, his many children would become wards of the state. No one wanted that, not even the men who had spent years hunting him.

Once the heat settled down, my father sued the state for an undisclosed record-setting amount. He won. My mother was a good woman. She was the only person capable of getting through to my father. Our family dynamic drastically changed when she was killed.

For years, I blamed authorities for the hell I was raised in. If the large, balding Russian standing in front of me hadn't convinced me otherwise, I'd still be avenging her death. A bullet from an agent's gun killed my mother, but that was only because my father pulled her in front of himself as a shield.

Why believe the Bureau over my own flesh and blood, you ask? Tobias had footage no amount of manipulation could alter. It was as gory and as terrifying as the video on a USB drive stored in my safe.

When I place Fien's photograph on my desk, Tobias continues with the conversation we were holding before her ransom note arrived. "I have strong intel on a new Castro compound popping up in the New Mexico region. A crew was deployed there last week."

"Where exactly in New Mexico?" The land there is rugged and spread out. I'm sure Smith would eventually unearth Rimi's location since he can't demand money without using some form of electronic communication, but I'd rather Tobias spell out the details for me. It will be quicker this way, although it could also be a heap bloodier.

Rimi isn't keeping Fien in one location. He's bouncing her around the country, constantly altering her location, so I can't get a solid lead for longer than a day, two at most.

"I can't tell you that."

The stiffness of my jaw is heard in my reply. "Then what can you tell me?" Although I'm asking a question, I don't wait for Tobias to respond. "Your department has been sitting on their hands for months. I've shared intel with you, trade fucking secrets, and what have I been given in return for it? Nothing. Not a single fucking thing."

Tobias doesn't rattle easily. "I placed men on your date to ensure she doesn't get snared by the same trap as Audrey."

I slouch low into my chair before making a teepee with my index fingers. Since my beard is thicker than I usually wear it, my jaw's tick isn't as obvious. "Don't act like you did that for me, Tobias. Your wish to keep Justine out of harm's way has nothing to do with me, and you know it."

There it is, the brutal pulse a vein in his neck gets any time I'm on the money. I don't know who fucked Tobias over, or how well he was fucked, but I guarantee you he doesn't look at Justine with the same set of eyes as me. I doubt he even views her how her brothers do. He sees a person, not an asset.

"Whether it's downright sinister or ingenuously brilliant, my plan is working. I received Fien's proof of life earlier this month, and the ransom is lower. Rimi is growing worried, which means he'll get sloppy."

Tobias breathes heavily out of his nose before slumping into the chair opposite to mine. Since our meetings need to be kept on the down-low, dust kicks up around him in protest to his large frame squeezing the last bit of air out of the chair's cushioning. "I agree. Impatience is one of Rimi's biggest downfalls. I just have a bad feeling about this one. The New Mexico region is the Castros' stomping ground. Rimi would only go there for one reason."

"To end things?"

When Tobias jerks up his chin, I take a moment to deliberate. Tobias's extensive knowledge on how the Cartel works is the sole reason I've continued to keep him updated on Audrey and Fien's case. He knows how these guys tick because he's been undercover in their organizations longer than some of the main hitters have been helming their reigns. If anything is about to go down, Tobias generally knows before it occurs. He tried to talk my father out of his failed takeover bid on the family now running New York. He didn't listen to him as I am tempted to do this time around.

"I can't let this go. The evidence is too overwhelming to discount."

"I agree," he says again. "But I also think you need to tread cautiously. Castro reacts stupidly when scared."

I shouldn't smile at the thought of Rimi quaking in his boots, but I do. What can I say? I like knowing he doesn't have one up on me. Tell me one air-breathing man who wouldn't? He's had my daughter for nearly ten months. Most men would have cracked by now.

Confident all is said and done, Tobias stands to his feet. "I'll try and get word to you before we make a move. In the meantime, stay out of Erkinsvale. Even with the security guard being shot in the back, his death has murky cartel smears all over it."

I slant my head to hide my smile. I shot the guard in the back to weaken the Feds' suspicions. I should have realized that wouldn't work with Tobias. He has an uncanny knack for knowing when his targets are coming out to play.

When Tobias's silence gets the better of me, I mutter, "He was going to rape that girl."

He shifts on his feet to face me. Even with him being close to sixty, his swagger is highly noticeable. "I know. Why do you think my cuffs are still shackled to my belt?" He waits for my gut to absorb his first hit before he whacks me with another. "Was he one of your johns?"

"Hypothetically speaking?"

His smirk matches mine. He isn't impressed with my negotiating skills, but he's aware we won't talk without them. "When aren't things hypothetical with you, Dimi?"

As my smile doubles, I shrug. "Hypothetically speaking, his kink was rape. He liked them un-bled and young—"

"Younger than the girl you left to clean up your mess?"

I shrug again. "Depends. How young is she?"

I'm seeking answers from the wrong person, but I can't fucking help myself. Even with my week being tied up dating Justine and praying Rimi is as stupid as he looks, the bleach blonde's sullied green eyes barely left my mind. I swear I've seen them before, but for the life of me, I can't remember where.

With his smirk as edgy as his mood, Tobias replies, "Young enough I shouldn't need to tell you to stay away, but I will. She doesn't belong in this life any more than Fien." Confident I'll adhere to his warning, he leaves the warehouse cloaked by a moonless sky, sidestepping Maddox Walsh on his way out.

Maddox's fists are balled tighter than they were when I

approached him at an underground college fight months ago, and fiery ambers are blazing through his icy gaze. I want to say the scum who tried to rip him off of five thousand cool ones last week is the reason for his anger, but I doubt that's the case. Rumors about me moving on aren't just reaching Rimi's ears. Justine's brothers have heard them too.

Although I know the reason for Maddox's visit, I try and downplay it. I've got a third date with his sister to organize. I don't have time to babysit men big enough to crawl out of their own shit. "The funds from last month's fights will be deposited into your account by the end of business Friday. I don't have any intel on the fighters being brought forward for next month."

"I'm not here about our arrangement." His voice is gruff like he's taken one too many jabs to the throat. I guess it's part and parcel of being an illegal street fighter. His skills are good enough not to get hit, but he knows the more strikes he takes, the bigger his prize will be. Even if it's rigged, idiots pay top dollar to watch two men come to blows for longer than a couple of minutes.

After planting his ass in the seat Tobias just freed up, Maddox locks his blue eyes with mine. "Is it true you're using my sister as bait?"

That wasn't close to what I was anticipating for him to say, but I keep a cool head. "Whatever do you mean?"

"Don't play the dumb card with me, Dimitri. You might have all the stupid fuckers around here believing you've got the hots for my sister, but I know there's more to it than you're letting on. You paid the dessert menu more attention last week than you did Justine, yet you're trying to organize another date. Why?"

I'll give it to him. It takes gall to call a man out as a liar on his turf. His valor sees me issuing him some leniency—just. I inconspicuously aim my gun at his stomach instead of straight-up pressing it to his temple like I usually do.

"She's not in any danger—"

"That wasn't what I asked." He winks, then leans forward, aware I have my gun on him but uncaring. If I gunned him down now, Tobias would be on my ass in an instant, and Maddox knows it.

Tobias isn't my friend. Only a fool would believe otherwise. We work together because we must, not because we want to.

"You're willing to die for your sister?" When confirmation flares through Maddox's eyes, I switch tactics. "How does Demi feel about that?"

Justine hinted that Demi and Maddox were going casual last week. I know it's more than that. Maddox isn't just fascinated with my cousin, he's wholly fucking taken by her. Enough for me to be confident in saying, "If Demi were taken by your enemies, how far would you go to get her back?"

I see the answer in his eyes—there's no line he wouldn't cross—but it doesn't mean he'll go easy on me, though.

Fortunately for me, I have another card up my sleeve.

"And what about that kid of yours growing in her stomach? The one you don't know about because you're ignoring all the signs. What if he or she were ripped away from you? How far would you go to keep her safe?" He's taken back by my suggestion his girlfriend is pregnant, but he doesn't deny my assumption, confirming he has an inkling that everything I'm saying is true. "My daughter was cut out of my wife's stomach. They butchered her like a piece of worthless meat. I don't care who I have to trample, I won't stop until they're forced to pay for their mistakes."

Maddox stands from his chair so quickly, he topples it over. "Justine is my sister. I won't have her used like this."

"And she's my daughter!" I thrust Fien's photograph onto

his side of the desk before lining up my pistol with the crinkle between his brows. "She ranks higher than anyone."

I discover the Walsh's don't just fight with their fists when Maddox draws a gun on me. It's clear it is one he picked up from a gangbanger in a back alley, but the quality of the weapon shouldn't enter the equation when calculating how much time you have left. The skill of its user is the only sum needed.

Do I think Maddox has the guts to kill me? Probably not. But he won't hesitate to maim me if it increases the odds of keeping me away from Justine.

If only the heat didn't get too hot for Tobias, then we would have found out. He interrupts our conversation long before I get the chance to prove nothing will ever come between Fien and me.

Not a woman.

Not the law.

No one.

"Lower your guns." When we remain standing firm, Tobias's voice rises as readily as his anger. "Don't make me repeat myself. I'll shoot you both before leaving you here to rot. Trust me when I say two less criminals in a sea of many won't be missed."

Unsurprisingly, Maddox lowers his gun first. He has the instincts of a killer, he just needs to hone his skills. I'd be happy to teach him if he weren't glaring at me like he wants my insides hanging out of my belly button.

"Stay away from my sister."

Stealing my chance to reply that I wouldn't be the only one licking wounds if I did that, he dumps his gun onto my desk, spins on his heels, then walks away.

You have no idea how satisfying it is when Tobias strays his eyes to mine to seek permission for Maddox to leave. Some would say it's because Maddox entered my premises with a loaded weapon, so Tobias is simply following the law. I know it's more than that. Tobias cares for me in his own twisted way. I guess that can be expected since he killed my mother.

Guilt does weird things to people.

As does vengeance.

I know that better than anyone.

Chapter Five

Roxanne

"Come on, Roxie, don't be like that. You were into it last time."

While rolling my eyes at Eddie's highly inaccurate statement, I continue down a dark alleyway. I can't believe I was so stupid to fall for his sob act. He doesn't care that my scholarship floated precariously in the wind for three months after the security guard was murdered, or that I sat at a police station for fourteen hours giving testimony about an incident I'm still struggling to comprehend.

Even the officer taking my statement was wary about my recollection of events, and I was as honest as Mother Mary. I even told him about the stranger watching Eddie notch his finger inside of me, aware that it could get me in trouble, but hopeful it would see me skipping a murder conviction.

It worked, however my life hasn't been the same since. My nanna is still angry at me, the dean at my school won't stop eyeing me like a freak since our emergency meeting to save my ass, and all my friends bar one up and vanished.

You'd think that would keep me on the straight and narrow, but no, I'm clearly a weirdo who gets off on danger. Why do you think I agreed with Eddie's suggestion for us to camp out in a dark alleyway on a rainy Friday night? It isn't the same alleyway as three months ago—Eddie was smart enough to pick one two towns over from the crime scene of our last farce—but I'm still striving to relive an event I should give anything to forget.

Someone call the mental hospital. A new patient is at the ready.

"Roxanne…" The clomp of Eddie's flip-flops on the wet ground irks my last nerve. "I wanted tonight to be special. Why do you think I bought you flowers?"

By special, he means he wants to slide to the home plate by doing something as simple as purchasing a bunch of gas station flowers. *If* he purchased them. I wouldn't put it past him to steal them. That's how cheap he is.

Too angry to let his bad taste slide, I say, "You left the price tag on the flowers, Ed. For future reference, $3.99 won't get you close to home plate." I let out a soundless whine before spinning around to face him. "Even if you did pay for them, which I'm highly skeptical about, I forked out fifteen dollars for *your* movie ticket, so if we're counting merit points, *I'm* coming out of this date shortchanged, not you."

"I tried to even the score." He slants his head so the moonlight can catch the speckles of yellow in his brown eyes. I'm a sucker for the uniqueness of his golden eyes. "But you weren't into it like you were last time."

If I were an honest, upstanding member of society, I'd tell him my lack of interest isn't his fault, it's the fact the mysterious stranger's watchful gawk was missing, but sadly, I'm not just a horrible person. I'm beginning to wonder if there's more wrong with me than an inclination for getting freaky in public.

"This isn't working, Eddie. I need…" *A guy who doesn't wear flip-flops and holey jeans on a date. Someone with hair darker than yours and eyes full of trouble. I need anyone but you.* "… to concentrate on my studies. If I lose my scholarship, I'll be stuck in our horrid town along with all the other geriatrics for the rest of my life."

Proof he doesn't know me at all shines through when Eddie replies, "That wouldn't be so bad, would it? Our families have lived in this region for decades—"

"Yet I haven't seen my parents in years. This isn't the life I want, Eddie. I want—"

"A stranger's gawk so you can come?"

I don't breathe for a good eight seconds. I had no clue he spotted the dark-haired man's stare three months ago.

None whatsoever.

"I don't need anyone to watch. I just—" I stop talking, having no plausible way to say I only want *one* man's gawk without making it seem as if I'm certifiably insane. I could barely see the stranger's face, yet here I am, basing all my hopes and dreams on him. "Can you please take me home? We'll talk more about this tomorrow, I promise. I'm just tired and hormonal, that's all."

"All right, I'll take you home." Eddie digs his keys out of his dirty jeans to authenticate his pledge. "After you answer one question." Although I can see in his eyes it will be a doozy, I dip my chin, agreeing to his request. "Did you orgasm because of what I was doing or because *he* was watching?"

My heart sinks as quickly as my mood. "Eddie—"

He cuts me off with a stern glare, reading me better than he should considering he doesn't know me at all. "As I thought. You're nothing but a gutter rat."

"Excuse me?" I snap back in shock. "You're expecting to

hook up in an alleyway. If that makes anyone ratty, that'll be you, Mr. Cheapskate."

After rolling his eyes with an immaturity you'd expect from a man with no class, he cranks open the driver's side door of his car, then slides inside.

My brows stitch when I attempt to mimic his movements. The passenger side door is locked, and he isn't leaning over to undo the latch.

"Eddie…" my words trail off for the second time when he plants his foot on the gas pedal. "Are you kidding me? It's late, and we're miles from home!"

When he continues rocketing toward the lot's only exit, I pick up the first thing I see and peg it at his car. My throat works hard to swallow when my swing is better than expected. The can of soup I thought was empty doesn't just smack into the rear window of his outdated ride, it smashes right through it.

It must have been as jam-packed as my anger.

I block the blinding rays of Eddie's headlights with my hand when he executes a U-turn. When he revs his engine like a deranged man, a normal person would run into the safety of the alleyway.

My efforts three months ago reveal I'm nothing close to ordinary. I watch his approach with wide, terrified eyes, only blinking when the bumper of his car buckles my legs out from underneath me.

My body's impact with the front window of his car causes as much damage as the can of soup did to the rear window. It cracks into a million pieces, sprinkling both mine and Eddie's hair with shards of glass.

I think the worst is over—I can't feel the lower half of my body, so how much worse can it get—but realize things are never easy for me.

With his narrowed eyes revealing how worthless he thinks I am, Eddie throws his gearshift into reverse before he whizzes back at a speed too quick for me to remain on his hood.

I fall to the ground with a thud, breaking more than my pride.

I also crack my head.

Chapter Six

Dimitri

Justine's eyes float up to mine when I order our meal in my native tongue. Although displeased I didn't ask what she'd like to eat or drink as I did our previous two dates, she's too shocked about me requesting a bottle of the most expensive wine to announce her annoyance.

I had wondered if she understood Italian when I took a call during our drive from her dormitory to this restaurant but played it off as inquisitiveness. I know better now. If the clipped tone I used on the waiter was a test, Justine just nose-bombed the finals.

Things are tense between us tonight. I guess that can be expected. Most of the women I bedded before Audrey had a three-date rule. Although it took me longer to convince Justine to discount her brothers' multiple warnings to stay away from me, tonight is technically our third date. It doesn't mean anything, though. I'm not looking to hook up. I just want my rivals to *think* I am.

While handing our menus to the waiter, confident Justine won't have the gall to go against me, I say in Italian, "I can order you something else if you'd prefer?"

Under normal circumstances, my pigheadedness would occur in private. Regretfully for Justine, I need it to be as apparent as possible. A bursting-at-the-seams restaurant in her hometown would have been ideal, but since I'm testing both Maddox's loyalty and those who share my blood, I altered our plans last minute. My family's restaurant will still have the effect I'm aiming for, just minus the glaring heat of Justine's brothers from across the room.

Usually, the fervor wouldn't bother me, however the past three months have been some of the longest in my life. The strain is prominent on both my face and my demeanor.

After Maddox left my warehouse minus a bullet wound, I was hit by one shitstorm after another. The gap in my dating schedule with Justine saw Fien's ransom requests returned to their original amounts. My father's wish to keep Miceli out of his realm resulted in four Arabian tycoons canceling their 'work' trips to my side of the globe this quarter, and Tobias's unusual quiet had nothing to do with him being forced to intervene on my 'conversation' with Maddox. It was because he was killed during a rogue operation two and a half months ago. The same operation he assured me would see Fien freed from captivity.

Tobias's death was the proof I've been seeking the past eleven months. Rimi isn't working alone. He doesn't have the means nor the ability to pull off the sting he did almost three months ago. He's getting help, and if the inkling in my gut is anything to go by, it isn't just from our side of the law.

The only reprieve I was given the past three months was news that despite her hankering for public hookups, the teen in the alleyway skipped prosecution. It probably helped that

Smith erased the surveillance footage from the security company's servers faster than Erkinsvale detectives drool their way through a box of glazed donuts.

Although Smith works at a lightning-fast pace, the quality of his work is never diminished. The fact he works fast *and* clean is the main reason he's on my team. Trust is a very close second.

My intuition about Justine understanding Italian is proven spot on when she mutters, *"Sono contento di quello che hai ordinato."*

"Ah, so you do speak Italian?"

The genuine surprise in my tone awards me my first smile of the night. "Amongst other languages," Justine replies as her smile picks up.

Her eyes shine as brightly as the diamond drop necklace I gifted her at the commencement of our date when I scoot to her half of our booth so I can lay her napkin across her lap. I'm bringing out all the charm tonight, hopeful the glitz will hide my wolfish insides well enough, she'll be convinced her brothers' worries the past three months were nothing more than them being overprotective ogres like all good siblings should be.

I can't say I don't understand their approach. I had a similar neurosis with my siblings before all but one of them perished. Roberto has been missing for a little over four years. Ophelia was killed in a traffic accident years ago, and CJ would rather live as a recluse than endure another two decades under our father's command. He says he's happy in his log cabin miles from the closest town.

Until Fien is returned, I'll never discover if he's telling the truth. My daughter is the only reason I've remained in this godforsaken town. Just like she was the very reason I strived so hard to leave it a year ago.

Part of me wonders if that was why Audrey was taken. Did

rumbles of my wish to cut ties with my family reach my enemies' ears that they were left with no choice but to respond before they lost the chance? Or did the rumors only reach my father's ear, and he did everything in his power to ensure his legacy lived on?

I don't want to believe the latter is true, but until I'm proven otherwise, I'm looking at everyone with the same tainted set of eyes—blood included. It wouldn't be the first time my father has gone against his children. I doubt it'll be the last.

My thoughts shift back to friendly territory when Justine runs her hand down my arm. "Are you okay?" She keeps her tone low, aware there are more than just her eyes on me. My family's reputation isn't what it once was, but that doesn't mean it isn't notable.

Fear is often more respected than gallantry.

"I'm fine." Needing to ease the tension strain creasing her forehead, I add, "I was just wondering whether we should eat dessert here or order it to go."

Although Justine shrugs like a nightcap isn't on the agenda right now, I know that's far from the truth. Her eyes aren't twinkling from the waiter setting down our scrumptious-looking hors d'oeuvres. Interest is responsible for some of their gleam.

While laughing at something wittingly intelligent I said, Justine dabs at her saucy lips with her napkin. Petretti's isn't as elaborate as the first two restaurants we dined at, but the quality of its meals and service is undeniable. If Justine wasn't seated across from me, I'd be convinced I was in Cefalù, a coastal city in northern Sicily. It's the only place I run to when I've had enough of life. I've not been back there since Audrey was taken.

Some days it seems as if I'll never get back there.

My moping isn't saved by Justine this time around. The waiter who's working super hard for an impressive tip has returned to our table to offer us the dessert menu. Although my earlier comment about us taking dessert home to eat was in jest, the slightest smell of Justine's heated skin has me reconsidering my objectives.

In my industry, the smell of a woman in need is sampled as regularly as a fresh brew of coffee. It's never had this edge before, though. Justine has a pure, unaltered smell, and although she isn't fawning for my attention, her interests are undeniable.

I slant my head to hide my devious smirk before asking, "Have you decided what you'd like?"

If she replies with one of the many options on the menu she's perusing, I'll continue portraying the gentleman I've been feigning the past three months. However, if her reply is anything close to the vulgar ones running through my head, all bets are off. Women have practically thrown themselves at me the past year. I've yet to accept a single offer. I want any exchanges to be on my terms, when I'm ready, and not because my father is convinced a woman's cunt wrapped around your cock is the answer for everything.

My mother's body wasn't even cold before he moved on. I'm not solely talking about sex, either. He married his favorite whore a month after my mother's death. Wife number three lasted exactly thirty-eight days. She no longer occupies my father's bed, but the rose garden at the front of my family's compound is well-fertilized.

I peer at Justine beneath lowered lashes when she mumbles, "Umm… I'm not sure what I want." I won't lie, when she returns my glance, my cock twitches. It isn't the same full-blown throbbing erection I got while watching the blonde get fingered in the alleyway three months ago, but it most certainly wouldn't have any issues getting the job done. Justine is beautiful, and although I can't replace Audrey, I can forget her for a night *or lose myself in someone with almost identical features.*

After handing my dessert menu to the waiter, I request him to place our meals on my tab. He almost shits himself when I suggest he add a hundred-dollar tip to the tally. His excitement is as high as Justine's when I scoot out of the booth before offering to help her out.

She accepts it, albeit hesitantly.

Little Red Riding Hood knows she's being stalked by the Big Bad Wolf.

While guiding Justine to the car I requested the valet keep close by, I silence my cousin, Demi's, third call of the night. She's most likely calling to gripe about the fight she had with Maddox earlier tonight—a fight I instigated with the hope it would keep Maddox off Justine's tail long enough for me to slip her away for a secret rendezvous.

Did it work?

Justine is being guided to my car, isn't she?

Once I've assisted Justine into my low-riding car, I jog around to the driver's side door a second valet is holding open for me. I gunned down a man in cold blood only a week ago, yet my heart rages more when I slip behind the steering wheel than it did back then.

Monogamy has never been my strong point, but it feels different this time around. My woman isn't holed up at home waiting for me in a toasty chiropractor-approved bed. She's most likely buried in an unmarked grave, her stomach still open and barren.

Since anger is surging out of me in hidden waves, I shut my door with more force than needed. Justine was supposed to be a ruse, a way to get my daughter back. My cock shouldn't be leading our exchange. Yes, it's been over a year since I've had a woman quiver beneath me, but that's part of my penance, isn't it?

I took my eyes off my wife to admire another woman, fascinated at how she could exude such beauty while thick black tears rolled down her face. She was more Gothically dressed that I would have liked, and far too young, but I couldn't take my eyes off her. She was too ravishing to deserve a half-scrutinized glance.

For over a year, I've failed to understand how Rimi got the better of me. Only now am I realizing he didn't blindside me. It was the unknown redhead on the corner of 29th and James street. She was so tiny, my body would have blanketed hers in an instant. The thought on how she'd respond to my big, brooding frame had me so mesmerized, I didn't realize Audrey had torn away from me until it was too late. My enemies had captured her.

She was carrying my daughter, my flesh and blood, yet, my wandering eye sees my daughter paying the price for my stupidity. I'd turn the knife on myself if it wouldn't make me as selfish as my father. For years, I craved his approval. I thought becoming his shadow would return our family's name to the stature it deserves.

Alas, he only taught me one thing. *Famiglia prima di tutto.* Fien is my family, she's all I have, so she comes before anyone —even me.

My focus returns to the road in just enough time to spot an overloaded truck heading my way. The driver flashes his lights, warning me the weight he's hauling is too heavy for him to stop our collision, leaving the task up to me.

I won't lie, my heart races more now with adrenaline than unease. The thrill zapping down my spine is maddening and addictive at the same time. I'm pissed I've gotten myself into a situation that could leave Fien to defend for herself, but I haven't had a surge of energy like this in months. It makes me feel alive like I'll can overtake the arrogant prick whose speedo has probably never been over thirty and make it back into my lane with a few seconds to spare.

"Dimitri…" Justine forces out through the panic clutching her throat when I flatten my foot on the gas pedal instead of the brake.

My car is a prototype designed to respond on demand, and I'm determined to see if its guarantees stack up. The needle on the speedo goes from thirty to seventy in one blurring second. The horsepower behind its motor glues me to my seat while the vibrations of the steering wheel mimic the spasms a woman's cunt does when I tease her clit with my tongue.

When we whizz past a brand-spanking-new Buick, the windows of my Hennessey Venom F5 rattle. My brutal speed isn't solely responsible for their shudders. Most of their tremors are compliments to the truck whipping past us a nanosecond after I slot into the minute space between the Buick and a chunky-tired Chevrolet.

Like a recently admitted mental patient, I commence laughing. I'm not talking a little, hey-that-was-fun laugh, I'm talking full-blown, cackling like a hyena who ate an entire dish of hash brownies. I had no idea how dead I felt on the inside until now. The adrenaline hit will wear off as quickly as it arrived, but the reminder that I'm alive will keep the blood in my veins hot for a few weeks to come.

Once my laughter dies down, I stray my eyes to Justine, shocked by the silence on her side of the cab. During our many hourly 'chats' the past three months, I couldn't shut her up, so her quiet is just unusual. It's a little unnerving.

Justine's back is one with her seat like mine and her eyes are wide. I can't tell if she's excited or scared. It could be a combination of both. She isn't asking me to pull over like Audrey did anytime my foot got friendly with the gas pedal, but is that because fear is clutching her throat too fiercely for her to talk? Or does she love the adrenaline hit as much as me?

If I were half the man I used to be, I'd ask her. Since I'm not, I slackened my pressure on the gas pedal before returning my eyes to the road.

For the rest of our fifteen-mile trip, I maintain the law. I blinker before turning, stay within five miles of the designated speed limits, and stop at pedestrian crossings.

It's the most mundane trip of my life.

Who buys a limited-edition sports car to drive it like a senior citizen in bad need of a bus pass?

The only good that comes from my slower pace is my ability to pay attention to other things besides how well my tires grip the wet asphalt.

We have a tail.

The lowness of my tailgater's ride assures me it isn't the Feds or a member of the local law enforcement, much less the heat of their glare. I should have known Demi wouldn't have called until *after* her fight with Maddox. Who stops an argument to make a call mid-crisis? Not any female I know.

With one plan out the window, I commence another. "Dammit, I forgot my place was being fumigated tonight. Do you mind if we swing by my father's house instead?"

As her jaw unhinges, Justine's still wide-with-terror eyes drift my way. "You want to go to your *dad's* house?" She cringes out 'dad' like most men do when their side dish brings up marriage during their first hookup.

"He's away for the weekend. Won't be back until Monday."

The width of her pupils double. I understand her shock. I pretty much just hinted that we should spend the weekend fucking at my dad's house. I don't have a cunt, but even I can comprehend how that would make most women want to close their legs instead of opening them.

"Other people will be there."

"Oh…" Justine's throat works through a hard swallow before she asks, "Like who?"

"Ah…" *Fuck, when did I lose the ability to lie on the spot?* "Friends and family."

"Oh." This one is much more approachable than her previous one. "That sounds nice."

Nice isn't a word I'd use to describe anyone in my father's crew, but with Maddox riding my ass, I've got no other option but to take his sister back to my family's compound. It has the means to keep Maddox out long enough that gossip will circulate to my enemies that I took Justine to meet the family.

In this industry, that's the equivalent of knocking a woman up with your kid.

With my foot once again becoming friendly with the gas pedal, I enter my family's fortified mansion approximately thirty seconds before Maddox. The window isn't wide, but it's long enough for me to request for the goon on the gate to commence full lockdown. That means no one comes or goes without my permission—not even the authorities.

After pulling up to the side of the mansion-like building, I switch off the ignition. "Things are usually pretty rowdy in the main quarters, so we'll head to the ones in the lower half. It'll be quieter down there."

"Okay," Justine says, hesitantly nodding.

Once I've assisted her out of my car, I commence guiding her inside. I can tell she's uneased about the ruckus we hear more than we see, but I pretend not to notice. She has four older brothers. I'm sure she's accustomed to the 'situations' most men find themselves in late on a Friday night. Even someone as mind-fucked as me prefers the cries of a woman in ecstasy over a wounded soldier being slain.

With my hand on the small of her back, I direct Justine past the den filled with drunken men and half-dressed whores until we reach the hallway that leads to the lower living quarters of the compound. If she was unaware of the lifestyle I was raised in, she isn't anymore. Men in this industry have no shame. If they want to fuck a whore, they do it wherever they please—including the very hallway we're walking down.

"Third door on the right," I tell Justine as my cell phone commences vibrating in my pocket.

My hand is only just hovering above her skin, but I feel the spike in her pulse when we enter my room. It's a large loft-type space with a separate seating area, mock-up kitchen, and grand bathroom, but the first thing everyone's eyes zoom in on is the four-poster bed. Although it was purchased as a joke, it's very much like me—designed for fucking. The handcuff grooves in the thick posts reveal this without a doubt, much less the leather straps that pull out from beneath the mattress.

Although I can drop the gentleman act since we're behind closed doors, I ask Justine if I can take her coat. I've never seen my daughter in the flesh, but that doesn't make me any less of a father. If Fien is ever allowed to date, I can sure as hell tell you her prospective partner better ask to take her coat. If he doesn't, he'll lose more than his fingers.

Justine's denial blasts through her eyes before she articulates. She's freaked, although if her scent is anything to go by, she's more uneased about where she is than *who* she's with.

I shouldn't like the thought, but I do.

With Justine looking for any excuse to leave, I stop ignoring my buzzing cell phone. "While I take this call, why don't you wash up?"

Not waiting for her to respond, I nudge my head to the

bathroom door on our right before sliding my phone out of my pocket and dragging my finger across the screen. Since I'm anticipating my caller to be Demi, I don't bother peering at the screen to check who's calling. I just growl down the line, "This better be good."

The voice that responds is much too gruff and manly to belong to Demi. "Where are you? I have current surveillance on the package."

"Fien?" I ask at the same time Justine whispers, "I think I should head off." She points to the door like it will magically zip her back to her dormitory that's almost an hour and a half from here.

"It's late, and I've got to…" Her words trail off when the sound of someone being pounded into submission overtakes her whispered words. It's clear the people in the room next to us are fucking. The droning "more, more, more" chant bellowing through the paper-thin walls is indicating enough, much less the sound of a headboard rocking and rolling with every thrust.

I'd tell them to keep it the fuck down if Smith didn't grunt out an agreeing hum. Now nothing but my daughter is on my mind. "How current are we speaking?"

When Justine attempts to interrupt me again, I hold my index finger in the air, rudely asking her to shut up for just a minute. Unless I've paid for the privilege, I haven't had a spotting of Fien since she was born. I can't sidestep this to walk Justine though a bout of unease because a couple is having a good time in the room next to us. I'm not asking her to join them, I simply need her to be quiet for a second.

My heart thuds in my ears when Smith says, "I'm looking at her now. It's a live feed."

"You can see her?" Even though I'm asking a question, I don't wait for him to reply. "Send me a link."

When a whoosh sounds through my phone, I drag it away from my ear. Like magic, footage automatically commences playing on the screen. I don't breathe while taking in the face I'd recognize no matter how grainy the image. I don't do anything for a good three or so seconds. I just absorb all the tiny features of my daughter's adorable face as she snuggles into the chest of an unknown blonde. She looks tired, and she's sucking her thumb like I have witnessed many times in her ransom photos the past twelve months.

"I'm backtracking the surveillance camera's footprints. I should have a location in thirty or so seconds…" Anything Smith says next is drowned out by the frantic thump of my pulse. Rimi doesn't have Fien out in the open for no reason. They're moving her. How do I know this? She's being carried on a large commercial-size private jet. Rimi would only order that size jet for one reason—he's going on a long-haul trip.

"I need to know her location, Smith, and I need to know it now!"

A keyboard being punished by tattooed fingers booms down the line along with Smith's accented voice. "I'm working on it. The fuckers are throwing up a ton of firewalls. I've never faced a security system this hard to crack…" His words are replaced with a groan. "I'll call you straight back." Not giving me the chance to tell him I'll kill him if he hangs up on me, he disconnects our call.

Since our connection is lost, my screen returns to its normal setting, losing me the image of Fien's sleepy face. I grip my phone to near death, both frustrated and as angry as fuck. It's good we have a lock on Fien, but how far and few between will that be if she's taken out of the country?

With my anger at a pinnacle, I forget Justine is in the room with me until she whispers, "I'm going to go," like it's impolite for her to depart without announcing she's leaving.

Believing it's best for all involved for her to do precisely that, I nod before digging my keys out of my pocket. "You'll have to take my car. I can't leave."

My cell works anywhere, but I don't have access to a state-of-the-art weaponry room in any old town. This compound isn't called The Artillery for no reason. Every weapon combination you can think of is here, and I've used them all at one stage in my life.

"Oh… umm, that's okay. I can call a taxi?" Justine suggests like it's perfectly normal to find your way home after a failed hookup.

Under different circumstances, I would organize her a ride with one of my crew, but since the rumblings of battle are vibrating under my feet, I jerk up my chin like a soft cock for the second time tonight. "I'll organize a cab while walking you out."

Relief crosses Justine's features. It's quickly chased by worry. Instead of her heart rate pelting my hand as it did during our walk to my room, mine thuds against her back when I guide her out of my room. My heart rate is so sky-high, I feel seconds from coronary failure.

Partway to the front entrance, my cell phone rings again. I'm so eager to dig it out of my pocket, I almost drop it. I inwardly curse, annoyed by both my fumbling hands and discovering how badly I work under pressure. I didn't need to fetch a cab for Justine. Her brother is being held up by the goons at the gate. The numerous texts they sent me requesting permission for Maddox to enter the compound assures me of this, much less the quickest peek of his Pontiac parked at the side gate.

Maddox can drive Justine home, allowing me to shift my guilt to a person it shouldn't have left for even a minute.

After sliding my finger across the screen of my phone, I

squash it to my ear. "Are you in?" When Smith whistles out an agreeing noise, I cup the speaker of my phone, then lock my eyes with Justine's. "Will you be all right from here?"

We're mere feet from the gate. Even a recently bled virgin would make it out of a house full of vampires unscathed in the distance she has left to travel.

Justine's chin barely dips an inch when I spin on my heels and race away from her as if she has cooties. It's a jerk-hat move, but as I've said before, Fien comes before anyone.

"Where is she?"

I stop dead in my tracks when Smith replies, "She's been under our nose the entire fucking time. She's in Ravenshoe."

Chapter Seven

Dimitri

As I race for the weaponry room to stock up on supplies, Smith advises why he had trouble tracking Fien's location. "You know the hold Isaac Holt has on Ravenshoe. His security personnel was never going to let me in without groveling." He scrubs at his hairless chin while disclosing, "I'm down a dozen favors, and he wouldn't even let me piggyback his trace. Fucker."

I'm not surprised. Isaac and I have met before. Let's just say things aren't amicable between us, so I don't see him letting his hacker work for me even if I offered to pay. "Did you ask him to cancel the flight?"

My jaw tightens when Smith's hum this time around isn't agreeing. "Tried. The airstrip is privately owned. Hunter agreed to throw up some server blockers to delay their departure. It'll give us thirty, forty minutes tops."

Thirty minutes works. I can get to Ravenshoe easily within thirty minutes. "Clover—"

"On his way with Preacher. He's taking the tank."

Smith's reply frustrates me to no end. "We can't go in heavy. Fien could get hurt." While weaponing up with my arsenal of choice, I take a moment to deliberate. "Tell Clover to wait. He's not to make a move until I've arrived."

I inwardly curse again, panicked I'm doing the wrong thing but also aware of how Clover works. He's a killing machine who craves a massacre no matter the cost. His passion for a bloodbath could get Fien killed. I'd rather lose sight of her for another year than lose her altogether.

"Monitor the situation with Hunter, if circumstances change, patch it through to the Range Rover feed. I'll take Rocco with me."

Confident he'll follow my orders to the T, I disconnect our call, stuff a second colt down the back of my trousers, then hotfoot it in the direction I last saw Rocco. He was the one getting frisky in the hallway when I guided Justine down it.

Rocco drives like a madman, has done two stints in prison, and has a murder count nearly as high as mine, and it was all achieved before his twenty-fifth birthday. His impressive stats aren't the reason I'm pulling him into this, though. It's because he achieved all of the above while under my watch.

I needed someone deep in the prison system for future plans. Dirty guards are always handy to have up your sleeve, but they've got nothing on true gangbangers. Despite what the warden tells you, he isn't in charge of anything that happens in the yard. He doesn't even have a hold on the cells. They've always been run by the Cartel.

The sweet smell of sweat-slicked skin streams into my nose when I enter the hallway where my room is located. Rocco is still going at it. I'm not surprised. He only has one whore on the go. He usually has two or three. "I need to get to Ravenshoe in under thirty minutes. We'll take the Range Rover most of the way."

To the disgrace of the brunette he's balls deep inside of, Rocco immediately withdraws, yanks his jeans up his stout thighs, then tucks away his cock. After winking at his whining counterpart to ensure her he'll be back to finish what he started later, he follows me toward a hidden bunker at the side of the compound.

My brutal speed slows a few seconds later when the quickest flash of galaxy black paint gleaming in the moonlight captures my attention. Maddox's pride and joy is still parked by the side gate. He's seated behind the steering wheel.

What the fuck? I thought he would have been long gone by now.

My brain is still striving to work out two plus two when India arrives out of nowhere. Her visits have been few and far between the past three months. I don't know if my almost choking scared her away or the fact Miceli likes smacking his girl around while she gives him head. She would have needed more than a stick of concealer by the time Miceli was done with her.

I shouldn't relish the thought, however I do.

Something about India rubs me the wrong way. She's supposed to be an innocent like Audrey, but her eyes reveal she's nothing close to that. They're as evil as mine, and it isn't just a hankering for danger firing them.

"Dimitri, quick. It's Justine." To a stranger, she sounds worried. In reality, she's just out of breath. The only exercise she does is running her mouth. She can't even tick sex off as strenuous activity. I haven't bedded her—much to her disappointment—but I've heard rumors. "Your father caught her on the way out. He isn't happy."

"Col is back?" Nothing but shock highlights my tone. I

wasn't lying when I told Justine he was out of town. I would have never brought her here if I had an inkling he was returning early. That's just asking for trouble. He has issues with anyone coming between him and his foot soldiers. It's one of the reasons I focused my search for the culprits of Audrey's kidnapping closer to home the past few months. There are too many missing pieces of the puzzle for me to believe the Castros are acting alone. They've had help, and I'm just really fucking praying it isn't someone within these walls. If it is, my family name will be tarnished more than it's ever been.

My gut twists when India nods her head. "He's sending her to the Gauntlet."

I curse out loud this time around. The Gauntlet is where my father sends people to die in the most inhumane way possible. Torture. Gang rape. The dismemberment of multiple parts of your body. He chooses his punishment on a whim. There's no rhyme or reason to his process other than undeniable proof that he's a madman.

India's eyes bounce between mine and Rocco's while asking, "Are you coming? I doubt she has long."

I jerk up my chin, commencing my lie in a nonverbal way. "Head down. I'll be right behind you."

She doesn't believe a word I'm speaking, but she's aware she'll take Justine's place if she dares to go against my direct order. "I'll do everything I can to delay things."

I wait for India to disappear in the compound before racing into the bunker to yank off a dusty tarp from an old minecart. It was stolen decades ago when Bronte's Peak was blasted into a cliff edge partway between Ravenshoe and Erkinsvale. We call it the Range Rover because it has the tags Clover swiped from my father's mint condition Range Rover last year.

Although the minecart is a rust bucket, it, along with the underground tunnel my father commenced drilling four decades ago, will get me to Ravenshoe in under twenty minutes.

I considered having my father's head examined when he unveiled the finished project after too many glasses of port when I was sixteen. Now I'm glad I encouraged his madness. I've only used this tunnel a handful of times, mainly to skip prosecution when shit went down at the underground fights we regularly hold on the outskirts of Ravenshoe, but you can't put a price on having an unknown escape route.

I'll never use it to hide from my enemies, but you can be assured I won't hesitate using it to sneak up on them unaware. When you're storming a compound, the last place you foresee being attacked is from behind. It will leave my enemies clueless while helping my empire grow.

While Rocco fills the Rover's tank, I yank my phone out of my pocket and call the last person I expected to speak to tonight. Maddox answers two rings later, and even over the phone, I can tell he's fuming mad. "I swear to fucking God, Dimitri, if you don't bring my sister out here immediately, I'm going to wring your fucking neck."

"If you want your sister to get out of tonight alive, I suggest you shut your mouth and listen to me." My brutal tone immediately gets his attention. I doubt he's even breathing. That's how menacing my voice is. Although I'm not technically prioritizing Justine over Fien—it only takes one person to fill the gas tank, so I'm more utilizing my time wisely than fucking around —I still hate that I'm in this predicament to begin with. "Tell the goon manning the gate that you need to go to the Gauntlet, give him the passcode 'cannon.' When you arrive, fall to your knees and fucking beg. Say anything and everything Col wants to hear—"

"Dimitri…"I don't know whether he pauses to catch his breath or to plot one of the many ways he plans to kill me.

Whatever it is, he's wasting time he can't afford. My father has no patience whatsoever. Once he's handed down a ruling, it is *immediately* executed. If Justine isn't dead, she's walking straight toward it. "What the fuck is going on?"

When Rocco nudges up his chin, wordlessly announcing the Range Rover is good to go, I say down the line, "You said you'd die for your sister, right?"

I hear Maddox swallow before he pushes out, "Yeah."

While slipping into the makeshift seat in the minecart next to Rocco, I mutter, "Tonight is your chance to prove that. Your life for hers, Maddox. I don't see Col taking any less."

Stealing his chance to reply, I press the end button on the screen of my cell, stuff it into my pocket, then tap on the roof of the Range Rover telling Rocco to floor it.

I never wanted to be a hero until I looked into the eyes of my daughter.

Tonight is my chance to become one.

My lungs wheeze in protest to the stuffy conditions, and I'm covered in dust, but as predicted, we make it out the other side of the tunnel in just under twenty minutes.

"Leave it uncovered, we don't have time," I tell Rocco when he commences sheltering the mineshaft cart with the camouflage netting he pulled off a real-life Range Rover. "Smith sent logistics to the Range Rover's mainframe. The airstrip is eleven miles from here." I lift and lock my eyes with his so he can see the urgency in them. "I need to be here ASAP. The jet is fueled and ready to go."

"Give it to me." After sliding into the driver's seat, he snatches my phone out of my hand. His eyes zoom over the screen as he calculates the quickest route.

Once he's confident he has his bearings right, he jabs his finger into the ignition button, fires up the engine, throws the gearshift in reverse, then peers over his shoulder. There's nothing but scrub behind us, which he parts like the Red Sea two seconds later.

Spotting my shocked gawk, he mutters out, "Why go around when we can go over?"

He flashes me a wink that has me forgetting the direness of the situation for a few seconds before he whacks the gearshift into first to commence our trek over sandy plains.

We pop out onto one of the many freeways servicing Ravenshoe a couple of minutes later. Since it's late, traffic is practically nonexistent.

The frantic beat of my heart slackens when I realize how close to the blue dot we are. Rocco's shortcut shaved a good three to four minutes off our travel time.

"Take the next exit," I advise Rocco when a message from Smith pops up on my screen. He's hacked into my system to advise us of the most direct route to take.

The further we travel up the ramp, the more the headlights of the Range Rover bounce off a figure coming from the other end. Although the ground is wet from a recent sprinkling, all the clouds have moved on, exposing a full moon. It adds to the deathly halo shrouding the petite blonde.

"What the fuck is going on here?" Rocco mutters under his breath when the brightness dims enough, we spot the streams of blood gushing down the blonde's face. She's barely walking, her wobbly strides more stumbling steps than polished strides. Her dress and boots are ripped like most punks pay out the eye for when selecting designer jeans, and her blonde hair almost looks red from how much blood it's absorbed.

She's either been in a car accident or run over by one.

Their list of injuries are about the same.

"Someone fucked her over good," Rocco summarizes, stealing the words straight out of my mouth.

He glares at me like I'm insane when I demand him to keep going. Although he didn't place his foot on the brake, he did loosen his pressure on the gas pedal, slowing our pace.

"We don't have time. Fien's jet could taxi toward the runway at any moment." I can see the lights of a control tower just over the horizon. We're almost there. "I'll send someone back for her once Fien is safe."

"All right." Although he's agreeing with me, he isn't happy about my decision. He has a soft spot for battered women since his momma was one. His dad used to beat the living shit out of his mother. Discovering the reason for her many bruises saw him facing his first stint in juvy at fifteen. His second was for his father's murder. I loaded the gun and handed it to him. He took care of business how I should have done with my father years ago. Regretfully, my surname means there are rules I must follow. Back then, Rocco didn't face the same issue.

With Rocco's jaw as tight as mine, he increases his pressure on the accelerator. The paintwork on my door gets friendly with the railing on the side of the road when he takes a wide birth around the stumbling blonde. I don't pay any attention to the brutal grind. I can't take my eyes of the one green eye popping out from a mattered mess of unbrushed locks when we whizz by the blonde.

I've seen that eye before—more than once.

"Stop!"

Rocco locks up the brakes so quickly, I'm winded when my ribs collide with the glove compartment. It'll teach me for not wearing a seat belt. Ophelia was killed when she was flung out of the windshield of CJ's ride. If she had been wearing her seat belt, she may have survived their accident.

With my mouth refusing to relinquish my words, it takes me a good three seconds to garble out, "Go back."

"Back?" Rocco double checks, not willing to risk death if he heard me wrong.

Although certain I'm making a mistake, I scream, "Yes! Now! Go!"

Rocco thrashes the living hell out of the Range Rover's engine after tossing the gearshift into reverse. We arrive at the bottom of the ramp in an instant, but the blonde is nowhere to be seen.

"Where the fuck is she?" My eyes go wild, seeking the reflection of her stark white hair. "We're the only people out this way. She couldn't have just up and vanished."

My eyes stray to Rocco when he mumbles, "Why go around if you go over."

When he spots the confusion on my face, he points to a section of the railing a few spots up from where we are. Bright red blood gleams off the silver material.

"Fuck." I throw open my door and sprint three solid strides to the portion of the blood-stained railing. My lungs react as if they ran a marathon when I spot the battered blonde at the bottom of the ravine. She's breathing, but only just. "Bring me a rope."

Nodding, Rocco pops open the back of the Range Rover before sliding out of the driver's seat. While he does as requested, I remove my suit jacket before rolling up the sleeves of my dress shirt.

I have one sleeve in place when Rocco arrives at my side with a used length of rope. How do I know it's been used? It's soaked with blood. Guns, knives, and Molotov cocktails aren't the Cartel's only source of weaponry. Everyday instruments can be just as useful in the right hands.

"Secure it to the railing."

I don't need to tell Rocco what knot to use. He knows all the tricks of this life, so he's more than aware the last thing you want is for a rope to snap when your boss sentences a man to be hung.

"I'll go," Rocco suggests when I wrap the loose end of the rope around my wrist so it can support my scale down the gorge. I don't need it to keep me safe, but it will come in handy to hoist the blonde out of the ravine.

Although appreciative of Rocco's offer, I shake my head. "I want to do this." I don't know why, and I'm reasonably sure I'll regret it at some stage in the near future, but I want to do this.

Rocco nods for the second time before he steps back, so I can swing my leg over the railing. It's slippery because of the recent rainfall, but I make it down the gorge relatively fast.

"Bring the car back around to the freeway. It'll be quicker to walk her out than pull her out," I shout after surveying the area. "I can see the interstate from here. It's about the same distance as the height of the gorge."

I wait for the lights of the Range Rover to disappear from above before kneeling at the blonde's side. A massive crack splits her head from the top of her skull to the middle of her forehead, she has a number of bruises and scrapes on her arms and torso, and her legs are all types of fucked up. The only part of her that looks untouched is her midsection, so that's what I toss onto my shoulder before hot-footing it in the direction I requested Rocco to meet me at.

The blonde grunts and groans with every step I thump, but it's better than her being silent. Silent would mean she's dead. Although she'd probably wish for that to be the case if I lose my daughter for the second time.

Rocco cranks open the back passenger side door. "Is she alive?"

"Just." I place her onto the back seat of the Range Rover as gently as possible before slipping in next to her.

When Rocco slides behind the steering wheel, I scream for him to go. I'm in two minds, torn between wanting to assess the blonde for injuries and causing her more harm.

Because I acted on impulse instead of the cruelness I was raised by, I wasted precious minutes I don't have—minutes that could have Fien torn away from me forever.

As Rocco races us back up the exit ramp, he strays his eyes to the rearview mirror. "Wrap your belt around her thigh. If the blood squirting out of her wound is a femoral artery, she'll bleed out in minutes. Trust me when I say no amount of scrubbing will remove her blood from your interior if you let that happen."

Under different circumstances, his murderous gleam would be entertaining.

Tonight, it's anything but.

While yanking my belt through the loopholes of my trousers, I hear my phone buzz. Naturally, I search my pockets.

It isn't there.

It's nowhere to be found.

I return Rocco's uneased gaze when he tosses my phone into my lap. "You left it in your suit jacket." I haven't been without my phone for a second over the past twelve months. Not once. It's my only form of contact with the people holding my daughter captive. I don't do anything without it being on me. Not a single fucking thing—*except this.*

Pissed at the fool I'm portraying tonight, I cinch my belt around the blonde's leg with more force than needed. Blood stops oozing out of the gash in her thigh, but she barely rouses. From experience, I can tell you her chances of surviving are low. When you stop feeling pain, you soon stop feeling anything.

Guilt for hurting her leaves when I read the message Smith sent. Fien's jet is taxiing toward the runway. My daughter is about to leave the state if not the country.

"Hurry the fuck up, Rocco."

Hearing the desperation in my voice, he mounts the curb edging the entrance of the private airstrip and drives through the steel security fence instead of going around it. While he creates his own path over rugged, sandy plains, I signal for Clover to move. It's fucked I have to warn him what will happen if he kills my daughter, but I'd rather him be cautious than go in bombs blazing like he usually does.

The scene replicates a stunt movie when our bumpy ride switches to a smooth one. We're at the far end of the runway. The jet is heading straight for us.

If playing chicken with twelve thousand pounds of metal isn't adventurous enough for you, you could always join Clover on the wheel of the jet. He's hanging on like a real-life action figure, unconcerned about the speed the jet picks up the further it careens down the runway.

"What's he placing on the jet?" I scream down comms when the placement of a metal box on the underbelly of the twelve-seater plane is quickly chased by Clover's huge ass rolling across the asphalt. This is usually when I'd plug my ears in preparation for a massive blast. He's a detonation expert as much as he is an assassin.

My heart stops punishing my ribcage when Smith's gruff tone barrels out of my phone's speaker. "Tracking device. Depending on the length of travel Rimi is planning to do, it may hold on."

Even though he can't see me, I jerk up my chin, understanding his objective.

Although I'd give anything to be handed a few minutes to

deliberate, things are progressing too quickly for that. I have to once again act on impulse.

Fingers crossed it works in Fien's favor as it did the blonde's.

"What will happen if I shoot out the window of the jet?"

Fingers fly over a keyboard before Smith replies, "On the ground, nothing much. No guarantees on her staying in the air if she takes off, though. All aircraft have holes in them, and the pressurized system is capable of taking an additional one or two, but if you blow out the window…"

When his words trail off, I fill in the gap, "I could kill Fien?"

"Possibly." He sucks in a big breath before continuing, "It's like all aspects of life, Dimitri, you either take a risk and hope you don't fail or sit back and let someone else control your life." Even aware his comment was more a personal reflection on his life than our current situation, it still hits me square in the stomach. First, I let my father puppeteer my life, and now I'm letting a weasel of a man like Rimi Castro get the better of me.

This needs to stop.

"Pull over."

Proof Rocco was born for this life is exposed when he yanks up the parking brake before he tugs on the steering wheel. He brings the Range Rover to a dead stop parallel with the jet still whizzing down the runway.

After grabbing an M16 stuffed behind the seat, I throw open my door, then climb onto the roof of the Range Rover. I'm not surprised when my glare down the scope has me stumbling on Rimi Castro in the pilot seat. He doesn't trust anyone, not even a qualified pilot. That's why he does everything himself.

I'm kind of the same, not that I'd ever admit that to anyone, especially not my enemy.

My target is locked and loaded, my finger is hovering over the trigger, but no matter how much my brain screams for me to fire, I can't. Firing at a moving target takes skill and precision. I have both of those, but what if Rimi pulls Fien into the line of fire a nanosecond after I take my shot? What if I kill her like my father killed my mother? He may not have fired at her, but he did use her as a shield. He *is* the reason she's dead.

"Five," Rocco commences counting down a short time later, warning me that the jet will be in the air by the time he reaches zero.

"Four…"

I recheck my scope before wetting my lips, my mouth suddenly bone-dry.

"Three…"

While inching back the trigger until the clip is close to releasing a bullet, I suck in a final breath. It could very well be my last if my shot shatters the cockpit's window, and Rimi still takes off. He's stupid like that. He'd rather die in a fiery wreck than give in.

"Two…"

The vibrations of the jet's engines overtake the shrill of my pulse in my ears.

"One…"

I take my shot.

My bullet perforates through the cockpit's windshield exactly where aimed, but I fail to hit my target. Rimi slanted his head with barely a second to spare. His life was saved by less than a millimeter, and I'm too late to take a second shot. The plane's wheels are no longer on the runway. They're zooming past my head.

When the jet disappears into the moonlit sky, I discharge the remainder of the bullets from the M16 into the tarmac. Several of them lodge deep into the blistering surface, however a handful ping off the rigid material, coating both my car and face with shrapnel.

The one that skims my cheek enough to scold my skin all but obliterates my last nerve. I'm fuming with anger and willing to take it out on anyone I deem responsible for the loss of my daughter for the second time in my life.

Seemingly having a sixth sense to my inner psyche, Rocco places himself between the back passenger door of the Range Rover and me when I leap down from the roof. "This isn't her fault."

"How is this not her fault? If we didn't stop to pick her up, Fien would be here!"

It's clear he has no desire to live when he replies, "Carrying her out of the gulley took about the same amount of time for you to line up your shot. If you want to shift the blame here, Dimi, you're gonna need to look in the mirror."

He smiles like a sadistic fuck when I dig the barrel of the colt under his ribs. I slant my gun upward, so it's facing his heart before getting to within an inch of his face.

Most men would piss their pants by now. Rocco isn't my number two for no reason. "You gonna shoot me, Dimi? You gonna gun down the only man whose *always* had your back?" He brings his face even closer to mine. "Who stood at your side when you buried Ophelia? Who helped you search for Roberto when he disappeared? Who has offered time and time again to pop bullets into your father's stomach because you can't?" The disappointment flaring through his eyes is as obvious as mine. "That was all me, D. Every fucking one of them was me. But if you want to kill me, go ahead because you ain't touching that girl."

"I need to kill." I can't put it simpler than I just did. The urge is so white-hot, it's burning me up on the inside even more than the truth of Rocco's statement. If I don't kill someone, I'll turn the gun on myself. That wouldn't just end things badly for me, it would leave Fien defenseless. The only time women in the industry are seen as valuable is when their womb is ripe with the next leader of the Cartel. Fien is years away from that age. If I die, she dies. There are no guarantees in my life *but* that.

"You can't have Rimi yet, so why not go after the next best thing?" My brows inch together when Rocco takes a step to the right, unblocking the visual of the almost unconscious blonde. Even with the roar of a private jet's engines barreling over her head and the discharge of a semi-automatic weapon, she's still out cold. "She didn't get banged up like that for no reason. Whoever did that to her is the person you should be taking your anger out on. She wouldn't have needed rescuing if someone hadn't fucked her over."

As my lips itch into a callous smirk, I snag my cell phone out of the Range Rover. "Smith..." Adrenaline thickens my veins when he hums a second later. "Do you have a spare laptop at the ready?"

The crack of a laptop screen being pried open sounds down the line before Smith asks, "What do you need?"

Rocco's grin matches mine when I say, "It's time to go on a scavenger hunt," but it sags when I add, "*After* we've dumped her far from here."

What I said earlier is true. Women are worthless in this industry, so I wouldn't do myself any favors adding another one into the mix. If the reports blowing up my phone are a true indication of how Justine encountered the Gauntlet, the nicest thing I could ever do for this unknown blonde is wipe the slate clean for her so she can start afresh.

If that means I have to remove *everyone* from her life, so be it. I'll do that. I'll do anything to ease the guilt tearing me up from the inside out.

Chapter Eight

Roxanne

My stomach swirls as violently as my temples thump my skull when I attempt to open my eyes. I don't know how long I've been out for, but if the dryness of my throat is anything to go by, I haven't had a drink in a thousand years. My mouth is bone-dry. I can't even conjure up the slightest bit of spit to moisten the burn of my swallows.

"Eddie…" That's the last thing I remember—paying for tickets to a stupid action flick Eddie wanted to see. If the price tag on the flowers wasn't a jarring enough reminder that we have hardly anything in common, his choice in movies should have been the icing on the cake.

Alas, I'm a sucker for his sweetly intense brown eyes.

Did I fall asleep during the movie? That could explain why my body is aching so much. The new theater complexes aren't as spacious as the out-of-date one in our hometown, and I couldn't afford premium tickets, so perhaps I'm kinked up because of the rigidness of the chairs in the theaters?

"Or not," I mutter to myself when I attempt to ease the throbbing of my temples with a quick swirl of my fingertips. My wrist is cuffed to a steel railing. I'm shackled to a bed like a convict at the start of the movie we watched.

"They said you murdered someone," whispers a shy, frail voice next to me. "That you cut him up into little pieces because he hurt you." After switching on the light hanging over her bed, a petite brunette with sunken, blood-stained cheeks and black eyes rolls over to face me. "Is it true? Did you kill him because he did that?"

"Did what?" I ask, truly confused.

My heart pains for her when she leans over to open a drawer next to her hospital bed. Her face isn't the only thing beaten up, so are her arms and torso.

"Who hurt you?" I ask when she hands me a compact mirror.

She tugs her nightwear in close to her body to hide her many bruises before lowering her eyes to her shoeless feet. "No one. I'm very clumsy. I often fall."

I want to reply, *headfirst into a fist by the looks of it*, but I keep my mouth shut. I'm not one to judge. I look just as bad as her, except my cuts and bruises can't be hidden with makeup. I'd need to grind out the stitches and staples running down my forehead first, and even then, I doubt the world's highest-rated concealer would help.

The only good to come from my battered and bloody appearance is the knowledge I can stop bleaching my hair. Its natural red coloring doesn't seem as bad as it did when I was a child. It gives me a unique edge not many women have.

It also may be the only way I can take the focus off the scar running down my forehead.

While licking my lips to soothe their deep cracks, I toss the compact back to the brunette's side of our room. I'd walk it over to her like she did me, but since I'm cuffed to my bed, I can't.

With that in mind, I ask, "If I'm so dangerous, why do I have a roommate?"

Her blue eyes widen to the size of saucers. "Umm…"

When she forcefully swallows, the truth smacks into me hard and fast. "We're not in a standard hospital room, are we?"

She only shakes her head for a second, but it's long enough for me to deserve the title of a mental patient. I scream like I'm in the process of being murdered while thrashing against the cuffs like I'll have the strength to break out of them. I don't. I'm too weak and pathetic for that, but my many pledges that I'm not insane does allow some clarity to form.

"We're not in a mental hospital," the brunette assures, pacing back to my side of the room. "We're in a special wing of a hospital. A *guarded* wing." Her next set of words take her nearly ten seconds to articulate. "It's where they put criminals awaiting trial."

"I'm not a criminal…" I stop talking when the first part of our conversation replays in my ears.

'They said you murdered someone.'

'That you cut him up into little pieces because he hurt you.'

"Who died?" I'm shocked I can talk with how hard fear is clutching my throat. Surely, I'm dreaming. This can't be real.

The brunette rushes a spew bag to my side of our room when her reply makes me heave. She didn't say any random old name. She said my boyfriend's name—his *full* name. Eduardo Emanuel Cordova.

"I didn't kill Eddie. I'd *never* hurt him," I blubber out through violent sobs. "I loved him…" My words fall short when the deceit in my tone reaches my ears. I cared for Eddie, but it was nothing close to love.

I raise my watering eyes to the mystery brunette. "What happened?" When she drags over a chair, preparing to settle in for the long haul, I ask a second almost just as important question, "And why am I the only one cuffed?"

Chapter Nine

Roxanne

Who knew straight-up murder rates higher than a measly manslaughter charge? My ex-roommate drove her car headfirst into a cypress tree with her abusive boyfriend in the passenger seat, however she only faced a manslaughter charge. I was 'allegedly' rundown by my boyfriend before being run over by him. Then, miraculously, I somehow got myself to his apartment two towns over from where I was left to die to, I quote, "Torture the complainant over a six-hour period." End quote.

Six. Hours.

That was the hole in my defense that had me transferred from the criminal wing of Erkinsvale Private Hospital to a standard ward. I was found in an ambulance bay by a medic going out to have a cigarette a little after one in the morning. Surveillance footage from my assault proves it occurred just after dusk. Despite wishing I was able to torture Eddie for six hours, it wasn't possible for me to be in two places at once, hence the reason my charges were dropped.

Do I feel bad about what happened to Eddie? Yeah, in a way. I'm more remorseful for his family than him. They have nothing going for them and will most likely never get off welfare, but they didn't deserve to lose their son the way they did.

I reached out to them a couple of weeks ago to offer my sympathies. When I got an automated message saying their number is no longer in service, I sent them a letter instead. Having their services cut is nothing out of the ordinary for the Cordovas.

"Are you ready?"

Ignoring the apprehension swishing in my stomach, I raise my eyes to my rock the past three months. My best friend, Estelle, grew up in the housing estate next to my nanna's ranch. With my grandparents refusing to sell no matter how elaborate the offer, housing developments popped up all around them. Now they have the only ten-acre block left in this area of Erkinsvale.

The executor in charge of my grandparents' will said I could make an impressive profit if I were willing to sell their decades of hard work. Sadly for him and his commission-seeking cousin, I missed my nanna's funeral because I was in a coma, so the last thing I'll ever do is see her legacy bulldozed.

She loved and took care of me when no one else would. Then she died alone.

I can't forgive myself for that.

The injuries that placed me in a coma for a month weren't my fault, but I do blame them for my nanna's death. She had told me time and time again that Eddie was no good. If I had listened, she wouldn't have been out searching for me when I failed to make curfew, and then she wouldn't have been knocked down a ravine by a drunk driver.

Mistaking my remorseful face as sympathy for Eddie, Estelle says, "Don't look so glum, Roxie. You survived for a reason." I roll my eyes when she chuckles out, "We just need to find out why that is." That's just like her. Even when we should be blowing snot bubbles out of our nose while in the throes of despair, she finds humor in every situation.

When I take a right out of the hospital room I've called my home the past three months, Estelle wraps her arm around my shoulders. "Nu-uh. Claudia isn't there anymore, remember?"

My sigh is soundless, but Estelle still hears it. My ex-roommate wasn't as lucky as me. Even with numerous witnesses saying they saw Claudia's boyfriend's hand on the steering wheel in the lead up to their crash, prosecutors pushed forward with their case. Claudia will give birth to her son in prison since she was served three years for involuntary manslaughter last week.

"We could visit her next weekend?"

I raise my eyes to my best friend, loving that she can read me like no one else. "Yeah?"

She bumps me with her hip, causing me to smile. "Yeah. You know me, always open for a three-hour drive to a maximum-security women's prison."

"How could you not when you say it like that?"

Laughing, she breaks away from my side to open the passenger side door of her beat-up Honda for me. Her car is a total write-off, but she loves it as much as she loves me. Nothing screams freedom like your own set of wheels. I'm hoping to scrounge up enough money for my own sometime this year.

"Your chariot awaits, m'lady," she says, all pompous like.

Giggling about my immature tongue poke, Estelle races around to the driver's side door. Because I forever admire her animalist grace, my eyes follow her trek partway around. My stare is incomplete because I'm looking at a pimped-out Range Rover parked across from the passenger loading bay. It's not often you see flashy cars like that in Erkinsvale, and very rarely is there a pair of piercing green eyes glancing out of the crack in the driver's side window.

"Roxie…" Estelle stammers out in confusion when I hotfoot it across the street without checking for traffic.

I almost get wiped out by a car traveling in the opposite direction. The whoosh of its outdated metal whizzing past my face is strong enough to add an extra hobble to my shaking strides, but it isn't to slow me down.

"Hey." I race faster when the engine of the Range Rover fires up. "Wait!"

It darts out of its parking space so quickly, the smell of burning rubber lingers in my nostrils long after it rockets out of the hospital's parking lot.

"Who the hell was that?" Estelle asks, out of breath. She isn't gasping because she followed my sprint. She runs miles every single day. She's as breathless about the eerie unease ridding the air of oxygen as me.

There's only one time I've felt this restless. It was when I was in the alleyway with Eddie. Not the time he ran me over, but three months earlier, when he brought me to ecstasy under the watchful stare of a pair of vividly beautiful blue eyes.

The pair that just rocketed away were nowhere near as entrancing as the ones that stared at me almost seven months ago today, but they were most certainly just as dangerous.

The knowledge shouldn't excite me, but for some reason, it does.

Chapter Ten

Dimitri

When Rocco places down his phone to make a quick getaway, I drag the timer on his live feed back a couple of seconds. I don't want the image of Roxanne Juniper Grace when she spotted Rocco's gawk half a block down from her apartment building, I want her reflection in the side mirror of the Range Rover Rocco's manning at my command when she chases him down like she did outside the hospital three months ago. The second in time when her big green eyes are wide and unconcealed.

Restless edginess thickens my cock when I find the footage I'm seeking, which is utterly ridiculous considering I'm in a boardroom with thirty of my father's closest confidants. He believes I'm in Sicily strengthening foreign ties. I'm here because it's the last confirmed place the tracker on Rimi's private jet was pinged. The Castros are either here, holed up at an unknown location, waiting for the heat to die down after their operation killed thirteen FBI agents and two CIA officers, or they took a secondary jet to another location.

Rimi's crew has been silent for over six months now—double the length of time Roxanne was an inpatient at Erkinsvale Private Hospital. I don't fucking like it. A ransom payment for Fien hasn't been requested in months. That makes me edgy because if I'm not paying to keep her safe, how can I be assured she is?

Although I understand the reasoning for the silence—Rimi now has both sides of the law chasing him—usually nothing stops business from progressing in this industry. Not even having my wife kidnapped and my daughter forcefully removed from her stomach saw me awarded any leeway. I work or die. I don't have any other option, so why isn't it the same for Rimi?

After grinding my jaw side to side, frustrated by the world I was born in, I restart the live feed just as Rocco's face fills the screen of my phone. "Satisfied?" he asks, sounding anything but.

Even with the eyes of thirty men on me, impatiently awaiting my verdict, I jerk up my chin. I don't know why I needed to see Roxanne move into a tiny one-bedroom apartment in the middle of Erkinsvale anymore than I needed to watch her walk out of the hospital three months ago, but for some reason, the urge wouldn't pass no matter how hard I fought it, so I gave in and let fate play its hand for once.

Will my indecisiveness see me scolded for the third time in my life?

Only time will tell.

"What now?" Rocco mutters, aware one task never ends without another one taking its place.

Hummed whispers bounce around the room when I reply, "Organize the jet to collect me. It's time for me to return home."

The sternness of my jaw doubles when Rocco mutters, "For your girl?"

His smile tells me his comment had nothing to do with my daughter, but I act stupid. "If you're referencing Fien, yes."

"What?" He pushes out a few seconds later, incapable of ignoring the wrath of my glare for a second longer. I've always been a temperamental prick with a short fuse, but it's grown substantially worse over the past six months. "You've had me stalking that girl for months. Justine's recovery didn't even get this much heat, and you take the blame for what happened to her."

I didn't think my mood could get any worse, however it just did. My father's verdict for Justine's 'supposed' disrespect was an hour in a room with a dog trained to kill. Maddox moved fast after I called him, but he was still minutes too late. Justine was torn to shreds.

I asked Rocco to keep me updated on the progress of her recovery. That surveillance wasn't as easy for him to conduct as it was Roxanne's because Justine has an army of people propping her up. Roxanne has no one. From what Smith tells me, her parents are alive, but she hasn't seen them in years. Her grandfather passed away a year before her grandmother, and she has no known siblings.

Do I feel sorry for her? Not. At. All. There are far worst things she could have faced than being forced to live with her grandparents. Her daddy could have sold her to his friends for the night like he has her mother multiple times when his drug supplies get low.

If a man pays to fuck you, he'll take it with or without your permission. Nearly every man around this table has done so in the past. The sex slave industry is rife at the moment. It's right up there with baby-making factories.

That's what my meeting today is about. A new baby-making facility is hoping to place footholds in the Sicily region. They want to take sex slaves, impregnate them, then sell their babies to the highest bidder.

Although this scheme isn't close to my predicament, I can't help but source similarities from it. Fien wasn't sold to the highest bidder, but is that because I can afford to keep her safe? What would happen if that changed? Would she be passed on to the next candidate? Or killed like her mother?

Just the thought has my mood souring to the lowest it's been. "Organize a meeting with my father within hours of my return," I say down the line after standing to my feet, hopeful the table's height will hide the raging pulse of my cock not even a bad mood could slacken. "I have some questions I'd like to ask him."

Rocco scrubs at the stubble on his chin. "I don't think it's wise to mingle with him right now, Dimi. He's knee-deep in some murky shit."

"Murkier than this?" His silence speaks volumes. The only time Rocco is ever quiet is when I'm right. If I'm wrong, he shouts it from the rooftops. "Although the journey to my takeover is miles away, at one stage, I must take the first step. That time is now, Rocco."

Since all is said and done, I disconnect our video chat, shut down my phone, then slide it into the pocket of my trousers. Despite the brief intermission, today is all about business, so I'm dressed to the nines—expensive suit, designer tie, diamond-encrusted cufflinks. If you didn't know any better, you could confuse me with a legitimate businessman. It's just the crooked people I'm forced to deal with day in and day out that would have you thinking differently.

"I gave your business proposal my utmost devotion the past week. The figures cited are impressive considering the lack of capital needed, and it appears as if you have infrastructure and clientele at the ready." The faces of the men seated around me gleam with hope, optimistic I'm about to approve their baby-making facility. "But…" I wait to ensure they have plenty of time to absorb the snip of annoyance in my tone before continuing, "Operations like this don't sit well with me. I want to drag my family's name out of the mud, not smear it with more dirt."

"But Dimitri, your father—"

"Lost the ability to make decisions for this sanction many moons ago," I interrupt, equally frustrated and shocked someone had the gall to speak against me. The day you lose respect in this industry is the day you retire.

I don't mean to an old folks home. I mean *eternal* retirement.

When my eyes stray to my contester, the reasoning behind his boldness becomes apparent. Cristo is one of my father's longest-known associates. He practically ran this chapter of Italy before I arrived. He didn't like handing over the reins, but he didn't have much choice. Names open doors in this industry, not decades of service.

"I said no—"

My nostrils flare to suck in a quick breath when Cristo defies me for the second time. "Your father approved our tender. Today's meeting is merely to tie up loose ends…" His arrogant words are gobbled up by a big swallow when I nudge my head an inch to the right, wordlessly demanding for Clover to move to his side of the room. Clover won't kill him. He'll just linger nearby in case he needs to muzzle his mouth. I'd hate for his throaty gargles to frighten his employees.

More times than not, a bullet to the head instantly kills you, but there are a handful of occasions where the bullet doesn't traverse through the midsection of the brain, leaving the victim gurgling on their blood for a good three or so minutes. It's rare but possible to survive a bullet wound to the head. I've seen it twice in my lifetime.

My lips twist when Cristo goes down without the slightest snivel. I wouldn't have minded hearing him sob. He was an arrogant prick who should have been taken out with the trash decades ago.

With my gun still hot from being recently fired, I place it on the tabletop along with my palms before roaming my eyes over the group of men staring at me with an equal amount of fear and respect. "This chapter is being placed into involuntary administration. You either let it die quietly or take the exit Cristo just took. The choice is yours."

Almost all of them hum out a collective agreement that I've made the right choice, but a handful aren't as eager as the rest. They're the ones I mentally jot down for execution, unforgiving that they could have wives and children relying on their 'income' to keep them feed.

Someone will hand their wives a few thousand at their funerals for food and expenses. By the time the money runs out, they'll have a new 'man' taking care of them. That's how fast things move in this industry.

"Luca, Davis, Porter, and Michel, you're free to go. The rest of you, place dinner orders with Gia. You're in for a long night." A ghost of a smile touches my lips when I drift my eyes to Clover. "Perhaps you can show our unneeded guests the way out?"

The deadly gleam in Clover's eyes reveals he understands what I'm asking—none of the four men named above will be breathing by the end of tonight—so I don't need to mention the hearty swallow they do when Clover opens the boardroom door for them. A paid killer only opens the door for you when he's planning to knife you in the back.

With Clover's mood appearing as tense as mine, I don't see

the men's deaths being handled quickly. If that's the case, I might join him later. Excluding Cristo's quick, unsatisfied kill mere seconds ago, I haven't witnessed the weakening of a man's pulse since I sentenced Eduardo Emanuel Cordova to death for his crimes.

Rocco and I took our time with Eduardo. His murder was more satisfying than Cristo's, especially when he cried while begging for his life to be spared, but it could have been better. He could have pleaded for forgiveness for what he had done to Roxanne instead of begging for his own pathetic life. We might have gone a little easier on him if he had shown an ounce of remorse. Alas, even bottom-dwellers think their lives are worth more than their female counterparts.

That's why my daughter was taken and my wife was killed, and it is the very reason I'm not leaving this boardroom until I find out exactly how deep my father's ties are with already established baby-making facilities.

I've wondered for months if my family had anything to do with Audrey's disappearance. Tonight I will find out. You can put your money on it.

Chapter Eleven

Roxanne

My race into the living room of the one-bedroom apartment I share with Estelle slows when I spot how she's celebrating Thanksgiving holiday weekend with her new beau. Braydon has her pushed up against a wall our tiny television doesn't come close to filling. Estelle's dress is wrapped around her midsection, and Braydon's hands are hidden in an area I'm going to act like I never saw.

They're creating their own things to be grateful for, and I'm insanely jealous.

Who doesn't want a hot, brooding man to pin them to the wall like they're not slumming it in an apartment that would only look more authentic if it were in the Bronx? A mattress would make things better, but since the only one in this apartment belongs to me, I'd rather they keep their hip-thrusting to the living room. I can sterilize a wall with a little disinfectant. I can't afford to steam clean an entire mattress.

"Wish me luck?"

When Estelle's lips drag away from Braydon's, mine pucker into an air kiss. I can't get mad about her getting freaky in our living room. She lost the only room in our dingy apartment in a rigged game of rock paper scissors—she always picks rock, by the way—and although I would have the means to rent something fancier if I were willing to sell my grandparents' ranch, Estelle has never once given me grief about that. As far as I'm concerned, that means Braydon could go down on her right now, and I wouldn't bat an eyelid. Our friendship is solid, and I don't see anything ever coming between it.

Despite Estelle being my rock, I've been in somewhat of a rut the last twelve months. I was the only witness to a murder, run over by my boyfriend, and accused of his murder. To say it's been shit is an understatement, but that is all set to change today. I have a job interview—finally!

A year of online courses and many *many* hours of free labor has been reduced to this. A permanent part-time position at a company I've never heard about in a town forty miles from here.

It could be worse. I could have been shortlisted for the position at the old folks' home. Even someone without a college degree knows that's a last resort for any twenty-year-old. I understand if you can't wipe your bottom anymore, someone has to do it for you. I'd just rather that someone not be me.

Estelle smiles a blistering grin when I whine, "I really hope Dimitri isn't as old as dirt. Momma needs some new pretties, but graveyard ready isn't the vibe I'm aiming for."

"Even if he's as fugly as Mr. Mugly, you're gonna get down on your knees and peer up at him with your pretty green eyes out in full force. This is the opportunity you've been waiting for, and it's offering thirty-five dollars an hour." Estelle exhales with a pompous flare. "I'd fiddle with a shriveled-up chunk of shrimp for thirty-five dollars an hour!" After winking off Braydon's stink-eye like it doesn't hold any steam, she meets her eyes with mine. The humor glistening in them exposes her dramatic performance was more to ruffle Braydon's feathers than mine, but it does little to hide her worry. "Are you sure you don't want me to come with you? I can sell ice to an Eskimo, so a college dropout with a partial credit for a double business diploma will be a walk in the park."

Although she can sell meat to a vegetarian, and I whole-heartedly appreciate her offer, I shake my head. "My interview is in Hopeton, and you're rostered on to work a double tonight. Our schedules are a no-go."

"Hold up, go back," Braydon interrupts, talking through his kiss-swollen lips. "You're going to Hopeton for an interview with a man named Dimitri?"

Nodding, I snag my purse off the kitchen counter before joining them in the living room. Our apartment isn't a loft. It just feels like one since it's so tiny. "Have you heard of him?"

"Have I heard of him! My God, Roxie, did your mama drop you on your head?" He grunts like his words jab his heart instead of mine. Even if every word he speaks is true, being truly, madly, and deeply in love won't stop Estelle from punishing him for talking down to me. Dropping me on my head would have been a kind thing for my mother to do to me. Estelle knows that, and now, so does Braydon.

After issuing his apologies to Estelle with only his eyes, Braydon shifts them to me. They're riddled with unwarranted guilt. "I'll come with you."

"No, Braydon, it's fine. You've got… *Estelle* to take care of." That was close. I almost reminded him he has nothing but a substantial inheritance to worry about. That wouldn't have been very nice considering he's not once shoved his money into my face.

I've reminded myself time and time again the past few months that he isn't one of the rich snobs I tussled with when trying to have my scholarship reinstated after my 'accident.' He's down-to-earth and kind, and on more than one occasion, he's offered for me to be his personal assistant even with him having nothing for me to do.

If life were about money, I'd accept his offer in an instant. Alas, I wasn't born fighting for no reason.

"Estelle has a double shift tonight, so I'd rather you ensure she gets home safely than worry about me. Hopeton is danger-ous, but it's safer than here."

Confident I have Braydon's worry honing in on another target, I snatch up my house key before hightailing it to the door.

"We'll talk about this more tomorrow," Estelle shouts through our rapidly closing front door.

By 'this,' she means me plopping her in the deep end without a life raft. It was deplorable for me to do, but what can I say? If an opportunity presents to shift the focus away from me, I'm happy to take it.

"The agreed price was forty-dollars." I thrust my iPhone toward the Uber driver's side of his car to show him our agree-ment. "We're still miles from Hopeton."

He shrugs like it isn't a big deal he's asking me to exit his car three miles out of town while wearing heels. It's chilly, and since his heating is as shitty as his personality, my toes are on the verge of snapping off.

"I didn't anticipate the traffic in Ravenshoe to be so thick."

"How is that my fault?" I argue back, beyond annoyed.

I didn't factor in traffic either since I've never driven through the town that was nothing but cornfields when I was a child. If I had, I would have scheduled for him to arrive an hour earlier. Not only am I late for my interview, if I'm forced to walk, the business I'm being interviewed at will be closed by the time I get there. The sun is already setting.

I fan the bangs I had cut specifically to hide the horrid scare on my forehead before issuing one final plea. "Please, Mr. Kind Driver Man. I'll do anything you want if you'll take me to my requested destination. I've got a few nickels in the bottom of my purse." I yank out the Starbucks voucher I got for my birthday last year. "This gift card still has eight dollars on it. That'll get you're a super frothy mocha latte. And…" I search my almost empty purse for something more appetizing than year-old mints and lint balls. When I fail to find anything, I say, "We could grab that latte together? If you want?"

I instantly regret my decision when lust flares through the stranger's dark eyes. I don't know where he grew up—which I'm guessing took place over five decades ago with how gray his ear hairs are—but inviting someone for coffee means you're *only* inviting them for coffee. This isn't Vegas.

While throwing open his back passenger door with a grunt, I snarl, "Say goodbye to your five-star rating, Mister. I'm going to one star your ass all the way to Uber headquarters."

I don't know what he replies. I can barely hear anything over the skid of his tires when his foot gets friendly with the gas pedal not even two seconds after I stepped out onto the road surface.

"And to think I was going to share my nanna's mints with you!"

I add a handful of expletives to my squeal before I commence my trek to Hopeton. I'll never make it in time for my interview, but Hopeton's bus station is closer than Ravenshoe's. My nickels might not have been on the Uber driver's radar, but I don't see a bus driver being as fussy. If he's lucky, I might even arrive on the scene with a super frothy latte for him.

Three painstaking miles later, I'm on the verge of deliriousness. My legs are quaking like they *never* have under any of my college boyfriends, and my mouth is bone-dry, but I've made it to my destination. Shockingly, the establishment my interview was to be conducted at is still open. It probably helps that it's an Italian restaurant bursting at the seams with clientele eager to get something more than overcooked turkey in their bellies, and it has the same last name as the man seeking a personal assistant. *Perfect!*

After twisting the Celtic ring on my thumb, so it faces the front, I throw open the door of Petretti's Italian Restaurant and make a beeline for the dining hostess. "Hi, my name is Roxanne Grace, and I'm here to see——"

"Booth or regular seating?"

I stray my eyes over the blonde's teeny tiny uniform and popping blue eyes before replying, "Excuse me?"

"Booth or regular seating?" she says again while dragging her eyes down my body in the same manner I just did hers. "Even if you're eating alone, I'd still suggest the booth. It'll save the clientele getting depressed when they see you eating by yourself on Thanksgiving weekend."

Ouch.

"I'm not here to eat."

She cocks a faultless brow. "Then why are you here? This is a restaurant."

Her pitied glare doubles my annoyance. "I'm aware it's a restaurant. I can read." *Unlike you.* "I'm here for an interview." I dig out the piece of paper I jotted my interview details on this morning before thrusting it the blonde's way. "I'm supposed to ask for Dimitri."

"You're here for Dimitri?" When I nod, her humored gaze extends to her collagen-filled lips. "Trust me, honey, excluding your hair coloring, you're not his type. One sideways glance, and he'll kick you to the curb. Save the bruise, leave now." She ushers me away from her podium with a wave of her hand like I'm worthless.

I'm not backing down this time. It's been a hard and long twelve months for me, and this blonde is about to be hit with the brunt of my annoyance. "I don't care if I'm not Dimitri's type." I air quote my last word an inch from her face, issuing her the same *snap-snap* dismissal her nails did when she waved me off. "I'm here to be interviewed for a position on his team, so I'm not leaving until Dimitri himself tells me to leave."

I fold my arms in front of my chest to hide the shake of my hands when the blonde says, "Okay." I hadn't expected her to give in so easily. "Dimitri's office is at the back of the restaurant. You need to go down the side alley and take the third door on the left."

"Side alley, third door on the left?" I repeat like I'm suddenly stupid. When she purses her lips with an agreeing nod, I say, "Okay. Thank you."

I won't lie, I strut like Catwoman under Batman's watch while following the restaurant hostess's directions. I'll never be picked as the demurest woman in a room, but for how many times my ass has been kicked the past year, I'm taking tonight's triumph as a win. Even if I don't get the job, I'll feed off the adrenaline of my victory for weeks to come.

The quickest flashback of a pair of golden-brown eyes flashes before my eyes when I'm partway down the dark alleyway. The food scraps on the ground make it obvious the restaurant receives most of its deliveries here, but because of the late hour and the early closure of businesses due to Thanksgiving, it seems shadier and more obsolete.

"Third door on the right," I mumble to myself when I stop in front of one that has 'Distribution' etched on the door.

Believing there will be a less-shady entrance past the graffiti-coated door, I push it open with only the slightest creak. The décor isn't any more inviting on the inside. There's nothing but scary shadows dancing across the faces of four middle-aged men.

The scene grows more confronting when I notice who their attention is fixed on. They're honing in on a smaller, more timid-looking man huddled against an outer wall. His face is bleeding, and his hands are held out in front of himself in a non-defensive manner. He's clearly scared.

My throat dries when a lone soldier breaks away from the pack of hungry wolves. He speaks to the frightened man in a heavy accent, his tone both demoralizing and angry. "The service you ordered was delivered as specified, so not only am I refusing your request for a refund, I'm anticipating a subsequent payment for your insolence."

Even with my business diploma unfinished, I'm not so stupid to believe this is a distribution disagreement. I've heard rumors about a mob mentality in Hopeton, but I've previously brushed them off as hearsay. I can't do that this time around. My potential employer is getting fleeced—fleeced of money that could possibly come from my thirty-five dollar an hour salary.

With my veins still hot with adrenaline from my clash with the restaurant hostess, I conjure up a ruse that will see both Mr. Petretti and me leave this room uninjured. I should be scared, but seriously, what's the worst that could happen? The men I'm about to confront are pushing sixty, if not seventy. I survived being run over by a car, so I can most certainly handle a mobility scooter.

Confident I've got what it takes to divert disaster, I blurt out, "I've called the police. They'll be here at any moment." I didn't call anyone. My cell battery died 1.8 miles from Hopeton. I just want them as scared as Mr. Petretti. "If you don't want to be arrested, I suggest you leave right now."

My gall takes a step back when the man in the center of the group pulls a large black gun out of the back of his pants. I was prepared to face a handful of bruises from the whack of a walking cane, not a maiming bullet from a semi-automatic weapon. "Or perhaps I'll just take care of business now instead of later."

The minute snippet of air in my lungs races out with a scream when he cocks back the hammer on his gun before he squeezes the trigger. He doesn't just gun down the man he was in the process of shaking down. He blows off his entire face.

Certain I'm next on the maniac's hit list, I mumble out, "Never mind," before pivoting on my heels and darting away.

I make it three steps before a bullet whizzing past my ear stops me in my tracks. "The next one I'll aim at your head." Confident he has me scared enough I will do anything he asks, the lone soldier requests that I spin around. "I want to see your pretty face one final time before I blow it away."

After forcefully swallowing the bile racing up my throat, I do as requested. My knees weaken halfway around. The elderly gentlemen circling the now-faceless man aren't the only men in the room. There are another four in the far corner of the dark space. They're all wearing black and have guns much larger and more capable of hindering facial recognition in their hands.

They appear bored until the only man seated rises to his feet. Unlike his mean-looking counterparts, he starts his assessment of my body from my snap-frozen toes to my whitened face. He takes his time, seemingly storing every little detail for future use.

I wonder if he does that to all his victims, or am I special in some sick, twisted way?

My hand unintentionally moves to flatten my frizzed hair when the stranger's narrowed gaze shifts from my eyes to my hair. It's longer than I normally wear it, and back to its natural red color. Waking up in a hospital room cuffed to a bed changed me. I'm not as straight as an arrow, but I'm most certainly trying to improve myself.

Being 'me' was the very first step.

I drop my hand like it's a bomb when the dark-haired man pushes off his feet to cross the room. He has an arrogant walk full of cockiness and self-assuredness. It matches his persona, which is almost as suffocating as my lungs' inability to suck in air when he stops to stand in front of me.

Goosebumps rise across my skin when he raises his hand to my face. I'm anticipating for him to wipe away the blobs of wetness rolling down my cheeks, so you can imagine my shock when he merely brushes away the bangs I had cut to cover a scar no amount of concealer can hide.

The room is cloaked by darkness—in more ways than one —but I can tell the exact moment the ugliest of my past rears its horrid head. The dark-haired man's discovery of my two-inch scar screws up the face of the elderly man behind him. He looks sickened like I'm suddenly as ugly as I feel.

I'd rather his disgust over the gleam his eyes held when they first landed on my face. Even someone with the purity of a saint couldn't have mistaken the longing in his heavy-hooded gaze.

I glance over the stranger's shoulder when the man behind him says, "You seem to have caught the eye of my son. I'm not surprised. He has quite the fascination for redheads." The man I'm guessing to be mid-sixties places himself between his son and me. His strut is as vile as the amused smirk on his face. "Is she one of yours, son? A little plaything for the night?"

My throat aches to release a frustrated scream when the man whose eyes seem oddly familiar mutters, "I forgot I ordered her. What can I say? The schedule of women coming and going from my life every week often gets confusing."

Everyone laughs except me. I know he's lying, but I can't tell if that's a good or bad thing. He's a little hard for me to read. He seems to be protecting me, but there's an undeniable amount of anger radiating from him. It's as if he's torn between wanting to soothe my panic or double it.

I stop seeking answers in his beautifully tormented eyes when the man with the gun points it at my head. "Unfortunately, you'll have to find another plaything for the night. This one knows too much."

I shake my head, assuring him I know nothing. "I won't tell anyone what I saw." I shakily cross my heart. "I swear to God."

"God can't help you now." He smiles a grin you should only ever see in hell. "But be sure to tell him I said hello."

I don't breathe for a second when he curls his finger around the trigger for the second time. His expression is so impassive. He shows no emotion whatsoever.

I can't cite the same thing.

The lady at the makeup stand lied earlier today. The mascara I paid twenty-two dollars for isn't waterproof. I can't see my cheeks, but I can feel the big black smears rolling down them. They're mixed with the saltiness of my tears, but the chunkiness that comes from applying three generous coats of mascara is highly obvious.

I stormed in here feeling as brave as a soldier.

Now I'm on the verge of peeing my pants.

That makes me ashamed of myself.

"Do it. Kill me." I step up to the man until the barrel of his gun digs into a dress too thin for this time of year. It makes the shudders reeking with my body more apparent, but has me proud I won't die a coward. "Put me out of my misery once and for all."

"Do you want to die, little girl?" asks the man with a thick Italian accent.

"No," I answer with a shake of my head. "But I'm not going to beg for my life to be spared. That would have me dying a coward. I'd rather die than be seen as weak." My words are strong, however my composure is anything but. I'm shaking so much, the black blobs rolling down my face quiver in the panted breaths when they cling to my top lip.

"You should be happy you made it this far. Usually, I would have shot you in the back." He shrugs like killing is something he does every day before he raises his gun to my head. "A change-up is as good as a holiday. I can see your eyes now."

I'm at a loss as to what he means, but his son has no issues understanding him. He grabs the barrel of his gun in an instant, shocking me so much my eyes bulge. "Let me." His voice is extra deep like his cock is hard just from the thought of killing me. I'm not surprised. He seems like a man who gets off on danger. "It's my fault she's here, so it's my responsibility to clean up the mess." When his father hesitates, the stranger adds more authenticity to his assurance. "Then I can get my money's worth during our trip to the woods. I paid good money for her, so I plan to find out if she was worth her price tag."

His father smiles a wickedly evil grin that has my stomach flipping even with him weakening his clutch on the trigger of his gun. "I understand your interest. She has such a feisty spark." My chest labors through a challenging breath when he angles his torso to face his son. He isn't peering at him in a loving manner. It's as if their family has as many issues as mine. "She reminds me a lot of your wife." He assesses his son's face for a response. Like he's hopeful his words will hurt him. "Is that what has you so fascinated, son? Or are you looking for a cunt to keep your dick warm for the night? Or a replacement spouse?"

"A man has needs." Even not knowing the dark-haired man, I'm confident in saying he's exuding mammoth self-restraint. His dipping tone is indicating enough, much less how white his knuckles are. His hands are balled so tight, even if his father were to yank back the trigger, the bullet wouldn't make it through the barrel. That's how fierce his grip is. "I had them long before I married, and I still have them now." His eyes are deadly, tainted with hate. "Do you have an issue with that?"

The tension in the room turns roasting. It hisses and crackles in the air even more than the energy that teems through me when the gray-haired man lowers his gun two heart-thrashing seconds later. "Fine. Do with her what you may, but be sure to have it done by sun-up."

Vomit scorches my throat when he fills the gap his gun no longer takes up. I never understood the term 'skin-crawling' until now. My skin does precisely that when he runs the back of his hand down my mascara-stained cheeks. If there weren't so much evil in his eyes, I could have mistaken his gesture as kindness. It's almost gentle, in a psychotic, mass-murderer type of way.

"Just don't be too gentle with her. I want to hear all about her screams." He waits for his son to dip his chin before he sidesteps me and exits the gloomy room.

I think I'm clear of danger.

It was silly of me to ever believe.

The door has barely banged closed when a white cloth is pressed over my mouth and nose. The scent vaping off it bombards me with horrendous nausea in less than a nanosecond, and even quicker than that, I black out.

Chapter Twelve

Dimitri

I hold my finger in the air, cutting off the scorn I see in Rocco's eyes before he can deliver. My mood is teetering on the edge of a very steep cliff. I'm the most unhinged I've ever been. Now is *not* the time for him to lecture me. I know what I saw, I know who Roxanne is, and I plan to make sure she takes responsibility for the death of my wife.

I knew I had seen her mesmerizing green eyes before. The change in her hair coloring and the maturity of her looks threw me off the scent for over a year, but there's no denying them now.

Her mascara stained-face is undeniable.

When she stood across from me minutes ago, riling my father like he wouldn't gut her where she stood, it felt as if I had stepped back in time. I was once again entrapped by her beauty, stunned she could emanate such appeal on her darkest day.

Roxanne was the woman standing on the corner of the restaurant Audrey was kidnapped from. The woman I gawked at for so long, I didn't see my enemies creeping up on me until it was too late. She's the reason Audrey is dead and the cause of me not laying eyes on my daughter in person since she was born. Now she must pay the penance for her stupidity.

I just need my cock to get the memo first.

It's as hard now as it was when I watched her being fingered in the alleyway almost a year ago today, pulsating with an equal amount of desire and adrenaline. Its response can't be helped. Roxanne's paper-thin dress is pushed an inch above her tiny lace panties, and her thigh gap allows an uninterrupted view of a cunt I'm sure tastes delicious.

Although her eyes are shut due to the strength of the chloroform Clover used to subdue her, I don't need them to be open to know they're the same emerald green color of her dress. I've studied them multiple times the past nine months in the many surveillance images Rocco took of her. I know every speckle and every flaw.

I also know them well enough to know they'll never be the same once I'm done with her.

I can't believe it took me this long to place all the pieces of the puzzle together. She's always been there in the background of every scene. At the restaurant Audrey was taken from, in the alleyway when I instigated my ruse to make it appear as if I were moving on, and on the very ramp that led to the airstrip that ripped my daughter away from me for another nine long months. I just stupidly saw it as fate instead of the intricate ruse it is.

My father left Roxanne's punishment to me. He never does that. If he has the opportunity of watching the light in someone's eyes be snuffed, he's there with bells on.

This time around, he walked away.

That can only mean one thing. He doesn't believe I have what it takes to kill her.

I'm more than happy to prove him wrong.

Chapter Thirteen

Roxanne

I wake with a groan, the punishing pound of my temples as noticeable as it was when I woke up in a hospital room with life-threatening injuries several months ago.

Although my eyes have yet to follow the prompts of my brain, I am aware I'm in the backseat of an expensive ride and that my hands are bound behind my back with a thick, scratchy twine. The coolness of leather upholstery caressing the back assures me of this, much less the sickening drone of four tires rolling over asphalt. They churn over the road surface as intensely as my stomach wishes to expel the contents weighing it down.

I don't recall ever feeling this ill, and I've had some horrific hangovers. That's why I rarely drink anymore. I'm not one of the lucky ones who wake up the next day feeling fine. For every drink I have, it takes me four hours to recover. That wasn't a schedule I encouraged while endeavoring to keep my scholarship afloat.

Sadly, I haven't had to worry about that the past nine months, meaning I should have had more than my share of drunken benders.

I couldn't be 'me' if I were a drunk like my father.

My eyes sluggishly open in just enough time to see the shadows of a city on the horizon. We're surrounded by sandy plains and overgrown bushes—an ideal spot to dump a body.

As my throat dries with worry, I divert my focus to the vehicle churning out the miles despite the bad conditions. Instead of the middle row of seats in the large SUV facing forward, they've been fixed to a privacy partition shielding the driver from the main section of the cab.

The configuration of the cab ensures I have no trouble locking eyes with the dark-haired stranger when I raise them front and center. He sits across from me with a tight smile and balled fists. He doesn't need to tell me where we're going. I can reach my own conclusion. I told them I had called the police, so it makes sense they'd move my murder away from their business premise. No one will find me out here.

Well, except the vultures, and that's only if they make my grave shallow.

If my death is anything like Eddie's, there probably won't be much of me to bury.

I stop praying for a quick, painless death when an accented voice ripples through the air. "You shouldn't waste your breath on him. He didn't mention you at all." When confusion crosses my features, the man with the evil, yet somehow appealing blue eyes says, "Eddie." He smiles at the widening of my pupils, loving my unease. "Or Eduardo Emanuel Cordova as he was known to us." When he says 'us,' he nudges his head to the men seated each side of me. Their shoulders are butted against mine like I'm the princess of their realm, and they swore an oath to protect me. "He didn't mention you once. He merely groveled for his own pathetic life, so why are you wasting your last words on him?"

Tears prick my eyes. I don't know if they're for Eddie or because the man glaring at me as if I am gum under a park bench just admitted I'm moments from my death. Eddie got what was coming to him, but still, the stranger's confession is a hard pill to swallow.

"I wasn't praying for Eddie," I force out through the sob sitting in the back of my throat. "I was praying for my death not to be as painful as his."

Humor flickers through the stranger's eyes like ambers in a fire. "Who said his death was painful? There's no body, so how would anyone know that?"

My nanna always said my mouth would get me in trouble, which it does precisely two seconds later. "They said he was cut up into little pieces. That he was tortured for hours." I lick my quivering lips before asking, "Is that true?"

He nods without shame, angering me further. "Why? What did he ever do to you?"

"He took my daughter away from me." The expression on his face turns menacing when he spits out, "As did you."

I balk, suddenly sickened. "I did *no* such thing. I don't even know who you are, much less know you had a daughter."

"Have. I *have* a daughter!"

Since my hands are bound behind my back, I have to use my legs to kick him away when he suddenly lurches to my side of the cabin.

Although I give it my all, his hand curls around my throat a mere second before his hot breaths batter my neck. "And if it weren't for you, she'd be snuggled in her bed. Instead, she's been bounced state to state, or worse, country to country."

When a dangerous gleam darts through his eyes, the reason behind their familiarity smacks into me. He's the stranger who stood outside the alleyway, the man who toppled me into ecstasy even faster than Eddie's hand. It was rainy, and my mind was blitzing about what we were doing, but I am confident he's the same man.

The already tight squeeze he's clutching my throat with doubles when a horrid thought enters my mind. Did my stunt that night prompt the kidnapping of his daughter? He was watching me as intensely as I was watching him, so there was plenty of time for his enemies to undertake a well-planned attack. It takes less than a second for evil to launch.

Oh, God, I feel sick.

"I didn't mean any harm. I was just fooling around. I had no clue about the controversy it would cause." He firms his grip around my throat for every word I speak. His hold is so fierce, I feel seconds from blacking out, but I push on, determined to make peace with my guilt before my life expires. "I liked you watching me, but I wouldn't have done it if I knew what would happen to your daughter. I'm sorry. So very, *very* sorry."

My apology seems to anger him more. His face goes red as the candor in his eyes fades to black pits of pure rage. "My wife is dead because of you. My daughter is missing. I should kill you now."

With my brain shut down due to a lack of oxygen, I ask, "Then why haven't you? It's been almost a year."

He must have a weird fascination for toying with his victims longer than necessary because I anticipated my question to increase the pressure he has on my neck, not weaken it. "My daughter has been gone longer than a year." Although his hand remains curled around my throat, slithers of air still manage to make their way to my lungs. It's only just enough to keep me conscious, but it's better than being dead. "She was cut out of my wife's stomach five days *after* she was kidnapped from the foyer of the Slice of Salt restaurant in New York." When my pupils unwillingly dilate, the furious pulse shooting through his palm turns rampant. "Have you heard of that establishment before?"

Even aware I'm adding a nail to my coffin, I nod my head, the pain in his eyes too intense to ignore. My honesty awards me the ability to once again breathe. I gasp in hurried breaths to pacify the scream of my lungs before straying my eyes to the pained ones still glaring at me.

"I met my father in a watering hole next door to that restaurant once. It was after my grandfather passed away. I thought he wanted to get to know me a little better." A flare I've never seen before darts through his eyes when I stammer out, "All he wanted to know was how much inheritance he was set to get from his father-in-law's death. He didn't care about me at all." Disbelieving of fate, and stupidly curious, I ask, "What date was your wife taken?"

The air I've only just gulped down rushes back out when the blue-eyed man replies, "February twelve."

"February twelve, last year?"

My throat works through a tough swallow when his twitching lips deliver his confirmation. He's placed his puzzle together the wrong way. I'm not to blame for what happened to his wife. I was near the restaurant he mentioned to meet with my father. Agreeing to his request was the only stupid thing I did that day.

When I say that to the dark-haired stranger, the furl of his lips turns nasty. "You don't have to whack someone across the temple with the butt of a gun to take part in their kidnapping."

He adds evidence to his comment by splaying his hands across his body. I'm bound in his car, at his complete mercy, however if you exclude him testing the heartiness of my pulse, he hasn't laid a hand on me.

"People can be manipulated in many ways. Take a pretty

redhead on a corner with thick black tears streaming down her face. All it takes is for a man to glance her way for a second, and *poof*, his entire existence is snatched out from beneath him."

The men seated beside me appear as shocked by his confession as me. They either didn't know the part he played in his wife's disappearance or they're damn good actors. It may be a combination of both.

Desperate not to be punished for something I didn't do, I mutter, "Just because you glanced my way that day doesn't make me responsible for what happened." I'd take the blame for what happened if his daughter was kidnapped while he watched my deplorable act in the alleyway, but this isn't my fault. "I've done nothing wrong."

"Yes, you have." His voice rises as rapidly as his anger. "You distracted me, you caught me off guard long enough for my enemies to get the better of me. That makes you responsible for Audrey's disappearance."

My retaliation is as loud as his, my determination just as robust. "I was merely in the wrong place at the wrong time. I am *not* to blame."

His hot breaths hit my lips when he snarls, "Confessing your lack of judgment is the only way I'll offer you *any* type of leniency. It'll do you best to remember that."

The anger surging through causes my usual levelheadedness to go askew. "Leniency for a crime I didn't commit, for a kidnapping I had nothing to do with. How can you expect me to confess to something I didn't do?"

"You distracted me——"

"Because you couldn't keep your eyes on your wife. That isn't my fault!"

He recoils like my words slapped him hard across the face. It's clear he feels guilt about his wife's kidnapping, but that doesn't mean he'll go easy on me. I'll have to work for every leniency I want him to give me.

"If I hadn't looked at you, my wife wouldn't be dead. If I hadn't stopped to find you, my daughter would be here. You're responsible for *everything* that has happened." His voice cools to that of a madman before he adds, "And I'm done playing nice."

"Dimitri…"

I don't get the chance to register the shock of learning my attacker's name. I'm too busy staring into Dimitri's soulless eyes, wordlessly begging for him not to shoot me with the gun he butts up against my temple.

I'm not a parent, so I'll never fully understand what he's going through, but I've often wondered what it would feel like to have a father who'd protect me no matter what. In my eyes, Dimitri's daughter is lucky, but she won't be if Dimitri doesn't learn to focus his anger on those deserving of his wrath.

When I say that to Dimitri, he cocks back the hammer on his gun. I'm about to die, and the man who brought me to ecstasy more times in my dreams than any man in real life is my executioner.

Chapter Fourteen

Dimitri

My back molars crunch together when Rocco fists my dress shirt so firmly, two of its buttons pop. I have a gun in my hand, and the itch to kill is skating through my veins.

He's a fool to fuck with me now.

Someone is about to die, and it's a close call on who the departed will be.

"Listen," Rocco demands my devotion with an authority I didn't realize he held. "She's telling the truth." He squashes my cell phone under my ear like I'm hard of hearing before requesting for Smith to repeat what he said.

"You're right. Roxanne was near the Slice of Salt the day Audrey was taken." The sheen in Roxanne's eyes doubles when he adds, "She paid the tab for the whiskeys her father had in an establishment next door before she arrived on an almost maxed-out credit card."

Even not knowing Roxanne any better than a hooker on a

corner, I'm aware Smith is telling the truth. Shame was the first thing that darted through Roxanne's eyes when Smith's words reached her ears. It was quickly chased by regret.

"But she left minutes *before* Audrey was spotted on surveillance being guided out the back entrance. She hasn't been back there since, and there's no chatter of any kind on her social media accounts or messenger apps. It truly seems as if she was in the wrong place at the wrong time."

Even though Smith can't see me, I shake my head. "There are too many incidents to discount." My gun is directed at Roxanne's head, but I act as if she's invisible. It annoys her more than anything. "She's popped up too many times for *any* of this to be a coincidence."

With my anger at a point it can't be contained, I push Rocco off me before sinking back into my seat opposite Roxanne's. The barrel of my gun is still aimed her way, but I'll have to pop a bullet through my second-in-charge if I want to take her down.

Rocco is protecting her like he failed to do his mother.

The fact I contemplate the carry-on effect Rocco's death would cause my empire reveals how badly I'm spiraling.

Tell me one man who wouldn't get a little fucked in the head right now?

I haven't had confirmation of Fien's well-being for almost nine months, then, suddenly tonight, a mere three hours before Roxanne shows up out of nowhere, a request for ransom drops into my inbox. Her proof-of-life video was grainy, and it was only four seconds long, but there's no doubt in my mind it was Fien.

Not in a million years would I forget her face.

After working my jaw side to side, I breathe out, "She didn't turn up tonight for no reason. Roxanne *is* a part of this."

"I'm not," she denies with a shake of her head at the same

time Rocco spits out, "Yeah, that's probably true. But is it via her choice? Or is she being forced into a fight she doesn't belong in?"

When confusion darts through my eyes, Rocco gets smug. "You're always racing ahead, Dimi, leaving nothing but a trail of destruction in your wake."

He said a similar thing when I told him I was marrying Audrey in a civil ceremony hours after she told me she was pregnant. He wanted me to hold off for a few months, citing there was no need to rush since Fien wasn't due for another eight months. I could have listened to him, but as he said, I'm always racing ahead.

"He could be onto something." Clover shifts the bulk of his heavy frame to the edge of his seat before he hands me a ripped piece of paper. "I found this in her purse when I rummaged through her things."

After gauging Roxanne's reaction to her privacy being invaded, which I'm shocked to say barely altered, I drop my eyes to a set of handwritten instructions on what looks to be part of a university letterhead. The word 'interview' scribble at the top has been underlined three times, revealing the person jotting down the details was excited they'd been granted one.

My anger shifts to confusion when my eyes skim the interviewer's name. It reveals I was supposed to interview Roxanne at my family's restaurant at the exact time Fien's ransom request landed in my inbox.

I drift my eyes back to Roxanne's watering ones. She's scared—there's no doubt about that—but she's also curious, and if I'm not mistaken, angry. Her emotions appear as uncontrolled as mine. "Who sent you this?"

The bangs I pushed aside when I was certain I was dreaming fall back into place when Roxanne shakes her head with a shrug. "An employment agency?"

Her blasé response agitates me to no end. The last time I took the focus off Fien for this long, I lost sight of her for nine months.

I won't let that happen again.

"You didn't think to ask who they were?"

Unsure where my fury stems from, Roxanne shakes her head. "I'm so desperate for a job, I don't ask questions. I just accept any interview offered."

Even with the rattle of her vocal cords chopping up her words, I'm confident she's telling the truth.

People are more honest when they're in fear of their life.

"Smith—"

"Already on it," he says down the line, his thick voice vibrating through my phone's speakers. "I'll have every number that's called her cell for the past year in five… four… three… two—"

My eyes snap to the side when Rocco blurts out, "It was me. I organized her interview."

Just as quickly as my eyes rocket to Rocco, they dart to Roxanne. She appears as shocked by his confession as me, meaning I can shift the focus of my gun to Rocco's head despite my gut begging for me to reconsider.

"*You're* playing *me*? *I* made you who you are. *I've* given you everything you have, but now *you* fuck *me* over."

Red hot anger scorches through me when I consider exactly how long he's playing me for a fool. We've been friends for over two decades. We skipped school together in the eighth grade. Was he a traitor back then? Or only when the gleam of money became too bright for him to ignore?

"Did you take my daughter, Rocco? Did you cut her from my wife's stomach!"

A numbed expression crosses his face. "No, Dimi, fuck! I

organized Roxanne's interview so you could see Fien again, so you'd have the chance to get her back."

Nothing he's saying makes any sense. How could forcing Roxanne back into my life help me get Fien back? She's the reason I lost everything to begin with.

I stare at Rocco like he's disturbed when he mutters out a name I never anticipated hearing right now. "Justine." Nothing but remorse is seen on his face when he adds, "Your ruse was working, Dimi. When you had Justine on the go, Fien's ransoms arrived like clockwork. They were *never* late, and you were given undeniable proof that she was safe every single month." He works his jaw side to side, his anger as noticeable as mine. "That hasn't happened in nine months, D. You haven't had a single ransom request—"

"I got one earlier today."

The truth smacks into me like a wayward missile a mere second before Rocco spells it out for me. "Because I organized Roxie's interview at your favorite hook-up location two weeks *after* placing a photo of you together on your social media accounts."

"Jesus Christ, Rocco, you didn't tell me it was for this," Smith says down the line at the same time Clover pinches his gun to Rocco's temple, aware he's more of a threat right now than Roxanne.

"I'm just going for my phone," Rocco assures Clover, frustrated and fighting the urge to retaliate. For the most part, they get along, but it hasn't always been that way. Clover is a member of my crew because he's paid for the privilege. Rocco is here of his own free will. He was here before the money came, and if I don't kill him for his deceit, he'd be here even if we lost it all. "See."

He swivels his phone around to face me. It has a photo of me carrying Roxanne out of the ravine. Because it was taken at an angle, it appears as if we're fooling around instead of Roxanne being on the brink of death. You can't see her blood-stained face or body, just the grip I have on her ass to keep her on my shoulder while sprinting out of the scrub.

My brows pinch when Rocco demands that I check my email. "What?" He smiles, clearly blind to how precariously his life is floating in the wind. "I want to see how fast they react. I bet your numerous requests for a better proof of life for Fien tonight has been answered now. My latest upload to the Dimitri and Roxie show has been in the wild the past ten minutes."

He shows me a second image. Just like the first one, the angle is badly deceiving. It looks like I'm about to kiss Roxanne instead of strangling her like I almost did ten minutes ago. "What's the bet an email dropped into your inbox within the last eight minutes."

Too curious to discount, I hit the email app on the screen of my phone. I know what I'm going to find before I discover it. Smith's silence is telling enough, much less the brutal drum of my heart against my ribs.

Rocco was right. My three requests for a better proof of life were answered precisely seven minutes ago. The footage is double the length of the last one, and it's crystal clear. It even has sound this time around.

I'm not going to lie. I was raised in a cruel, hard world that's only grown crueler the longer I've sucked the life from its veins, but my daughter's tired giggles are enough to bring the strongest man to his knees. It's perfectly balanced like she isn't being raised by a group of dead men walking amongst the living.

Although I could stare at Fien's smiling face for a lifetime, hearing her laugh for the first time doesn't dampen my wish to find her. If anything, it triples my determination. "Smith—"

"On it. I'll pass on any findings ASAP." Eager to get to

work, he disconnects our call before remotely logging into my phone.

I take a few minutes to gather my bearings before locking my eyes with Clover's. Roxanne's sigh of relief is more audible than Rocco's when I wordlessly instruct Clover to lower his weapon. He isn't happy about my request, but he does as he is told.

All hired hitman do.

Once Rocco has slipped back into his spot next to Roxanne, I ask a question no amount of anger could have me setting aside, "How did you know they'd respond so fast?"

Rocco's lips twitch in preparation to respond, but before he can, Roxanne gabbles out, "Because your daughter's captor is a woman."

Chapter Fifteen

Roxanne

Dimitri stares straight at me. Even in the shadows of a near moonless night, I can't miss the tight clench of his fists and jaw. His aura is unnerving, but since his menace isn't directly focused on me this time around, it doesn't make me quiver like it did earlier. The shudder of my thighs is now more a positive shake than a negative one. He's watching me like he did in the alleyway a year ago, appearing as if he wants to join in but never will.

At least now I understand the reasoning behind his withdrawn demeanor. He isn't just dark and dangerous, he's fighting not to be as cruel as the people holding his daughter hostage. I doubt he'd hold back the urge if she were safe and in his arms. He wants to maim the people responsible for the scars no number of good looks will hide, and in all honesty, I can't blame him. After hearing his daughter's giggles, I want to do the exact same thing, and I haven't even seen her yet.

"How do you know her captor is a woman?" Dimitri asks

while staring at me as if I'm the only person seated across from him.

"She's jealous and acting out. All traits of a scorned woman." I wet my dry lips before asking a question I guarantee he's never been asked before. "Did you cheat on your wife?"

"This isn't a custody dispute." His words are fired out of his mouth like bullets. "I saw Fien removed from Audrey's stomach in a dirty, unsterile room. No amount of money would have a mother putting her child in danger like that."

Although I agree with him, his skirting of my question won't get us anywhere. "I didn't ask if the kidnapper was your wife. I asked if you cheated on her."

He's pissed about my line of questioning, but since the safe return of his daughter is more important than anything, he lets it slide. "Yes, I cheated on her. Multiple times."

"Did she know?"

I have no clue why I asked that question. It will make no difference to my assumption whatsoever. I'm just curious to discover if he's a man who cheats and lies about it, or does he parade it around for the world to see.

Dimitri adjusts the expensive-looking cuffs on his sleeves, something he seems to do when frustrated, before muttering, "It wasn't something we openly discussed, but she was aware of my inability to keep my dick in my pants."

"And the woman you cheated with? Did they know?" This set of questions has a direct correlation with the theory I'm running. If any of the women he slept with while married experienced half the jealousy I'm being bombarded with now, they could have gone as far as kidnapping his wife and taking his daughter. I want to stab a bitch, and Dimitri isn't even mine.

"Know what, exactly?" His voice is so menacing, I peer

down at his gun, anticipating for him to curl his finger around the trigger at any moment.

When that fails to happen, I answer, "That you were married and expecting a child. Some women are very possessive. They may not have taken the news well."

I'm talking from experience more than assumptions. My high school boyfriend's strut was never the same when I caught him kissing Belinda McCotter in the bleachers during the homecoming week game.

I begin to wonder how many women Dimitri has slept with when he pauses to consider a response. I can't see the women he's mentally ticking off, but I can see the flicker of his eyes as he scrolls through his little black book of bed companions. It makes me insanely jealous.

"Most were aware, but some were not," he answers a short time later.

"Do you think any of them would be capable of doing something like this?"

His lips furl at the corners. "I don't know. I wasn't with them to conduct a psych exam." His eyes snap to Rocco's so quickly, he misses my scoff. "I thought you said she was a double business major."

Rocco's scrub of his jaw to hide his grin is pointless when I mumble, "I can be anything you want for the right amount of coin."

With his eyes back on me, Dimitri arches his brow. "You want me to pay for your help?" When I nod, he slouches low in his chair before shaking his head. "Why would I do that?" I'm about to sell myself in a way that would make Estelle proud, but he continues talking, foiling my attempt. "I don't need to pay you to do anything. I can just *force* you to do it."

"It wouldn't be authentic." I take a mental note to have my head examined after this. I just witnessed a murder, and I'm reasonably sure the timer above my head is minutes from expiring, yet here I am, negotiating with a mobster. I've been in such a rut I'd do anything for an adrenaline high, but still, this is ridiculous. "It would be more believable if I were there via my own choice."

"*Where* of your own choice?" Dimitri asks, humoring me with fake interest.

He isn't laughing on the outside, but I can see the chuckles he's struggling to hold in his rising and falling chest. It's heaving the same way it did when Eddie 'milked my loins of their nectar.'

Usually, any type of laughter would have me backtracking on every decision I've ever made. I can't do that this time around. We're still heading toward the woods. My life is on the line, so I either sell my soul to the devil or relinquish it for nothing.

I don't know about you, but I'd rather go out fighting.

"On your arm. By your side." I swallow the brick lodged in my throat before muttering, "In your bed."

My lungs fail to follow the prompts of my brain when Dimitri scoots to the edge of his seat. He moves so close to me, even if I wanted to press my thighs together from his hot, heated stare, I wouldn't be able to. His knee is wedged between them. "Once again, why would I pay you to do that when I could make you do it for free?"

My ability to reply is lost by the thick, accented voice of the heavily tattooed man sitting next to me. I haven't caught his name yet, but he has a tattoo of a clover on his cheek. "It's the curse of the golden pussy, boss. All girls think they have one." As he sucks his bottom lip into his mouth, he drags his eyes down my body in a slow and dedicated sweep. "It's rare to find one who does, but she might have one. Her smell is sweet enough." He releases his lip with a pop before straying his eyes to Dimitri. "Maybe you should give her to the boys for a few rounds, see if they think her pussy is worth paying for."

I don't breathe while snapping my eyes back to Dimitri's. He wouldn't do that, would he? He wouldn't risk his daughter's safety because I insinuated I'd only sleep with him if he paid me. Only an insane man would let his pride get in the way of his daughter's well-being. Dimitri isn't one of them.

My eyes pop open when the truth smacks into me. He watched me come via the hand of another man before he murdered the security guard who interrupted his show, then he tortured my boyfriend for six hours straight. Those events could have seen him facing thirty years to life in a maximum-security prison. He's far from sane.

"I'll do it for free!" My eyes dance between Dimitri's frozen ones when I join him in sitting on the edge of my seat. "On the agreement you let me go once your daughter is found."

I doubt I'm getting through to him, but am denied the opportunity of hoping when our negotiation is interrupted for the second time. This time it isn't from the large brute on my right. It comes from the front of the car, from the driver. "We've got a tail. They're a few spots back, but they've been with us the last two miles."

"Fuck," Dimitri curses under his breath after cranking his neck back. The moon is barely a slither in the sky, meaning even someone with poor eyesight would have no trouble seeing the curved headlights of a sedan in an almost pitch-black night. "Pull over here."

I watch nervously when our break is closely mimicked by the car tailing us. They're close enough for their presence to be felt but far enough away, they won't see the sweat that beads on my temples when Dimitri throws open the back passenger door and slides out. He doesn't approach the vehicle three hundred yards back. He heads straight for the trunk where he removes two shovels and a tarp.

Oh my God. I'm about to be buried where I'll never be found.

"Please," I beg when Dimitri dips the lower half of his body into the cab so he can pull me out a few seconds later. "I can help get your daughter back. Rocco proved I'm worthwhile. You just need to give me a chance."

Since my arms are bound behind my back, it takes Dimitri no effort at all to pluck me from my seat and drag me to the front of his sleek ride. Not even digging my heels into the rugged terrain slows him down. In a matter of seconds, I'm kneeling on the tarp he laid out, and his gun is aimed at the petrified crinkle between my brows.

"Please," I plead to the man who stood in the rain to watch me climax instead of the maniac standing in front of me. "I'll do anything you ask. I can cook," I groan about my inability to lie, "Not very well, but it's edible… for the most part. I'll clean, wash your clothes. I'll do anything you want as long as you don't kill me. I don't want to die." The dusty conditions make the tears welling in my eyes feel like sawdust. They scratch my eyeballs as well as a sudden urge to live warms my veins. "I've barely lived. Please, Dimitri. I'll do anything you ask."

"You're the reason my wife is dead."

His words are barely heard over the drumming of my heart, but I cling to them as if they're a life raft, and I'm in the middle of the Indian Ocean. "I know, and I'm sorry. I'd take it all back in an instant if I could." When my words appear to break through Dimitri's cold, hard exterior, I keep blubbering. "We'll be good together. I saw the way you looked at me in the alleyway. You liked what you saw." I pause to see if truth registers on his face before continuing, "If we had that much spark from a distance, imagine what we'll have when we're close together. Your enemies won't doubt our connection. They'll truly believe you're moving on."

I'm not one hundred percent sure what Rocco meant when he said Justine's ruse worked, but I'm so desperate to live, I'm willing to give anything a shot. "If you want your daughter back, you need me. You can be angry at me, you can hate me, but you still *need* me." I bounce my drenched eyes between his. "I'm no good to you dead, Dimitri. I'm worth more to you alive than dead. I can be what you want me to be. I can be *anything* you need."

After running the back of his hands down my mascara-stained cheek, he smiles as if I flashed him my tits. I didn't, but it was pretty damn close. I offered myself to him, wholly and without constraint. I'll be his *if* he doesn't kill me.

"Please, Dimitri. I'm begging you for mercy."

His smirk shifts to a full teeth-bearing grin, full of angst and confusion. I understand things drastically changed for him from the last time we stood across from each other, and that he's most likely only holding on by a very thin thread, but his anger shouldn't be projected at me. It should be rained down on the people holding his daughter captive, and the ones responsible for his wife's death.

When I say that to Dimitri, the muscles in his neck bunch. "Why do you think you're here, kneeling before me?"

With his lips arched at one side and his eyes locked on mine, he curls his finger around the trigger and takes his shot.

Chapter Sixteen

Dimitri

As the scent of my recently fired gun lingers in my nostrils, I stray my eyes to the black sedan idling a few spots back. The brightness of the Audi's high beams ensures I'll never see the occupants inside, however my gut has no issues identifying him.

My father doesn't trust anyone. He is who I got my neurosis from. He's so distrusting, I'm surprised he didn't request to helm our trip to the woods.

I'd be lying if I said I didn't understand his concern. Roxanne saw him murder Old Man V for a measly ten-thousand-dollar dint in his profit margin. That's an instant one-way ticket to a graveyard. I'm seeing things differently now, though.

Although Roxanne was a witness to one of my father's many mistakes the past three months, unfortunately for him, she wasn't his *only* witness. He's made an incalculable number of costly blunders during his reign, but tonight's was by far his most senseless. He showed his hand way too early, and now this wolf is primed with anticipation.

I've been seeking answers for months, and it came in a way I never predicted. Because my father was as distracted by Roxanne's tear-stained face as I was on that night almost twenty months ago, he fucked up in a way he can never come back from. He ruined his legacy with one little word.

He said, 'wife.'

Not plaything.

Not whore.

Not a cunt to keep me warm throughout the winter as he called Audrey many times the seven months of our marriage.

He said wife plain and clear for all to hear.

I failed to join the dots together until Roxanne peered up at me with mascara smeared down her cheeks mere seconds ago. She once again had me trapped, blinded to everything happening around me that didn't include her. I was so caught up by her beauty and determination to live in spite of her horrid upbringing, I played her re-entrance into my life on repeat until the clog in my mind spilled away.

Roxanne *is* to blame for my wife's disappearance. She *is* the reason I haven't laid my eyes on Fien in over nine months. But she *is* also responsible for my father's slip up. If it wasn't for her, I'd still be trying to push a four-pronged puzzle piece into a three-pronged spot. She freed my mind from the torment, and she did it all the while offering herself to me.

I catch sight of my unforgiving smirk in the fender of my modified Range Rover when the headlights of my father's chauffeur-driven Audi shift to the right. This is a one-way track, so his driver, Mario, either executes a three-point turn in atrocious conditions or squeezes by the minute snippet of space my Range Rover isn't taking up.

My father would never allow the latter to happen. He'd

rather risk being bogged than show weakness. It's another unwanted trait I inherited from him. We're more alike than I'll ever admit, but there's one difference between us—I'm willing to show weakness if it's for the greater good.

This is for the greater good.

Roxanne's eyes lift to mine when the taillights of my father's car disappear into the black abyss of an almost moonless night. They're wide and terrified and have my cock tapping at the zipper in my trousers like it did when she placed herself onto the table during our unrequired negotiations.

They were unrequired because if I wanted to fuck her, she'd be splayed across the hood of my Range Rover now, being thoroughly pounded as my cock has begged to do since I spotted her in the alley. However, that isn't what this is about. For once in my life, my libido isn't part of the equation. This is about placing my daughter before anyone—even me.

"You will do what I say *precisely* when I tell you to do it, or we'll come back here and settle the score. Do you understand?"

She has nothing to fight with except her looks, which she uses to her advantage when she dips her chin. It isn't the rake of her teeth over her plump bottom lip I'm paying attention to, it's the fat, salty blob rolling down her cheek. It's stained with blackness and has me recalling the color of the blood that runs through my veins.

It wasn't always that way. Before my heart was scolded beyond repair, my blood used to run red. Now it's stained with the murkiness of my dark, bleak existence—an existence Roxanne is now a part of.

Chapter Seventeen

Roxanne

Rocco's hand falls from my face when the gravelly voice of Dimitri rolls across the cabin of his car. "Let it be. It's just a graze." He locks his eyes with mine. They're as tormented and beautiful as they were when he took his shot. He fired at me as predicted, but instead of the bullet burrowing deep into my skull, it skimmed past my right cheek, leaving a slither of a burn. "The more you pick at it, the more it will scab. If you don't want another scar, leave it alone."

The heat from the graze on my cheek is barely noticeable until he returns his eyes to the scenery whizzing by his window. He's been detached since our negotiations were finalized during the first forty minutes of our trip like his mind is far from here.

I discover that's the case when he tugs his cell phone out of his pocket. Although he doesn't dial a number, he speaks down the line as if he did. "I need my father's schedule synced with mine as soon as possible." The man he's speaking to attempts to interrupt him, but Dimitri continues spraying out orders, faulting his effort. "His movements the past three months are to be on my desk before dawn, and any upcoming functions over the next two weeks should be forwarded with them."

"On it," says a man with a uniquely distinctive accent. It's either British or Australian. It could even be a combination of both. "Anything else?"

"One last thing." My pulse twangs in my neck when Dimitri shifts his eyes to me. They're as hot as ever, even with them being the color of ice. "Call Alice. I want to see her tonight. Offer her double for the late hour."

It's deplorable to comment on the jealousy roaring through me, so I won't. We're not friends or lovers. I am his property until he says otherwise. His stipulations during our one-sided talk were as clear as glass. I'm to do what he says, when he says, for exactly how long he says. If I do that, I'll come out of the exchange with my life intact. If I don't, I won't want to know the consequences of my stupidity.

His threat would frighten me if I had more family than I do. If it weren't for Estelle, I may have let him kill me.

My eyes float up from my clenched fists when the man on the other end of the line says, "Consider it done."

Dimitri's eyes remain on me even with his focus being devoted to his caller. "Tell her I want the works." When my eyes unwillingly roll, his lips do their favored half-smirk. "No holds barred."

I imagine the gleam in Smith's eyes matches Dimitri's when he replies, "Alice knows what you like, so she won't let you down."

Their call ends just as the Range Rover pulls onto the curb across from my building. You'd think the embarrassment I felt begging for my life would keep my annoyance on the down-low. Regretfully, my hair isn't red for no reason.

It matches my fiery personality.

I slip out the back of Dimitri's car so fast, even if he wants to follow me, the brutal slam of his door in his face won't allow it. I'm not running. I know the terms we agreed upon during the first half of our trip. My ass is Dimitri's until his daughter is returned without a scratch. But that doesn't mean I have to continue displaying the weak, pathetic woman I did in the woods an hour and a half ago.

I hate that I begged at Dimitri's feet. I've only ever pleaded for one thing in my life, and that teary wish was never answered. I want a redo of my last conversation with my nanna. If I knew how things were going to end, I would have hugged her fiercely instead of storming off in a huff the way I did. I was angry she was still treating me like a child, having no clue she was only treating me that way because I was acting like a child.

My eyes snap to the door of the outdated elevator in my building when a tattooed hand shoots out to stop it from closing. I'm anticipating for Rocco to join me inside, although quiet, he seemed more on my side than Dimitri's during our negotiations, so you can imagine my shock when Dimitri enters the confined space in his place.

After pulling across the rickety gate that's meant to keep us safe in this death trap, he jabs his finger into the 'close door' button multiple times in a row, obviously impatient.

Once the elevator shudders into action, he shifts on his feet to face me. He looks set to remind me of our agreement, but instead, steers our conversation in a direction I never saw coming. "Stay away from Rocco." His gruff tone gobbles up my scoff. "He has a soft spot for battered women, but that isn't what *this* is about." While saying 'this,' he shifts his hand between us. "If you want to fuck him after this is over, that's your choice, but I won't allow it to occur under my watch. I won't be made to look like a fool."

"Like your wife was?" I snap out before I can stop myself.

Mercifully, the elevator car arrives at my floor a nanosecond later, saving me from being scolded by the wrath of his anger in a tight confinement. I barely survived it in his car the past hour and a half, so I don't see me faring well in a much tighter space.

Incapable of breathing through the sternness of his glare, I mutter out, "I understand your request. I'll keep my mitts to myself."

I break into the hallway before he can see my mouth's arched response to the hesitation firing through his eyes. He was satisfied with my response until he realized that means my hands won't go anywhere near him, either.

It's as if he yanks out the electrical cord responsible for my snippy attitude when he says, "I wasn't lying about Eduardo. He didn't murmur your name once. You weren't on his mind at all when I punished him for hurting you."

Aware he only said his comment to return my serve, and a little unsure how to react to his confession he killed Eddie because he hurt me, I stab my house key into the rusty lock on my apartment's front door before pushing open the water-damaged wood.

"We're behind on the electric bill. There's a torch on the kitchen counter," I advise Dimitri when his multiple flicks of the light switch fail to illuminate the room.

It's the fight of my life not to let my laughter be heard when he crashes into the entry table I purposely forgot to warn him about. He can't bitch-slap my attitude back to next week because he didn't look where he was going.

After lighting a candle on the dresser in my room, I head for my overflowing closet. One of the benefits of stunted growth is the ability to wear clothes from my teen days. My height hasn't altered since I got my learner's permit, and despite my budget only affording me the privilege of grease-laden food, my waist is around the same size as well.

I sense Dimitri's presence before I hear him rummage through the bag I've just commenced packing. With Estelle at work, it isn't hard to miss the disapproving huff of someone hating my sense of style.

"You won't need any of this." He upends my bag onto my bed before he drags his narrowed gaze over my candlelit room. The further his eyes travel, the more disgust crosses his features. "You won't need *any* of this."

I sound like a whiny brat when I snap out, "You said I could pack my things."

"Yeah, things you need. Not *this* junk."

Heat creeps up my neck when I struggle to hold in a blood-curdling scream. "These are *things* I need. They're all I have."

My anger shifts to confusion when he replies, "Then we'll get you new *things*." He slants his head to the side and arches a brow. "Better *things*."

I thought begging for my life was embarrassing, but this is ten times worse. "I can't afford new *things*. That's why I have these *things*."

"Sorry. Let me rephrase." Think of the most arrogant man you've ever seen in your life. His attitude wouldn't be one-third of Dimitri's right now. "*I* will get you new *things*."

"Fine." He's shocked by how quickly I cave, but I'm done arguing for today. I'm cold, hungry, and hormonal. If anyone should be in fear of their life, it shouldn't be me. "But I'm taking this."

I snag the most hideous-looking dressing gown you could imagine in your life off the end of my bed. It's a replica of the one Fran Drescher wore on *The Nanny*, one of my all-time favorite sitcoms.

"And them."

I snatch a pair of panties out of Dimitri's hand that I only ever wear when I'm worried about exploding tampons.

"And this."

My voice is nowhere near as punchy as it was when I snag my nanna's photograph off my nightstand. Even with her death still not feeling real to me, I miss her so much.

"Is that it?" My brashness isn't the only thing taking a back seat, so is Dimitri's bossy demeanor. He doesn't know who the lady in the frame is, but the wetness filling my eyes makes it obvious that she was important to me.

My head bobs up and down two times before it switches to a shake. "One last thing."

After blowing out the candle, so we don't start a fire, Dimitri follows my walk to an ancient tape recorder on the entryway table, taking a wide birth to ensure his crotch doesn't once again become friendly with its poky edges.

Once I've exhaled to clear my voice of nerves, I push record on the device before lifting it to my mouth. Dimitri almost jumps out of his skin when I scream at the top of my lungs. "I got the job! Thirty-five smoking big ones an hour for the next four weeks minimum." I have to be over-the-top dramatic, or Estelle will never believe my ruse. "The thing is, the ridiculous amount is because it's a live-in position. Mr. Petretti is graveyard ready." I drift my eyes to Dimitri when I feel the heat of his rising blood pressure. "He's old, like hideously archaic. He has wrinkles and gray hair. I doubt even Viagra can help him now." After hitting Dimitri with a frisky wink, hopeful it won't see me murdered where I stand, I get back to the task at hand. "Anyhoo, I just wanted to let you know why I'm AWOL… because I'm wiping an old dude's ass like we always knew I would. Ciao, chica. I'll see you in a few weeks."

With a hard swallow, I hit the stop button before placing the recorder back into its rightful place. Even with me seemingly exuding a ton of confidence, my hands shake when I tie a red ribbon around the recorder's overused exterior. It's our equivalent of a blinking red light on the answering machine we can't afford.

I want to believe Dimitri will uphold his side of our agreement once his daughter is returned, but a part of me is worried he's never been taught the principle of honesty. He said it himself, he cheated on his wife multiple times, so why would he be honorable to a woman he hardly knows?

I'm snapped from my dreary mood by Dimitri's curt tone. "Let's go." He nudges his head to my partially cracked open door as he's over the depressing environment I call home as much as me.

After a final glance at the dim and dreary space, I shadow his walk to the elevator cart, my steps slow and lethargic. This place might be a dump, but it's the only true home I've ever had.

We ride the elevator in silence. I wouldn't necessarily say it's uncomfortable, it's more foreign than anything. Silence isn't something I often crave. I did it many times before my parents dropped me off to live with my grandparents. Even something as simple as breathing too loudly got me in trouble when Mother woke up angry. That was more often than not when I was a child.

I safeguard my grandmother's picture under my dressing gown when our trek through the foyer of my building reveals the heavens have opened up. It isn't pouring rain like it was the night I first crossed paths with Dimitri, but it has the possibility of wrecking the only photograph I have of her.

I'm just about to dart through two parked cars when my arm is jerked out of its socket. I'm about to give Dimitri an ear full, but the brutal roar of an SUV whizzing past my face stuffs my words into the back of my throat.

"Jesus Christ, Roxanne! You almost got yourself killed." My eyes bounce between Dimitri's when he pins me to the back of an outdated minivan with shaky, splayed hands. "You need to start paying attention to your surroundings, or one day, it won't be a close call." My dress is soaked through, but I don't feel the cold. There's too much fury radiating out of Dimitri for me to feel the slightest chill. "Did your near-miss at the hospital teach you nothing?"

"That was you?" Shock highlights my tone. The eyes peering at me through the crack in the window all those months ago were undeniably dangerous, but they didn't have the risqué edge Dimitri's have, so I was confident it wasn't him. "You were outside the hospital when I was discharged?"

My confusion augments when Dimitri shakes his head. "It wasn't me."

He sounds honest, but I'm done acting as if I have air for brains. "Then how do you know what happened? I didn't tell anyone, and I doubt Estelle shares her friend's stupidity with the customers at her work."

Before he can answer me, I spot some truth in his eyes.

"You had someone following me?" Another flare darts through his eyes before the cut line of his jaw turns fascinating. "I told Estelle I wasn't making things up. She thought I was going crazy, that I needed my head examined." I laugh like I'm in desperate need of a psych workup. "But that wasn't it at all. I was being followed... by you."

Dimitri's anger picks up right along with his clutch on my arm. "It wasn't me."

The way he speaks down to me doesn't deter me in the slightest. "But it was someone *you* ordered to watch me. Why were you watching me?"

"I don't know."

My eye roll matches my maturity level. "You know why, you just don't want to tell me."

"I said I don't know!" He pushes me back with enough strength to crack the rear shield of the van before he hightails it to his sleek ride. "Get your ass in the car before your promise of being away for a month won't see your roommate sleeping in your bed." He peers back at me for the quickest second. His eyes are deadly and black. "Not even reformed Goths like sleeping on their friend's blood-sodden mattress."

He's hoping his underhanded threat will have my knees knocking together. That might have been the case if I hadn't spotted the tiniest flicker of light beaming out of my apartment in his narrowed gaze. It isn't the shimmer of a recently lit candle. It's too bright and breath-stealing for that. It's a beacon of hope that the man I sold my soul to isn't as malevolent as he wants me to believe.

Besides Estelle and me, Dimitri is the only person who knows we've fallen behind on our bills. Braydon only visits during the day, and Estelle keeps his thoughts far from the fact our television's standby light is never on or that our microwave's clock has been on the blink for months on end.

Furthermore, despite his impressive bank balance, I doubt Braydon has access to a computer genius who can find a credit card transaction I fought tooth and nail to have reversed from my card in less than a second—my father didn't say goodbye to me, so there's no way I wanted to pay his bar tab—but Dimitri sure as hell does.

Are Smith's skills impressive enough to have electricity reconnected to a property in under five minutes? If you had asked me that very question two hours ago, I would have said no. Now, I'm confident it was him. Dimitri's phone's screen wasn't lit up when I joined him in the elevator to ride it to the lobby, but that doesn't mean anything. He used it to communicate with Smith earlier tonight without touching a button. Who's to say he didn't do the same thing this time around?

My clue hunt ends when my name snaps out of Dimitri's mouth in a thick, accented roar. He's standing at the side of his vehicle, holding open the back passenger door for me. Although his expression is as impassive as it was when he held his gun to my head, something in his eyes has changed. He's either shocked how quickly Smith works, or he's hoping I missed his handiwork.

I'm leaning more toward the latter.

He'd hate for me to think I have more power than he deems necessary because even mobsters know there's no greater strength than a woman determined to prove a man wrong.

Chapter Eighteen

Dimitri

The *click-clack, click-clack* of Roxanne's inexpensive shoes tap along the marble floors in the foyer of my home when she shadows my walk into the quiet space. Her heels aren't the only disturbance. Her hot breaths as she takes in empty room after empty room are just as meddling. They hit my neck as they did my face when she slid past me to enter the backseat of my Range Rover idling at the front of her apartment building.

I had hoped she wouldn't notice the illumination of her living room since it was eight floors above. Regretfully, she's as nosy as she is attractive. I should have instructed Smith to wait until we had left Erkinsvale before remotely connecting Roxanne's electricity. Alas, I hadn't anticipated a near-fatal to occur within seconds of exiting Roxanne's apartment.

That woman should be dead. She's a klutz who speaks without thinking and leaps in front of cars without a single consideration for her safety.

The hate that's bred in me since I was born usually craves a bloodbath. If it had been anyone but Roxanne, my hand wouldn't have darted out to clutch her arm. I would have watched the carnage, smirked, then moved on.

Things are starkly different this time around. I'm not seeking a cape, nor do I want the title of hero. I merely want my daughter back, and as much as this kills me to admit, I believe Roxanne can help me achieve that faster than planned.

She was right when she said our spark is undeniable. It was blistering when we went toe to toe in the elevator, and it didn't dampen when I insulted her idea of style. It will make my ruse more authentic this time around, and if I keep her off my father's radar, everyone will come out of this agreement in one piece—including Fien.

"Take off your shoes. Their clicking is driving me bonkers."

I don't give a shit about the noise Roxanne's shoes make while we walk. I just need to notch up my asshole radar a few decibels until the sly grin she's been wearing since we left her apartment is gone.

She isn't here as my guest.

She's here as my slave and will be treated so accordingly.

After tugging off her shoes in a manner that reveals she knows they're worthless, Roxanne follows my trek up a long curving stairwell. I purchased this property the month Audrey was kidnapped. It wasn't to be our family home but more a means to ensure our family would forever live in comfort.

This property is where I host my foreign dignitaries. The events here range from one-on-one meetings with the clients' favorite prostitutes to all-in orgy fests. Tomorrow night's festivities will be milder than previous guests' level of kink, but it will be the perfect place to commence plans I've had in the works for months. My father will be in attendance along with hundreds of men we class as both competitors and allies. It's ideal and has me hopeful I'll see Fien in person sooner than I'm hoping.

"This time tomorrow, these rooms will be filled with important members of my association. You're to treat them with respect and to be courteous at all times."

When the sweet smell of Roxanne's heated skin streams into my nose, I half the length of my strides. The fear her body coats itself in is so intoxicating, I'm tempted to throw her to the wolves just to see how engrossing it can be.

Regrettably, if I want my enemies to believe my ploy that I'm moving on, I need to be the jealous, neurotic prick I was when Audrey's beauty caught the eye of an admirer.

I cheated on my wife, but if someone so much as looked at her in the wrong manner, they would have lost an eye at the very least.

"The event is black tie. Hors d'oeuvres will be served in the parlor at seven. Main festivities will commence at nine."

My pace slows even more when Roxanne garbles out, "At night?" When my brow props high into my hairline, she nods. "Night. Right."

"I'll meet you in the foyer at six forty-five sharp."

"Okay." Her eyes flicker like she's mentally jotting down everything I'm telling her. "Will we be doing dress shopping before or after noon? I want to know whether I should hit the carbs at lunch or breakfast."

She's joking. However, I'm not amused.

Now is not the time for jokes.

"Sorry," she apologizes for the umpteenth time tonight. "I blubber when I'm nervous."

I want to say she's nervous because we're alone in a very big house, but alas, that would be a lie. For some absurd reason, she isn't afraid of me. She knows I could end her life in an instant, and that she's under my control until my daughter is returned, but fear isn't the sole emotion that passes through her eyes when she spots my inconspicuous glances. Desire is there as well.

She fought for her life not because she believes it's worth fighting for, but because of what she hopes it could be.

That's the exact reason I've fought so hard for Fien. Her video earlier tonight showed she's a happy, well-adjusted toddler, but that doesn't mean her life couldn't be better. I can give her more than she's ever had because only I can give her a father's love.

With my mood teetering toward the negative, I push down on the handle of the master suite's door with more aggression than needed. Roxanne's deep exhale fans my nape like Justine's did when I opened the door of my room in my family's compound, except her exhale is more in exhilaration than fret.

A similar-size four-poster bed sits in the middle of the back wall, a private seating area/reading nook is on its left, and an office/library is on its right. With my room used more for business adventures than sexual conquests, my desk looks more original to the space than my rarely used mattress. I'm one of those people who catches sleep on the fly. Little power naps here and there keep me going well into the wee hours of the morning where I usually crash on the couch or in my office chair.

I'm about to give Roxanne the standard old you-can-wear-one-of-my-shirts routine, but the lowering of my eyes to the hideous sleeping ensemble she's clutching for dear life stops me. At first, I was shocked she'd pack something so warm, our nighttime temperatures never get close to freezing, but when I sent Clover and Rocco home, it made sense. We're not in winter, but the iciness of untouched waters is always a little cool.

Roxanne's emotions don't know which way to swing when I

say, "While you shower and change, I'll conduct my meeting with Alice before grabbing you something to eat." She's excited about washing up and being fed, but her eagerness waivered during the middle portion of my sentence.

Good. That's exactly how my competitors should see her. Wide-eyed about everything I do, terrified she could lose me at any moment, and seemingly under my thumb—the perfect Cartel wife combination.

"In you go," I say with a smirk, praying a smile will hide the yearning roaring through my veins. I'm not thickening below the belt because she appears to have the makings of a mafia kingpin's wife, it's from the way her pupils widen when she spotted Alice standing at the top of the stairs waiting for me. She's being hit with the same crass feelings that swamped me when the dweeb she called her 'boyfriend' located her clit. I didn't want him touching her, but for the life of me, I couldn't stop him. It was like seeing a family sedan stuck on the tracks as a train barrels toward them. I shouldn't have watched, but I did, and I devoured every second of it.

As I do again now.

The tint Roxanne's eyes get when she's jealous is even more intoxicating than when she comes. It makes them a murkier green like they're too tainted for me to corrupt.

The thought alone has me the hardest I've ever been. If Alice wasn't at the end of the hall staring at me as Roxanne is staring at her, I may not have been able to set aside a craving so strong it has me wanting to fall to my knees.

Mercifully, Alice doesn't just have impeccable timing, she's a sure-fire knockout. Big brown eyes, glossy blonde hair, and an hourglass figure that could turn over revenue like seconds on a clock if she had the gall to sell herself to more than one client a night. She's a perfect ten out of ten, and I'm not the only one noticing.

Roxanne could only be greener with envy if she were forced to watch us fuck.

"Don't make me ask again, Roxanne. I do *not* like repeating myself." There's an urge in my voice I can't contain. It's thick and hot and as potent as the blood surging to my cock. It has me listening to the head between my legs instead of the one on my shoulders.

With the grunt of a man with holes in his heart, I shove Roxanne into my room. When she falls onto her knees, the situation goes from bad to worse. She's in the perfect position to take my dick between her lips, to suck me down as I've dreamed about her doing more times than I should have the past twelve months.

I could order her to as threatened earlier tonight or remind her of the pledge she made to be on both my arm and in my bed, but I won't. She won't have the look needed to make my ruse authentic if I can't control myself around her within an hour of us being left alone.

Furthermore, she got one up on me when she noticed Smith had connected the electricity to her apartment. I can't let her get more leverage because despite what my cock thinks, she's enemy number one, and it will take more than a roll in the hay to change that.

Chapter Nineteen

Roxanne

I curse at the soap as if it's my stupid lust-fired brain when it slips from my grip for the second time the past five minutes. I'm scrubbing my skin like one of the many dangerous thoughts that flared through Dimitri's eyes when he shoved me into my room occurred instead of him locking me in the palace-like setting before he moseyed to his hookup for the night.

Well, I'm assuming it's a one-night-only fling. They had a familiarity with each other like they know each other's kinks. Alice didn't bat an eyelid when Dimitri shoved me into my room, nor did she flinch when he cockily strolled her way.

How do I know her response, you ask? I peered through the keyhole of my bedroom door like a freak who can't get her rocks off without watching another woman get hers.

There's nothing wrong with voyeurism until you realize you don't want to be the watcher, you prefer being watched.

When that tedious bit of information curdled my stomach,

I gathered myself up from the floor and drudged to the bathroom. My room is so opulent, it should have taken care of the massive knot in my stomach straight away. Regretfully, no amount of glamour can hide ugly truths. Estelle has hot water, electricity, and a bed to sleep in for the next God knows how long, but I have no way of contacting Estelle to tell her I'm safe, no way to check if she made it home from her double shift okay, and no way to tell her I miss her even though we've only been apart for hours.

The very first thing Dimitri confiscated when he let his goons off for the night was my phone. It occurred a mere second after he told Smith to disconnect all the home servers and landlines. He promised I would have a way of contacting Estelle during my stay, but I won't be given the privilege until I've proven myself worthy.

I'm not exactly sure what he wants me to do to prove my worth. I all but begged for him to answer one of the thoughts in his head when I toppled onto my knees, and I was still turned down.

Don't judge. Until you're in my predicament, you can't say how you'd react. I can't bribe Dimitri with money. By the looks of his house and the expensive cars I saw in the driveway, he has plenty of it. The cheap weed I've occasionally bought from my long-lost cousin wouldn't come close to the stack of foiled bricks I saw when shadowing Dimitri's walk through his home so that only leaves me one option. Sex.

If it were with his father or any of his gun-toting elderly friends, I'd cringe at the idea, but I'd be lying if I said the faintest trickle of hope didn't race through my veins when I considered how I could make Dimitri realize I'm worth my weight in gold.

When it dawns on me that scrubbing my skin raw won't stop my ears from working when I exit the bathroom, I shut off the faucet before stepping out of the steam-filled space. My nanna was a fan of letting your skin dry naturally, so I slip into my dressing gown instead of drying myself with the gold 'P' embossed towel on the heated towel rack.

While scrunching my hair to encourage natural waves, I use my spare hand to wipe away the condensation on the gold-framed mirror. The ring I inherited from my grandmother clinks against the foggy surface.

Once it's all cleared away, I take a step back to get a better overall picture. The girl peering back at me doesn't look as frightened as she should. I don't look like a slave of a notorious gangster. My eyes are a darker shade of green than they usually are, and my hair appears more a reddish-brown since it's dripping wet, but my lips are extra plump from the number of times I've dragged my teeth over them, and the smears of mascara my shower didn't remove give my eyes a smoky look. For the most part, I look okay, somewhat desirable.

Just not enough to save myself without praying for a miracle.

I want Rocco's plan to work. If it does, Dimitri's daughter will be safe, and I'll get to go home to my one-bedroom flat, in a town I hate, to the endless job applications at old folks homes where men like Dimitri's father can't wipe their own bottoms.

Can you understand why I'm so conflicted? My edges have always been more frayed than my friends. I'm as daring as I am stupid, but shouldn't I be seeking my cheap thrills anywhere *but* here? Dimitri has almost killed me twice. He tortured my boyfriend before killing him, threatened to harm those I love if I don't comply to his every request, then tossed me out with the bathwater when his late-night party favor arrived as scheduled, yet, I'm more jealous than I am angry.

That proves how insane I am—no evaluation is needed.

My lunacy can't be helped. Every time I look at Dimitri, I remember what I experienced when he watched me in the alleyway. It's the most alive I've ever felt, and it has me willing to take heedless risks to see if I can recreate it.

With a grumbling stomach and still soaking wet hair, I enter the main part of my room preparing to settle in for the night. I'm not a diva. I shower within the four-minute water restriction guidelines brought in years ago when droughts occurred miles and miles from here, so I'm confident I have a good thirty or more minutes before Dimitri returns with the food he promised.

Since my annoyance is higher than my wish to sleep, I'm startled to within an inch of my life when the entrance to my room has me stumbling onto Dimitri standing just inside the bedroom door. He's still dressed in his powerhouse-ready suit, but his jacket and tie have been removed, and the sleeves of his dress shirt are rolled to his elbows.

"Back so soon?" I say before I can reprimand myself for being petty. I'm not upset he has returned early. I'm too gleaming with happiness to feel any type of disappointment. "I thought you'd be gone for hours."

My smugness gets snuffed when he drops his eyes to my dressing gown as he grunts out, "Remove it."

"W-w-what?" Don't ask if I'm stuttering in fear or excitement as I wouldn't be able to answer you.

Once I'm confident my voice will resemble some sort of normalcy, I ask, "Why? Didn't you get your kicks from Alice?"

My heart thrashes against my ribs when Dimitri pushes off his feet to stalk my way. His walk matches the one I've dreamed about time and time again the past year. His hands just aren't moving for the belt of his jeans as my fucked-up head recalls the security guard doing. I hardly took my eyes off Dimitri, so why do flashes of the guard's hands moving for his belt constantly pop into my head when I'm daydreaming?

I'm drawn from my thoughts when Dimitri asks, "What was our agreement, Roxanne?"

"You can call me Roxie. All my friends do…"

My offer to fake niceties fades to silence when the gritting of his teeth overtakes the shrill of my pulse in my ears. "What was our agreement, Rox-*anne?*" He overemphasis my name to prove a point.

"That I am to do what you want, when you want, for how long you want," I chirp out like an obedient little bird.

Dimitri slants his head as his eyes flare with an unknown glimmer. "And what did I ask you to do?"

"You asked me to remove my dressing gown." Knowing this is a test, I unknot the cord around my waist, toss open my dressing gown as if I'm wearing a onesie underneath, then let the material fall to the floor. I don't care if this is a credit for my double business diploma or a sick, warped mind-fuck, I refuse to have another 'F' marked against my name.

The fluffy, static-loving material descended to the floor with a whoosh. Its breathy drop has nothing on the air that whistles through Dimitri's teeth when he takes in my naked form for the first time. He can deny me all he likes and have his staff tell me I'm not his type, but the crotch of his pants isn't so lucky. It's fatter in an instant, and I'm not the only one noticing.

After adjusting his footing so his erection isn't as prominent, Dimitri cranks his neck to the side of the room. When I follow the direction of his gaze, my mouth falls open. We're not alone. The owner of the woman's name I spat out as if it was vomit is seated in a leather chair behind a bulky desk. She's taking in my naked backside as eagerly as Dimitri did.

"Leave it," Dimitri shouts when I bob down to gather my dressing gown off the floor.

I freeze like a statue, aware of the repercussions if I ignore his direct order. Rocco barely survived Dimitri's wrath when he demanded he switch places with the driver partway back to Hopeton. It ended with a gun being drawn and Rocco grumbling that Dimitri is a surly bastard who couldn't see a good thing if it slapped him in the face.

Even with the heat of two beady eyes on me, I keep my hands balled at my sides and my eyes planted on the floor. I'm adventurous, but I am not comfortable with this. Estelle hasn't seen me naked, and she's been my friend for a hundred years.

"What do you think?" This question came from Dimitri, but it wasn't directed at me. It's for his gawking, bug-eyed friend.

"She's a little skinny, and her hair could use a trim, but I don't see any issues. Her body has a nice symmetry between her hips and breasts, and she's very attractive. She'll turn heads no matter the notoriety of your guests." Alice has an accent like nearly every other person in Dimitri's crew. It isn't as strong as the others but still noticeable.

My eyes float up to Dimitri when he asks, "And her scar?"

In the corner of my eye, I spot Alice making her way across the room. She either sees naked women regularly, or she isn't interested in anything I'm offering. Her eyes never leave mine—not once. She saw what she needed of my body, and now her focus is elsewhere.

Through twisted lips, Alice asks Dimitri, "You don't want to keep her bangs?"

"No, it hides her face. It's one of her best assets. I don't want it hidden." His reply is almost a compliment until he adds, "I just need to get rid of her scar."

I inconspicuously drape my arms in front of my breasts when Alice stops in front of me to brush my bangs off my forehead. She doesn't cringe when she takes in the scar I got from hitting the ground headfirst. She hums out a moan.

"I agree with your assessment. Even pinning her bangs

back will give her face more appeal. And her eyes…" There she goes with her inappropriate moaning again. "They're perfect." After dropping her hand from my face, she shifts on her feet to face Dimitri. "Are you sure you don't want her to become an asset? The men will love her."

"I'm not interested in selling her." When relief darts through my eyes, Dimitri is quick to shut it down. "Yet." Leering at my pout, he nudges his head at me like he hasn't been ogling the shadows between my legs the past five minutes. "Get your measurements. I need outfits by morning."

Alice's smile matches Dimitri's hidden one when she replies, "No need. I have everything I need right here." She taps her faultlessly perfect nail on her even more faultless head. "Six or eight? I can't do seven because Lucy has a Skype session with her father. The warden would only agree to a morning session." A pfft vibrates her lips. "Anyone would think he was running the show around there."

Dimitri laughs. I don't know his laughs, but I'd register this one as being sixty percent fake, even with him seeming friendly with Alice. "We'll do six. Roxanne is about to head to bed, so she'll be well-rested." He commences walking Alice to the door. "And if you want me to talk to Ashton, let me know. He's new, so he still has a lot to learn."

"I've got it, but thanks for the offer." A stupid rush of jealousy scatters through my veins when she presses a kiss to Dimitri's mouth. She doesn't do the air kisses the rich folks do. She presses her mouth so firmly to his, even though I can't see Dimitri's lips, I know they're coated with lipstick. "Until tomorrow."

When she farewells me with a wiggle of her fingers, I snatch up my dressing gown from the floor. I have one arm in and the other just about to burst through the opening when Dimitri demands me to 'leave it' again.

I don't listen this time around, too mortified with embarrassment to care about being punished. Not only did he parade me in front of a woman who has more plastic than a Barbie doll, he made me feel hideously ugly while doing it.

"Why do that? Why agree to my help if I'm not up to your standards?" After tying the dressing gown's belt around my waist like it will take more than a set of hands to undo the knot, I air quote my last word.

"Tomorrow's guests are very important to my overall plan. They'd never believe my ruse if you showed up in a Ross Dress for Less dress."

I stare at Dimitri, wondering how the hell he knew my dress was from my favorite discount clothing chain.

He douses my curiosity in an instant. "Your dress tag had the infamous last season strike through it. It wasn't showcased at Fashion Week this season." He snickers in a way the men for *Queer Eye for a Straight Guy* would be proud of. "It probably wasn't featured in the last two decades."

My anger is lessening, but I still scoff, not over the jabs he hit my ego with just yet. "And your revulsion of my scar? What's your excuse for that?"

Air whizzes out of my nose when he has the audacity to laugh. I'm glad he's finding amusement in our exchange. I'm anything but humored.

"I'll do what you ask. I will follow your plan. I'll even let your over-polished bozo make me look like a gleaming piece of plastic, but the next time you look in the mirror, ask yourself how you'd feel if your daughter ended up with a man like you."

Ignoring the furious heat bounding out of him, I drag down the bedspread on the king-size bed I'm standing next to, then slip between the sheets.

"You need to eat before sleeping." His words are ground through clenched teeth and a pulsating jaw. Right here, right now, he wouldn't care if I starved to death. The only reason he's acting like he gives a shit is because he wants his daughter back, and Alice's visit filled him with hope that I could help him with that. "Roxanne——"

"I'm not hungry."

His roar nearly shudders my heart straight out of my chest. "I don't give a fuck if you're hungry or not. You heard what Alice said. You are far too skinny. You need to eat."

When a stretch of silence passes between us, he growls out my name again. Unfortunately for him, my hair coloring matches my personality.

Lately, I'm as stubborn as I am stupid.

"Fine. Don't fucking eat. You can starve for all I care." Although he sounds more frustrated than vindictive, his words still kick me in the gut.

My ego hasn't gotten over his earlier battering.

It didn't need another walloping.

My wallowing in a self-pity party is bookmarked for another date when the sound of someone getting undressed trickles into my ears a few minutes later. Too curious to discount the odd noise considering I'm in the room with a stranger, I slant my head to the left before glancing across the room.

My parched throat becomes a thing of the past when my eyes lock in on Dimitri's half-dressed form. His dress shirt has been removed, and he's in the process of yanking a wife beater over his head.

The number of tattoos on his hands, forearms, and neck should have clued me in on the fact he has an extensive collection, but I had no clue it was this vast. Black artwork covers almost every inch of his body—even the top of his thighs which I get a bird's-eye view of when he toes off his shoes before tugging down his trousers.

It's a beautiful collection that grows more exquisite when

you take in how they accentuate the cut groves of his body. I doubt he works out, but his body proves he doesn't leave the heavy lifting to his goons. He gets in on the action as often as possible.

"Sweet Mother of Jesus," I whisper on a moan when he leans across his desk to dump a set of cufflinks into a silver dish. His backside is divine, an ass worthy of a top-rated centerfold.

When Dimitri suddenly freezes, no doubt feeling the heat of my stare, I snap my eyes shut and pretend I'm sleeping. In less than a second, it dawns on me that my ruse is futile. Not only do I feel the heat of his eyes on me as I ogled him only moments ago, I hear his sock-covered feet indenting the thick carpet pile. He doesn't cross the room with his infamous cocky strut. He takes his time, moving slyly like a fox, forever on alert, yet somehow easily distracted.

"I had wondered if your refusal to eat was because your hunger had nothing to do with food." His voice is thicker than it usually is, twanged with his Italian heritage. "But since I always double-guess myself around you, I once again brushed it off. Silly me." He's at the side of my bed now, so close the fine hair on the tops of his legs brush the arm draped across my body. "Everything you want to see is right in front of you, so why don't you open your eyes, Roxanne?"

Either determined to prove he doesn't scare me or that I'm downright stupid, I pop open my eyes at his request. The visual is ten times better than the one in my head. I don't know where to look first—at the thick rippling of muscles in his midsection or the sturdy thighs holding up the incredibly mouthwatering package.

Perhaps I should start at his bulging biceps before finishing at a hardness more than a spark of attraction would be required to instigate?

His cock is thick and hard, meaning the stretchy material of his trunks is being put through the ultimate durability test. They're a quality brand, however they look seconds from fraying under the pressure of his pulsating rod of flesh.

My eyes slowly float up to his face when he says, "All it takes is a few seconds of distraction and *poof,* your entire existence is over." I'm confused as to what he means until I attempt to stop him from uncinching the belt holding my dressing gown close to my body. My hands are bound above my head, secured by a set of cuffs that have been used often enough to leave notches in the bedposts.

"Let me go." Just the thought of any woman being cuffed to his bed has my voice the most unhinged it's ever been. It's fueled more by anger than fear, peeved as fuck that even when my life is in danger, jealousy is still my most paramount emotion.

I couldn't understand Eddie's anger about me climaxing over another man's watch, yet here I am getting blistering mad over a man I hardly know playing sex games on the bed I'm resting on.

I'm certifiably insane.

Dimitri's smile is as white-hot as the surge that bolts through me when he shakes his head. "Not until you say please."

With his eyes locked on mine, he undoes the knot in my dressing gown cord faster than I can snap my fingers. His chest rises and falls in rhythm to the throb in my throat when he pries open the material. He doesn't part the seams far enough that my nipples become exposed, but the heat from his hooded-gaze makes it seem as if he did.

The friction his meekest touch causes is unbelievable. It has heat blazing through me, and its fiery response grows in intensity when he glides his index finger through the galley between my breasts. He's barely touching me, but every inch of my body tightens, anticipating more. *Wanting* more.

When his hand stops near my chin, my head naturally slants so I can nuzzle my cheek into his palm. It's as sticky as the mess between my legs, his body temperature too high to discount.

Dimitri's body isn't the only thing warming up. Heat burns at my cheeks, just not all of their redness can be blamed on desire. Some of it is shame. Shame he killed my boyfriend, and I don't feel the least bit bad about it. Shame his touch should revolt me when it doesn't. Shame that even after he made me feel as tiny as an ant, I'm on the verge of begging him to touch me.

"Say please, Roxanne," he grinds out through clenched teeth. "Say please before I remember you're the reason my wife is dead, and my daughter is missing. Say please before I remember for every hour of every day that *you* are responsible for everything that has happened." He locks his eyes with mine. They're dark and tormented, but oh so beautiful. "Say please before I remember no amount of pleading will *ever* see me sparing your life. Say please, Roxanne." He lowers his hand from my cheek to my neck. "Say it now before it's too late."

The last of the air in my lungs rushes out with a moan when he grips my throat with enough strength both my clit and my lungs award his aggression with their utmost devotion. They both scream with need, one is just slightly louder than the other.

"Please."

Chapter Twenty

Dimitri

Although Roxanne's one word is as breathless as her lungs, and the itch to kill is skittering through my veins begging me to ignore her request, I tamp down the debilitating restlessness I was born with before weakening my grip on her throat.

Her gasps as she fights to fill her lungs with air excites me even more. It's a genuine need that spreads through me like a wildfire as hot and heavy as the blood feeding my cock. She has so much attitude, so much spit-fire—the very thing Audrey was missing.

My wife's attitude didn't live up to her brash hair coloring. She was always the quieter one in the room. She didn't raise her voice or fight for the top position in the room. As long as it kept her out of the spotlight, she was happy to let anyone take the lead. She could see another woman's lipstick on the collar of my shirt, smell her perfume on my skin, and she did nothing —not a single fucking thing.

Her inability to fight for me saw me fucking around on her more. I wanted to see her cheeks inflamed with jealousy, for her to tell me she hated me before vowing to kill the woman who dared to slip between our matrimonial sheets.

I wanted to feel needed.

I *never* got that from Audrey.

Not once.

The same can't be said for Roxanne. She didn't ask me to stop because she's sickened at the idea of me touching her. She did it because she's angry at herself.

Even the risk of dying isn't enough to offset her desire for me. I killed her boyfriend, threatened her family, and told her I'd bury her alive just to hear her screams suffocated by the dirt clogging her lungs, yet she still wants me to fuck her, lick her, kiss her, and claim every single inch of her.

She wants me like my wife never did, but in a way I'll never be able to fulfill.

I can learn from my past, however I can't forget it. Fien deserves more than to be set aside for a woman who infuriates me as much as she intrigues me. She's my daughter, my blood. She comes before anyone—even me.

With that in mind, I snatch my hand away from Roxanne like her scar revolts me as much as she believes before heading for the attached bathroom.

The agony between my legs worsens when I flick on the faucet in the freestanding shower. Roxanne's scent is stronger in confined spaces. It's why I couldn't keep a cool head when her breast continually brushed Rocco's arm during our drive to Hopeton.

I could have blamed the bumps in the road for their constant contact, but my fucked-up head refuses to play nice when it's spiraling out of control. One more brush and I would have popped a bullet between Rocco's eyes like he hasn't been my friend for the past two decades.

While waiting for the water pumping out of the shower-head to turn blistering hot, I shred off my all-black trunks before moving to stand in front of the mirror. I briefly consider returning to my room when I take in how red and angry my cock looks. He's throbbing with need, his thickness solely reliant on the woman handcuffed to my bed.

My lips curve to the side when I recall how easily I distracted Roxanne. Not even the clanging of the cuffs when I removed them from my bedside table shifted her eyes off my body. She dragged them over every inch of me, heating my skin with the same frantic buzz of a tattoo gun.

Her distraction should give my guilt some leeway. Unfortunately, that's far from the truth. I stopped seeking excuses months ago. I fucked up, I looked away, and now I'm paying for the consequences of my actions.

When I step into the steam-filled space, my hand stirs to drop to my engorged cock. I want to squeeze it a little to release some of the tension causing its agony, but since I refuse to let the fiery little wildcat mere feet away know the hold she has over me, I lean into the scorching hot water, praying it will scold her touch from my skin as effectively as it will drain the blood from my cock.

Usually, my cock reacts to burning heat the same way it would if I plunged it into an ice bath. It isn't having the same effect today. I like the passion that comes from a fiery response. Whether the death of an insolent man or the slap of a scorned woman, there's an emotion attached to every response, a thrill you can't get from wrapping your hand around your cock and batting one out. It requires a woman's touch. Her heated breaths on my neck. Her silky-smooth skin under my hand. Her cunt wrapped around my cock.

Jesus. I should have taken Alice up on her offer. Wanting Roxanne to experience the inane stupidity that pumped through me from Rocco's protectiveness, I overexerted my words when requesting Smith to organize a late-night appointment with Alice. He must have conveyed my request to Alice in the same manner. She came over ready to suck my dick. Her logic that penetration isn't cheating always sees her ready to get on her knees.

I told her no. I walked away.

I'm regretting it more than ever right now.

Perhaps I can be quiet? Maybe Roxanne is already asleep?

No! I release my cock from my hand before grabbing a bar of soap from the soap dish. I scrub my skin until it's raw, then attack it with the same amount of intensity with a towel.

By the time I walk back into my room, my anger is as high as my dick rests against my stomach. My fury hasn't weakened its pulse in the slightest. Its hardness is fed by the same gall firing in Roxanne's eyes when she spots my naked stalk across the room. She doesn't speak, she just raises her brow that exposes her red hair color is natural while silently stalking me.

"You should be sleeping. Alice is *never* tardy." She learned what happens to slackers the hard way seven years ago. "She will be here at precisely six."

Roxanne waits for me to pull on a pair of sleeping pants before she raises her eyes to my face. Although her hooded-gaze is brimming with lust, they reveal she's still scared. "I can't sleep." She chews on the corner of her plump lips before half-heartedly shrugging. "I'm kinda hungry."

Air whizzes out of my nose as I fight not to roll my eyes. "Of course you are."

I gather up a plain white tee before marching to her side of the room. I pretend not to notice the blistering of goosebumps racing across her skin when I adjust the angle of her head so I can see if my earlier anger left a mark. Her neck is a little red where I gripped her, but for the most part, she's relatively uninjured.

Mistaking the annoyance in my eyes as sorrow, Roxanne frees her lip from her menacing teeth before saying, "It's more frustrating than sore." She jangles the cuffs circulating her wrists. "Kind of like these." As she bounces her pretty eyes between mine, she asks, "Can you please take them off?"

Her cutesy act gets side-swiped when I shake my head.

She's back to her feisty self in no time.

"Why not?"

Although I don't appreciate being interrogated, this line of questioning doesn't bother me. "Because that's only something that will occur *once* you've gained my trust."

"How can I gain your trust while cuffed to a bed…" Her words trail off as her throat works hard to swallow. She noticed how thick I was when I re-entered the room, so her thoughts immediately deviate toward wicked territory.

So do mine, but I pretend otherwise. "You can start by answering some questions for me."

When she hesitantly nods, unsure how she could possibly have any information I need, I gather a manila folder from my desk and the chair from underneath it. While I set up a makeshift command center on Roxanne's half of the room, she maneuvers herself into a half-seated position. It's no easy feat considering she's cuffed to the headboard, but she makes it appear easy.

"Ready?"

Ignoring the dangerous drape of her dressing gown, she dips her chin.

Feigning the same level of calmness, I drop my eyes to the stack of paperwork Smith delivered during our commute from Erkinsvale to here. For the most part, it's my father's movement sheets for the next several months, but there are also snippets of the information he shared about Roxanne's movements the day Audrey was kidnapped.

"Do you recognize any of these men?" I show her a photograph Smith pulled from the FBI's database several years ago. It's the last known group shot of the Castro crew.

"Look longer," I demand when Roxanne shakes her head within a few seconds of drinking in the group shot. There are over thirty men pictured. It isn't possible for her to have scanned all of their faces in that short amount of time.

When I say that, Roxanne scoffs. "I don't need a longer look. They all have dark, ethnic appearances. I grew up in Erkinsvale, so you can trust me when I say we've never crossed paths."

"What about when you met with your father in New York, did you see them, then?"

Her cheeks whiten when reality dawns. "Are these the men who took your wife?" When I nod, she scoots as close to me as her cuffs will allow. "Can you hold it a little closer? I don't have the best vision."

Unappreciative of the humor in her voice, I hold it to within an inch of her face.

After a period long enough to ensure me she scanned each face with precise detail, she inches back before once again shaking her head. "I'm sorry, none of them ring a bell." The anger making my skin sticky eases when she adds, "But I've seen him before."

When her eyes drop to a surveillance image of my father, my breath comes out in a rush. "He killed Old Man V earlier tonight. You don't get any credit for that."

My brows fetter in confusion when she replies, "Not tonight. At the bar next to the restaurant your wife was taken from. I swear he was seated at the end of the bar, although he looked a lot younger back then than he does now." She lifts her eyes to mine, even though confusion is clouding them, I can tell she's being honest. She has truthful, wholesome eyes. "His hair was darker, and his stomach was a little rounder, but I remember him because he was wearing a St. Jude pendant, but instead of it being on his necklace—"

"He wore it on a leather bracelet on his left wrist?"

When her pupils dilate in confirmation, I feel like I've been punched in the gut.

"Was it him?" I ask after gathering a photo frame from my desk and clearing away the dust coating it. It's a photograph of me with three of my siblings—Roberto, Ophelia, and CJ. It was taken by Rocco at my twenty-first birthday, a mere month before everything went downhill for my family.

"Yeah," Roxanna answers with an unsure nod. "But he had put on some weight and aged by almost a decade. Who is he?"

"He's my brother," I answer, too shocked to think up a lie. "My brother, who's been missing for almost five years."

Roxanne raises her eyes to mine. Worry, I think she's leading me astray, is seen all over her face. "Maybe it was your father, then? My head was all types of muddled that day. I was eighteen and in the big city alone for the first time. I could be mistaken."

I know she's lying, and so does she. She either saw Roberto or his biological twin. Either way, I need to know *exactly* who he is because there's no way my missing brother being at the same restaurant my wife was kidnapped from could be classed as a coincidence.

"Smith…"

Forever on alert, Smith's voice comes through the speaker of my cell phone two seconds later. "Yeah?"

Roxanne arches a brow when I ask, "Are you still friends with the composite sketch artist at Ravenshoe PD?"

"Yeah, but I don't see her coming out at this hour." His snickers out a laugh before continuing, "She might if you were willing to offer her some kind of incentive."

By incentive, he doesn't mean money. The male counterparts of Ravenshoe PD are all about favors, money, and uncut blow. The female half are all about the D.

You can have anything you want around these parts if you're willing to toss a few orgasms at the depraved women running this place. Even the chief of police's daughter shared trade secrets when I was balls deep inside of her.

I'm about to tell Smith to get her here no matter the cost, but the faintest trickle of a whisper stops me. "I can draw." When my eyes stray to Roxanne's, hers roll at the shocked expression on my face. "If you don't believe me, tell Smith to take a look at my Instagram page."

"She's telling the truth," Smith chimes in as image after image pops up on the screen of my phone.

I hear Roxanne's throat work through a hearty swallow when I move to gather my phone off my desk. Although her confidence is hot enough to blister my skin, she's nervous about what my response will be to her drawings.

She has no reason to fret. She has an immense amount of talent.

"You drew these?" The drawings range from portraits of dogs and cats with their tongues hanging out to couples in various stages of erotic content. The detail is undeniable. Even with the sketches being black and white, I can see the texture of the dog's shiny coat, and I'm not going to mention the realistic veins in one of her model's cocks, or he'll have a bounty on his head by the end of tonight.

"The animals were commissioned pieces on Fiverr. People emailed me photos of their animals, and I turned them into sketches for five dollars a pop." She drags her tongue over her plump lips. "And the people are from the images in my head." Shame burns on her cheeks when she mutters, "If I dream about them, they end up in the pages of my sketchbook."

I'm torn between wanting to explore the shame in her eyes and getting back to the task at hand, so instead of picking, I do both. "Send someone out to purchase a sketchpad and pencils." When Smith hums an agreeing noise, I send him a quick message about a request I can't articulate in front of Roxanne before devoting all my attention to her. "Do you think you can sketch the man you saw that night?"

A current I haven't experienced in years trickles into my veins when she once again dips her chin.

Chapter Twenty-One

Dimitri

His face is rounder than I remember, and his stomach is almost double in size, but there's no denying the man Roxanne saw at the Slice of Salt is my brother, Roberto. His eyes are the same wintry blue coloring as mine, his bushy brows hang heavily over his eyes, and the faintest of scars from where I accidentally jabbed my stick-sword into his right cheek is present in Roxanne's sketch.

It's Roberto. I'm one hundred percent confident of this. The only thing I can't work out is why. Audrey was taken less than two years ago. Roberto has been missing for almost five years. The math doesn't add up. Roberto, along with Ophelia, CJ, and I wanted to leave the family behind, but we were meant to do it together. We were a team, a unit, and we pledged never to leave the other behind, so why did he? And does his reasoning have anything to do with Audrey's kidnapping and Fien's disappearance?

There's only one way to find out. "Pack everything up. We leave in an hour."

Roxanne's eyes dart up to mine, seeking answers, but I'm out the door before a single syllable can be fired from her mouth.

"What do you make of this?" I ask Rocco, who leaps up to his feet since my unwarranted jealously saw me stationing him outside of Roxanne's room instead of inside of it.

When I thrust Roxanne's drawing into his chest, his lips purse. "What does Roberto have to do with this?"

"That's exactly what I'm trying to work out." He follows my fast pace down the hall. "Roxanne saw him around Slice of Salt the night Audrey was kidnapped."

"Shit." Rocco drags a hand across tired eyes before pushing out a set of words I never anticipated for him to speak—especially when it comes to Roxanne. "Are you sure we can trust her? Maybe you should hold back for a moment and take a good look at the evidence."

I freeze partway down the hallway before glaring at him with steely, annoyed eyes. He forced Roxanne into my life believing she could help me get Fien back, and now he's asking me to tug on the reins just as things get interesting. Is he brain dead?

"I'm not saying she's untrustworthy. I just need you to be cautious." When his roundabout excuse fails to hit its mark, he tries straight-up honesty instead. "Smith sent me to collect Roxanne's sketchpad from her apartment as per your request." That was what I texted Smith about earlier. I didn't want Roxanne knowing how fascinated I was to see if I had featured in her dreams, so I didn't vocalize my needs. I sent them via a text message. "There was more than one sketchpad. They went back years. This one is from when she was in primary school." He thrusts a cheap, flip notepad into my chest. "From the dates, I'm guessing she was around eight or nine."

The already brisk cantor of my heart jumps up a notch when I flick through the extensive collection of drawings. Although Roxanne's talent isn't at the level it is now, there's no denying she was a skilled artist even back then. But the thing is, the sketches are too graphic for a child, far too erotic. The images only adults should see, and even then, they'd be paying top dollar to see them. I know this because my empire was built on this type of filth.

After handing the notepad back to Rocco, I ask, "Roxanne said her drawings are based on dreams. Could that have been the case back then?" My question is a woeful waste of time. I've never seen Fien in the flesh, but even I know this type of behavior isn't normal for a child.

Rocco shifts from foot to foot while nervously breathing out of his nose. "Smith said her mother dropped her off to live with her parents when she was only a child." He lowers his eyes to the notepad holding graphic images of couples in various stages of raunchy sex. "Could this be the reason?"

I shrug, truly unsure. The information Smith unearthed about Roxanne's family months ago reveals her parents are fucked in the head, but come on, this is beyond that. You can be dependent on drugs, but that doesn't stop you knowing the difference between right and wrong. A parent is supposed to protect their child, they're supposed to love them like no one else can. They are *not* supposed to make them a mental case like my father did me.

Although my jaw is tight and the wish to kill is doubling the width of my veins, I can't let this slide. "What if she isn't wrong, Rocco? What if she did see Roberto that night? If I ignore that, and it turns out she was telling the truth, I'll never forgive myself. I need to know if she saw Roberto. I need to know if he's a part of this." I bounce my eyes between Rocco's. I'm incapable of recognizing the man glancing back at me but I know one day he will eventually expose himself. "Then once I know, I'll deal with *this*. I'll make *this* right." The way I say 'this' reveals who I am speaking about. "Just not until Fien is home. She has to come first, Rocco. She should have always come first."

"All right," he agrees with a frantic bob of his head. "Tell me what you need and where you need it, and I'll get it there for you."

I slap his shoulder, grateful for his understanding. "I need the jet fueled and ready to go. It's time to head back to New York."

I halt flicking through one of Roxanne's many sketchpads when Rocco enters the plane without her. Although something isn't sitting right with my stomach, the longer I peruse Roxanne's collection of artwork, the more my curiosity is piqued. There are no faces on the people she sketched during her childhood, no identifiable marks or features that would help Smith track them down. There are just arms, torsos, legs, and pelvises in various stages of movement. The detail of each piece is so vivid, I can imagine the positions each couple made during their intricate tryst.

If I were unaware the sketches were drawn by a child, I'd purchase every one of them like a crazed collector, aware the artist would be big one day. But since I know that isn't the case, I'm tempted to burn them all until they're nothing but chunks of charcoal Roxanne could use to start all over again.

With my emotions not knowing which way to swing, I place

the overloaded notepad into my suitcase before raising my eyes to Rocco. "Where's Roxanne?"

My head slants to hide the tick of my jaw when he answers, "She isn't coming."

"What do you mean she isn't coming? She doesn't have a choice." I drift my eyes to the Range Rover parked at the side of the plane. I know Roxanne is sitting inside of it because not only did I buckle her into the seat in more ways than one before our thirty-mile trip, the lights illuminating the hangar are shining into the back seat, lighting up Roxanne's already bright hair.

My eyes rocket back to Rocco when he mutters, "She said she'd rather be buried in a shallow ditch than forced into a sex trafficking circuit." When shock crosses my features, he chuckles out a breathy laugh. "Think about it, Dimi. She has a point. How is nearly every white American female lured into the trade these days? Fancy mansion, top-of-the-line Range Rover, and a private jet, then, before you know it, *boom-shaka-laka*, you're eating porridge from a dog bowl in a cage. If I were a chick, I'd be gripping the door handle as hard as she is now. You wouldn't get me in here for shit."

Neither amused by his humor nor having the time for it, I snap out, "You don't *ask* her to join us, you *force* her to join us."

He holds his hand out in front of himself like I ordered for him to suck my dick. "You know that isn't me, Dimi. I don't do that shit." My foul mood worsens when he adds, "Especially not to Roxie. I ain't got no beef with her."

Needing to leave before I pop a bullet between his quirked brows, I unlatch my seat belt, clamber down the stairs of a private jet, then throw open the door opposite to the one Roxanne is clutching in fear for her life.

"Don't you want to come to New York with us?" It's the fight of my life to keep the surprise off my face. I'm stunned by how calm and collective my question came out considering my veins are being obliterated with blackened rage.

Roxanne takes a beat to consider my question before she timidly shakes her head.

"All right. Then off you go."

The shock I'm struggling to keep off my face jumps onto Roxanne's. "I'm free to go?"

Her 'duh' face is cuter than I care to admit. "Uh-huh. You did as asked. You gave me information I needed to identify Fien's kidnappers."

"But I said her captor was a woman. Roberto isn't a woman." She pauses to reprimand herself for trying to talk herself out of going. "I guess he could be working with one?"

"Perhaps, but I won't find out here. I need to go to New York."

"Okay." Her constant licking of her lips shouldn't be sexy, but it is. "Then go. I can find my way home from here."

I almost smile at her cunningness. "When I leave, this vehicle, along with my possessions inside of it, will return to the Petretti compound. If anything is removed from it without my permission, it'll be classed as theft. Theft is a big no-no in this industry, Roxanne. Do you know what happens to people who steal from me?"

Her pupils don't dilate in the slightest when she answers, "They die."

"Uh-huh. Is that what you want to happen to Maio?"

Her eyes lock with Maio's in the rearview mirror for the quickest second before she shakes her head.

"Then, you need to leave this airstrip before me."

A smirk begs to notch my lips higher when she once again shakes her head. I should have known she's too smart to fall for my tricks. She might only be twenty, but she's lived a harsh life that matured her at double the rate of her peers.

It's the same for me. I'm barely notching twenty-six, but it feels like I'll be seeking an assisted living facility within the next year or two. That isn't surprising considering hardly anyone in this industry lives past thirty.

When Roxanne's knuckles remain white from her death-clutch on the door handle I cuffed her to for our trip, my bad mood gets the better of me. "All right. Then, I guess I may as well shoot Maio now."

Before Roxanne can blink, I blow Maio's brains out. He slumps forward, the honk of the horn announcing to the rest of my crew that the trash has been taken out.

I didn't just kill him to scare Roxanne out of my car. His sneaky hands were stirring one too many pots, and don't get me started on the comments I heard him whispering to my men when I guided Roxanne to his car, or I'll discharge my entire clip into the space of air his brain should have been taking up.

Respect for Roxanne's determination whizzes out my nose when she throws open the door she's been clutching the past ten minutes, slips out, then hightails it away from me. She doesn't look back my way once, her focus solely on escaping.

I could threaten to shoot her if she doesn't stop, or chase her down, but why exhaust myself if I don't need to? She's running straight toward the marshlands Clover hid in while waiting for us to leave so he could take care of Maio.

She isn't going anywhere but to New York with me.

After dumping my gun onto the floor of the Range Rover so Clover can clean up my mess—the Petretti run on the 'no bodies, no time for our crimes' theory—I return to the private jet.

Rocco eyes me with confusion slashed across his features, shocked I returned without the package I went to collect. His bewilderment is alleviated two seconds later when a kicking and screaming Roxanne is walked into the plane over Clover's shoulder. She's fighting him with everything she has, which only doubles the amusement on Clover's face. He's so big, I doubt he's feeling the slightest twinge of pain from her fists whacking him in the back.

"Did someone order a redhead with a slice of feisty?" Clover asks with a chuckle.

As the men around him laugh, my jaw tightens. There are too many hungry eyes watching Roxanne's every move. It has me itching to kill even more than Maio's attempt to bite the hand that fed him.

Rocco's eyes snap to mine as quickly as Roxanne stops pounding the shit out of Clover's back when I say, "Take her to the bedroom."

Knowing better than to double-guess my direct order, Clover immediately commences moving Roxanne to the lower half of the jet.

Rocco doesn't follow his obedient lead. "Dimi—"

I shut him up with a stern sideways glare. "Tell the pilot I want wheels up in no less than five minutes. We're already behind schedule."

Too tired to answer the many questions his narrowed eyes are throwing my way, I sidestep him before shadowing Clover's walk.

I've only just entered the compact yet luxurious sleeping quarters at the back of the jet when Roxanne lands on the bed with a thud. She springs back onto her feet in under a second, but my stern grumble telling her to sit stops her bounce off the springy mattress.

"We had an agreement. You have not yet fulfilled your side of our agreement, so you're not free to go."

"This was *never* part of our agreement." She peers past my shoulder to the men I feel watching her. There's no doubt they're interested, but since they'd have to get through me to touch her, she has nothing to worry about.

The pounding of my heart matches the vein working overtime in Roxanne's neck when I request for Clover to disembark the jet. She watches his exit, her eyes only returning to mine after I've fastened the latch on the only bit of safety between her and my thirsty crew.

"If you think I brought you here to fuck you, you're wrong." My next set of words are hard to articulate when the late hour has me confusing the flare darting through her eyes as a disappointed one. "If I wanted to fuck you, you'd already be fucked. If I wanted them to fuck you…" I nudge my head to the door I just locked, "… they'd be lining up for round two. But that isn't what this is about. *None* of this is about you. It's about Fien, my daughter. I'm trying to protect her as your daddy should have protected you. I'm trying to keep her safe."

For the first time tonight, the wetness in Roxanne's eyes isn't from fear. She's remorseful, although it has nothing on my guilt when I ask, "Did your father fuck with your head or his druggo friends?"

This isn't a conversation we should be having now. I doubt it's even one we should have in the near future, but for the life of me, I can't hold back my interrogation. The knot in my gut won't lessen until Roxanne gives me the answers I'm seeking, and even then, I'm certain it'll take more than words to fully smooth it out.

"What?" I can see how badly she wants to deny my claim, but with her mouth refusing to relinquish another lie, she could only get one word out.

"You have the markings of an abused child, a fascination with the man who watched you get off in an alleyway." I didn't just feature in her latest drawings. My rain-soaked, cloaked-by-darkness form is the *only* thing she has sketched the past year.

"The sexual maturity of someone much older and wiser." I lock my eyes with her watering ones. "And your nipples bud every time you feel threatened or scared." She can deny my accusations all she likes, but the straining of her nipples against the thick material of her dressing gown is undeniable. "So that leads me to believe your daddy either fiddled with you, or he sold you to his drug-fucked buddies like he did your mother."

Her hands ball as tightly as mine when she shakes her head, denying my accusations. "He never touched me."

"So, his friends did?"

"That isn't what I said." Her words are as icy as the color of my eyes and just as lifeless.

With anger clutching my throat, every word I speak is delivered with a gravelly growl. "You didn't deny it either, Roxanne. So what is it? Did they touch you? Or did your sweet ole Pa treat his daughter like a dirty little whore?"

"It was neither of those things!"

When she attempts to race by me, I grab the tops of her arms and drag her to within an inch of my face. "Then... What. Was. It?" My voice is as loud as hers, my anger just as palpable. I'm not angry at her. I'm fighting the urge not to track down her father and slit his pedophile throat.

This kills me to admit, even more so since Ophelia's life was cut short right around the age Roxanne is now, but Roxanne's eyes hold the same dark, gleaming secrets Ophelia's did any time our father returned home after a long stint of absence. They were badly stained, but not enough to have you believing they were wholly broken. They could be fixed if the right person was willing to put in the hard yards.

I thought Isaac Holt was that person for Ophelia. I was wrong then just like I could be now, but I can't stop pushing. I need to know who hurt Roxanne. I need to know more than my lungs need their next breath.

"Did he touch you, Roxanne? Is that why you were sent to live with your grandparents? Did your mother try to protect you *after* your father already fucking hurt you?"

"No," she denies again, even with her eyes screaming the opposite. "He didn't touch me!"

"Then what did he do? Why do you act as if he doesn't exist?" I crowd her against the door of the private jet just as its engines roar to life. "Why do you hate him so much that just the thought of saying his name has you wanting to vomit."

"He made me watch!" she shouts before she can stop herself. "He made me watch what they did to my mother." Tears roll down her ashen face unchecked as she repeats, "He made me watch."

I want to kill, I want to go on a rampage, but instead of doing either of those things, I do the last thing anyone would ever expect. I pull Roxanne into my chest, hopeful her tears will cool the rage burning me up inside.

If they don't, I'm sure I can find another means to dispel my anger.

Torturing her father will be a good start.

Chapter Twenty-Two

Roxanne

Sighing, I rest my cheek onto the top of my knees. The meal a member of Dimitri's staff is placing on the bedside table smells as divine as the previous three, but no number of excited rumblings from my stomach will pull me out of the slump I'm in.

I cried in the chest of a man who'd rather kill me than bed me.

If that isn't bad enough, it seems as if that was the beginning of my punishment.

I've been shunted from activities. Left out in the cold like the naughty child I am.

The confession Dimitri forced out of me three nights ago on his private jet isn't to blame for my disturbing ways. I was barely a child when my father found humor in my pink cheeks and wide eyes. He wanted to embarrass me, where in reality, he sparked a sinister curiosity for sex.

I didn't see the men sleeping with my mother—I didn't

even see her—all I saw was two bodies becoming one, the gripping of flesh, and harmonic sounds I'd never heard before. I saw how the simplest movements could change the light in someone's eyes in an instant.

I saw beauty when all I should have seen was darkness.

When my grandparents discovered the reason for my almost erotic drawings in grade five, my grandfather contacted the first shrink he found. He was mortified like Dimitri, confident there was something horrendously wrong with me.

Mercifully, my grandmother saw past my chipped exterior and overstimulated curiosity. She understood my vividly graphic drawings weren't to recreate acts I should have never seen. I wanted to recapture a unique beauty I hadn't seen since I went to live with my grandparents, not live in wickedly naughty thoughts.

My nanna was light years ahead of her time. She taught me it was okay to be sexually inquisitive as long as I wasn't being forced against my will to explore it nor encouraging others to experiment in ways they weren't comfortable. She slackened my lead with things like reading novels not recommended for my age but retightened it when she believed my curiosity couldn't be curbed in a non-physical manner.

Her system was faultless until that night in the alleyway a year ago. There was no beauty in my previous exchanges with Eddie, no crackles in the air, or breathy, wordless moans. There was nothing but lackluster, lifeless exchanges that had me wondering if the memories of my childhood were as jaded as my devilishly immoral compass.

Then he arrived out of nowhere as dark and dangerous as ever. When I spotted Dimitri, the faintest trickle of desire floating through my veins switched to a full-blown pandemic of heated rushes and core-clenching tingles. Every inch of my body tightened in anticipation. I was trapped, mesmerized, and finally free from the chains that had held me down for years.

It wasn't just him watching me that heightened my senses to beyond belief. It was wondering what he'd do to me if he weren't a spectator, how I'd react if his hand were to replace Eddie's. Would the light in my eyes change like they did for my mother, or would they fill with tears like hers did every time my father's friends left?

Although the thought of discovering the truth should have haunted me more than it did, my nanna's constant reminder that I'm a perfectly balanced and normal person kept it on the back burner.

I'm an adult now, so it's perfectly okay to be fascinated with sex. I just had to find the right person to spark a response out of me.

Dimitri does that. He just wishes it wasn't true.

He hasn't looked at me the same since Thursday night. Other than ordering for my hair to be peroxided back to the blonde coloring it had been in the alleyway over a year ago, he enters our shared room well after the noise in this fortress-like bunker dies down and exits long before a member of his staff enters with my breakfast.

It feels as if I could stand in front of him naked, and he wouldn't notice me. He hasn't even checked to see if the chemical peel a well-known dermatologist placed on my scar worked, and he paid out the ass for an emergency appointment.

I guess his rejection should be expected. If someone repulses you, the last thing you'd ever feel for them is desire.

With another sigh, I shift my eyes to watch a middle-aged European woman exit my room. The brittle beat of my pulse notches up a little when I fail to hear the lock latching into place before her shadow disappears from underneath my door. I'm usually confined to my room, the order to keep me under lock and key handed down from above. No one here would ever do anything to defy Dimitri because they fear him as much as I do. There's just one difference. Their fear is that he will kill them. Mine is that he'll never look at me like he did in the alleyway over a year ago.

Forever curious, and somewhat willing to break the rules with the hope of forcing a response out of Dimitri, I throw my legs off the bed I'm sitting on before tiptoeing across the room.

My heart rate jumps into a cantor when the lowering of the door handle isn't hindered by a reinforced latch. I'm uncuffed, and my door isn't fastened by prison-like bolts.

After a quick breather to ensure I don't collapse from a lack of oxygen to my brain, I carefully peel open the door. This could be a test, however failing has never scared me. As long as you get back up, you can fall as many times as you'd like.

The party-like atmosphere I've heard through the floor of my room the past three nights booms into my ears the more I move down the corridor. The ambiance gives off an elegant, ritzy feeling compared to the grittiness of a nightclub. It probably helps that this fortress is more suitable for a king than rough-and-ready mafia men. The drapes are thick and expensive, and all the fittings are top-of-the-line. So much detail has been placed in every inch of this hallway, I'm confident in saying it's better fitted than my apartment building and ten times more expensive.

Although I'm not dressed as flashy as the people milling around, they let me slip by with only the quickest glance. There's too much beauty to drink in to worry about little ole me ruining the glamourous atmosphere.

"Hello," I murmur to a couple getting friendly against the wall leading to the curved stairwell.

Who am I to judge their hookup location? At least they're under the privacy of someone's residence.

When I leap off the final stair, I take an urgent step back. Dimitri is in a formal sitting area to the right of the stairwell. He's swirling an amber-colored liquid around a whiskey glass while talking to a group of men. Although the closest women to him are several feet away, an intense rage of jealousy blasts through my veins. All the women are topless, and their pleated miniskirts leave *nothing* to the imagination. I'm not going to mention how they can't take their eyes off Dimitri, or I might do something more stupid than cry into the chest of a cartel kingpin.

Certain I'll be booted from festivities the instant Dimitri spots me, I head in the direction opposite to the room he's seated in. Even with most of Dimitri's 'guests' not speaking English, it appears as if they're having a good time. The gaming area is overflowing with men placing bets at a line of craps tables while smoking cigars. Unlike the room Dimitri is in, the topless women in this part of the compound are either seated on the men's laps or accepting their bets.

The further I travel, the more excitement slicks my skin. This is unlike any party I've ever been to, but it doesn't make it any less exhilarating. Think of the dirtiest, riskiest, most all-out naughtiest event you've ever wished to attend. Now double it. That'll give you an idea of the 'festivities' Dimitri and his guests are being wooed with.

It's as if Vegas and Times Square had a baby. Everything you could possibly want is in the one space—scantily dressed women dancing in crystal birdcages, acrobatic gymnasts daringly floating above your head, bloody men fighting bare-knuckled in a UFC-authentic cage, and gambling is in abundance.

There's even sex if you enter the right room.

Hot, raunchy, sweat-producing sex.

I hesitate for a beat before entering the square box with

only one solid wall. Although the couple going for it in clear-view for all to see are too engrossed with each other to pay me any attention, I can't help but wonder if I'm walking headfirst into a trap.

With how much sexually stimulating content this party is pumping out, I'm not surprised a viewing area I've only ever read about is empty. I'm more disappointed than anything. The priciest artwork can't compete with the beauty of two bodies intimately joining.

After wetting my dry lips, I enter the sex-scented space, willing to take a risk even if it kills me. With three out of four walls being floor-to-ceiling glass, I'm soon awarded an unimpeded view of three couples in various stages of undress. The cube on my right has a topless blonde on her knees about to suck the cock of a man whose mask is shielding half his attractive face.

The couple directly in front of me is ticking off every office romance novel checklist. A brunette with lace-topped stockings and black-rimmed glasses has her thong-covered backside planted on a desk covered in papers while an almost still fully clothed dark-haired man in a fiercely cut suit pounds into her. She calls him 'boss' on repeat while he refers to her as his 'naughty little secretary.'

Although the two exchanges I just told you about are appealing to the eye, the couple on my left is far more interesting. They're not just producing a feast for the eyes with needy grabs and fluidly precise rocks of their hips, they have my ears satisfied as well. They're the most vocal of the group, and if the way the orange-haired man has his partner bent over the couch is anything to go by, this isn't the first time they've fucked. They move together so well, I'm mesmerized by them in under a minute. It's a beautiful scene of pounding flesh, light-altering eyes, and moans I've only heard leave my mouth once before.

If I had a sketchpad and a chunk of charcoal at the ready, I'd be in my ideal fantasy. I don't care that they're fucking or that I'm sneakily witnessing them at their most venerable. It's the raw magnificence of the exchange I'm paying attention to. The way sweat rolls down the blonde's temples every time the man plunges his veiny penis inside her, how the light above their heads enhances the wetness on his thick shaft, and then there's their undeniable connection. It's so blistering hot, my skin perspires as if I have just ran a marathon.

The heat bouncing off them has my temperature rising as rapidly as my panic when the only shroud of light lighting up the room is suddenly blanketed by a large, brooding frame. The poor condition means I can barely see an inch of my approacher's face, however I don't need to see his features to know who he is. His aura is telling enough.

"I kept your name off the guest list to ensure you didn't end up in this room, and where do you venture to the instant you're freed from captivity?" I can't see Dimitri's face, but I can imagine his scold when he answers his question on my behalf. "In the very room you have no right to be in."

When he enters the space now feeling ten times smaller, the sound of skin slapping skin fades into the background. I can't hear anything but my raging pulse. His eyes are holding the same murderous gleam they had when Eddie found my clit, and his jaw is so firm, I'm afraid it's about to crack.

I discover the reason for his fury when he slants his head to the side and growls, "Get out."

Sickness rolls through my stomach when a man I hadn't noticed in the corner of the black space stands from a chair. Even with conditions being poor, my eyes have adjusted enough to the dark to understand his intentions. The crotch of his trousers is extended past the length of his zipper, and his belt is undone and hanging loosely in front of his stout thighs.

Although he's as tall as Dimitri and almost as wide, he appears the size of a dwarf when he commences shimmying past Dimitri's ominous frame. Dimitri could take a step to the side to give him a clear passage, but he won't. He won't do anything that will risk him taking his scorning eyes off me. He's pissed the stranger witnessed my immorality, and he's more than happy to make sure I'm aware of that.

His scorn makes me all types of hot. It also tells me why he's arrived out of the blue. I disobeyed him. As far as he's concerned, that's cause for punishment.

I'm tempted to follow the stranger's flee when he squeezes through the minute portion of air Dimitri's menacing frame isn't taking up, but lose the chance when Dimitri takes another step. My feet root into the floor, both mesmerized by the fury radiating out of him and scared. I don't think he will hurt me, but in a way, that's as scary as the thought of him never touching me.

"Do you know what this room is, Roxanne?" His voice is low and husky in the quiet of my wickedly dreary thoughts. It demands my attention even more than the couples fucking around me. I don't pay them an ounce of attention. My focus is entirely gobbled up by the brute of a man in front of me.

When I nod, Dimitri *tsks* me like I'm a child. Determined to prove I'm not as stupid as he thinks, I fold my arms in front of my chest to hide the rattle of my hands before mumbling, "It's a viewing chamber. They're usually found in BDSM clubs or fetish dungeons. They're for people who enjoy watching others have sex."

"Close." He takes another step my way, trapping my perception as well as smarts. My clit is buzzing more now than it was when the ginger-haired man bent his date over the two-seater sofa to take her from behind. "This is a play space for people who like being watched." The dark, shiny locks framing his face fall away when he peers up at the ceiling. "The voyeurs are up there."

Like magic, the black ceiling that appears to be made out of glass turns transparent. It unveils a group of thirty to forty people glancing down at us with hungry, wanton eyes.

Shit.

"They…" Dimitri's eyes are still on the people watching our every move, "… pay good money to watch people have sex." Once his eyes are back on my face, he drags his teeth over his lower lip. "However, you can hire these pods for other *things*." The ceiling shifts back to its original setting when he takes another step closer to me. "You can suck your brother-in-law's dick without guilt, fuck your secretary without your wife knowing. You can even celebrate your fifth wedding anniversary if that's your kink." His eyes shift to each couple he's referencing before he returns them to me. "You can even be punished here when you don't do as you're told."

The coolness of a wooden desk brushes my backside when his next step sees me taking a giant one back. I'm not scared of the menace in his tone. I need something to balance on to ensure my legs remain upright. That's how smoking hot his voice is when its fueled by undeniable anger.

"What did I tell you to do tonight, Roxanne?" he asks after taking in the faintest press of my thighs.

"You said—"

"Louder."

I swallow the saliva threatening to pool in the corner of my mouth before trying again. "You said I was to stay in my room until you returned."

He smiles like my submissiveness is hardening his cock.

If the bulge in his trousers is anything to go by, it is.

"Is this your room?"

When I shake my head, he arches a thick brow, demanding a voiced response.

Bossy bastard.

"No. This isn't my room."

Another step is closely followed by another squeeze of my thighs. "Then why are you here?"

With this the simplest question to answer, I reply, "I wanted to join in—"

"Louder."

"I wanted to join in," I almost shout. "I don't like that you're excluding me."

His smirk would have you convinced I said what I really wanted to say. That the more he ignores me, the more I crave his attention. I'm like a disobedient child who doesn't understand good attention far exceeds bad attention. I want it in any way I can get it.

I guess that's why my father's endeavors to embarrass me didn't work?

With my mood not as chipper as it once was, I attempt to sidestep Dimitri. "I'll go back to my room."

He grips the top of my arm before I'm halfway to the door. It isn't a painful hold, but it's most certainly a domineering one. "If you want to be included, Roxanne, I'm more than happy to include you."

I don't know whether to gleam with shock or horror when he requests me to lean over the desk and raise my ass high in the air.

"W-w-what?"

I realize the spectators can hear us as clearly as we can hear them when he repeats, "Lean over the desk and stick your ass in the air." They're as turned on by his domineering command as me, they just vocalize their excitement, whereas I remain as quiet as a church mouse. "Don't make me repeat myself, Roxanne. I am not a patient man."

I'm torn. I don't want to agitate him more than I already have, and I'm super curious to see where he's going with this, but only now am I realizing I don't want to be fucked in front of spectators. I don't want anyone but the person I'm sleeping with to see if the light in my eyes changes. It isn't something I want to share.

With that in mind, I shake my head. "No."

Dimitri balks like I slapped him. "What did you say?"

"I said no." I run a shaky hand across my cheeks to ensure they're still dry before adding, "I want to be a part of the festivities, not fucked like a whore."

He lowers his head until we meet eye to eye. "Who said I was going to fuck you?" He cages me to the desk by bracing his tattooed hands on each side of my hips and leaning in really close. The strong smell of whiskey bounds from his mouth when he whispers in my ear, "These rooms are only rented for an hour." He locks his eyes with mine. They're as blistering as ever. "I'd need a lot longer than that to work out all your kinks." I don't know if he's sucking in the scent of my arousal or fear when his nostrils flare during his next statement. Either way, it doubles the width of his pupils. "But your punishment for entering this room with another man won't take an hour. I'll have your ass as red as your cheeks in not even five minutes."

I respond to the jealousy in his tone as if it's legitimate. "I didn't know he was sitting there. I would have never entered if I knew he was there."

"These rooms are for fucking, Roxanne. You only enter them to be fucked or to fuck someone." When he takes a step back, the mask he was wearing when he entered the room slips back over his face. My closeness didn't calm his agitation. It made it worse. "Mitis thought you were here for him, and he was prepared to make you his no matter how many times you begged him not to." The expression on his face reveals he isn't lying. This isn't a room where 'no' is acknowledged. "That alone deserves punishment for both of you."

I have a feeling I'll leave this exchange less scarred than Mitis. The vicious glint in his eyes assures me of this, much less the murderous smirk etched on his face when his eyes shifted to the door Mitis snuck through only moments ago.

My eyes snap to Dimitri's when he growls out, "If I'm forced to repeat myself, you won't leave this room until your ass is dribbling blood like the bullet hole between Mitis's brows." He shifts on his feet to face the only solid surface in the room. "Chest flat on the desk, ass high in the air. I won't ask you again."

Ignoring the tremble of my thighs—which I'm confident are shuddering with an equal amount of excitement and worry —I spin around to face the desk. Spit seethes through Dimitri's teeth when I curl over the sturdy material. The high rise of my dress is already indecent, but my stretch to reach the other side of the desk makes it outright immoral.

My butt cheeks are showing, but no matter how hard I try, I can't force my hands to tug at the hem. I could use the excuse that Dimitri is towering over me, so even the spectators who paid top-dollar for a prime spot will leave tonight grumbling about bad seats, but what excuse do I have for the wetness between my legs?

Unexpected hotness races through my veins when Dimitri lifts the hem of my dress, so it sits on the lower half of my back. He doesn't take the time to notice the only underwear Alice supplied me with for the next four weeks are lace thongs, he just takes a step back, breathes noisily out of his nose, then spanks my right butt cheek.

The brutal crack his palm makes with my backside verifies

he didn't hold back with his hit. It doubles the heat teeming between us and has me torn on whether I should sob or curve my knees inward.

I've never been spanked before, but I'd be lying if I said it was more painful than enjoyable. It's an odd feeling that rapidly explains why people crave it along with hairpulling. It's naughty but oh so good.

"Grind your pelvis against the desk, Roxanne. I don't want to miss." Dimitri's voice has me wondering if he's enjoying this as much as me. It's hot and edgy and has me so eager to reacquaint his hand with my ass. I stretch my toes to the max, seeking the hand he's pulling back in preparation for his next smack.

I call out when his second hit has perfect aim. It doesn't just add to the fiery burn racing across my butt cheeks, the tips of his fingers encroach an area thudding as fast as my heart rate.

By his third spank, I've forgotten we have an audience.

By his fourth spank, the fact this is supposed to be a punishment has slipped from my mind.

By his fifth spank, I'm grinding against the desk as per his earlier request, needing something to take the edge off the tension in my clit. It's buzzing like crazy, verifying my madness. I'm being used as a gimmick like my mother was, showcased as if I'm a dirty whore, yet, I feel the most alive I've ever felt.

I'll do anything for this to continue, anything at all.

I will even beg.

"Again. Please."

My words are separated by big, needy breaths, but Dimitri has no issues hearing them. He spanks me again, his hit so exquisite, an orgasm crests at the peak of my core, threatening to topple at any moment. I just need one more spanking, one more brief touch of his fingers on my drenched panties, or better yet, the quickest flick of his thumb against my clit, and I'll be done.

But instead of doing any of those things, Dimitri lowers the hem of my dress, demands for me to immediately return to my room before he pivots on his heels and exits the sex chamber without so much as a backward glance.

Chapter Twenty-Three

Dimitri

Damn Smith and his ability to reach me at any time. Damn foreign dignitaries who prefer to watch instead of participating.

Damn my whiskey-soaked veins that had me refusing to listen to a rational thing my brain has to say.

And damn Roxanne and her delectably fine ass.

When she begged for me to spank her again, my cock sat so snugly against the zipper in my trousers, it took everything I had not to whip it out and plunge it inside her drenched cunt. She was so wet, every spank had evidence of her arousal glistening on the top of my fingertips.

Even smacking her ass six times didn't see its redness overtake the wanton heat on her cheeks. She wasn't embarrassed I was punishing her in a room full of spectators, she was too turned on to care we had an audience.

Roxanne's non-existent morals had me wanting to forget my objectives. I almost took her right on the desk, as destitute of standards as her greedy cunt. If Smith's desolate tone hadn't snapped me from my trance, I guarantee my cock would be coated in her juices right now. I only went into the sex pod because of the urgency in his tone, just like I left it for the exact same reason.

He doesn't interrupt me unless it's urgent. Saving Roxanne from a man who'd cut her up like an animal was urgent. It better be the same case this time around as my patience is stretched as thin as the thread struggling to hold my cock's reaction to Roxanne's moans.

My fucking God, my cock twitches just recalling how delicious they sounded. They're as delectable as the scent of her skin mingled with mine, and the very reason I need to put more distance between us than I have the past three days.

Pulling Roxanne into my chest four days ago was one of the stupidest things I've done. Ever since then, instead of my focus remaining on freeing Fien from her nightmare, it continuously shifts to ways I can eradicate Roxanne's. I'm not prioritizing my time on the right person, and the injustice is both souring my mood and worsening my daughter's chance of survival.

That's why I stepped into the room with guns blazing. I was mid-conversation with a man who knows the whereabouts of every gangbanger in the country when Smith updated me on Roxanne's location. I tried to tell myself she's a big girl who can get herself out of the riskiest exchange, but the longer the movie on how that would go down rolled through my head, the higher my blood pressure spiked.

It was within danger territory, only two stomps away from the man who could possibly know Roberto's location, and it wasn't going to settle until I took my annoyance out on the person responsible for its incline.

A public spanking seemed like the ideal punishment.

Roxanne's multiple sketchpads should have told me differently.

If I was being honest, I'd say a part of me knew how she'd reply to my arrogance. Her willingness to please would usually stop my eagerness in its tracks. However, there have been a handful of times my cock has overruled my head. Roxanne has been in the picture for every one of those days, so who's to say it wouldn't have been the same this time around?

"Roxie was right—"

I hold my finger in the air, halting Smith's update midsentence before shifting my eyes to Rocco. He's standing in the corner of the command center. His fists are clenched at his sides, and his jaw is tight, wrongly believing I used Roxanne's fucked-up childhood against her. He's all for fucking, has been from the age of thirteen, but if it involves marking a woman's body with anything but his cum, it's a no-go for him.

He wasn't up in the viewing chambers watching Roxanne's punishment firsthand, but Smith has eyes and ears over every inch of this compound, meaning he didn't need to be in the room with me to get a bird's-eye view of Roxanne's punishment. He just needed to hack into the camera in the button of my shirt.

The tightness of Rocco's jaw slackens when I say, "Make sure Roxanne gets to her room in one piece. I'll be up to check on her in a bit." I don't know why I added the last half of my statement. Most likely as a warning to Rocco that he won't have time to nurture her like he's hoping.

It won't stop him from ribbing me about the possibility, though. "Want me to rub some cream into her welts for you, too?" He doesn't wait for my growl to work its way up my chest. He just smirks, gives me a one-finger salute, then exits the room with a pompous flare I usually relish more than hate.

It doesn't have the same effect tonight. I'm hard, pissed as fuck, and fighting not to shake off my funk with a few lines of coke and an endless number of whores. Returning to the drug-fucked idiot I was before I became a father won't help anyone, but some days, I wonder if it would make life a little easier to take.

Do you have any idea how gutting it is to know your enemies have been fucking you in the ass for almost two years? Weak. Pathetic. An incapable man. There are a few words I'd use to describe myself when the negativity enters my mind with a refusal to leave until I've killed a man. Considering it's almost daily lately, you can imagine how high my death count now sits. Trying my hardest not to become the monster my father wanted me to be, sees me becoming exactly that.

After working my jaw side to side, I shift my focus back to Smith—for the most part. "Put Roxanne's room up onto the main feed." It's playing on a smaller monitor on my left as it has been the past three nights, but I want to avoid eyestrain while stalking her to see if goosebumps prickle her skin when Rocco is within sniffing distance. They've become close the past three days, and I don't fucking like it. It agitates me to no end, much like my continuously deviating mind.

"What was Roxanne right about?" My clipped tone warns Smith I'm at the end of my teether. If his findings tonight aren't associated with Fien, we will exchange blows. No fear.

My attitude gets sliced in half when Smith replies, "Roberto. He was at Joops like Roxie said." He twists his laptop screen around to face me. It has a still image of a much older and fatter Roberto on the screen. Just like Roxanne's composite drawing, I'm confident it's him. "As you know, we couldn't get anything off the restaurant's surveillance cameras. They were wiped before you realized Audrey had left your side." His comment isn't an underhanded swipe at my stupidity, he doesn't do anything underhandedly, he's merely relaying the facts as he sees them. "I worked credit card transactions for Joops. I didn't get anything significant, so I shifted my focus to cell phones."

"Which also came up blank?" I interrupt, pushing him along. We're having this conversation with my dick pressed up against the zipper in my trousers. The sooner it's over, the better it will be for all involved, and I'm not going to mention the jumping of my blood pressure from watching Roxanne's arrival to her room. Rocco doesn't drop her off and leave, he walks her inside like they're returning from an intimate date. It frustrates me more than it should, but there's no denying the obvious.

Even Smith has noticed a change in my temperament. He tugs at the collar of his shirt as if his temperature is rising as rapidly as mine before moving at a steadier pace. "Yeah, they didn't come back with anything either, but I was working off pings for pre-2010 circuit phones, assuming not even six-year-olds get around with flip phones these days. I should have realized the rules don't apply for some people." He tosses an outdated and cracked phone onto the desk between us before nudging his head to a bank of monitors on my right.

This kills me to admit, but it takes me a good three to four seconds to shift my eyes from the monitor broadcasting Roxanne's room to the one Smith wants me to look at. Roxanne and Rocco are moving toward the bathroom—the only room in this compound without a motion-activated camera.

When a bloody and bruised man bound to a rickety chair in a dungeon-like room confronts me, my annoyance deepens. Rocco wouldn't have roughed-up Roxanne's dad unless he has some sort of feelings for her. He gave me that exact same line when I ordered for Ian's whereabouts to be unearthed. This is what I meant when I said Roxanne is distracting me from what really matters. The absence of the two men I sent out to bring her father in was barely felt, but the time I put Smith on the case to discover his current location was most certainly notice-able. Every second he hunted the demon of Roxanne's past added a second to my daughter's captivity.

Can you understand now why I can't tell which way is up?

"What did you find on Ian's phone?"

With the smile of a man at the top of his game, Smith nudges his head to Roberto's photo. I'm about to ask for further information, but within two keystrokes, Roberto's blurred image zooms out until he's nothing but a speckle in the background, and Roxanne's big green eyes take up a majority of the screen. Because she cried off most of the gunk she had coating her lashes, the greenness of her eyes is mesmerizing.

"Who did he send that to?" The image is attached to an outgoing text message. I don't give a fuck who may have seen Roberto in the background of this image, it's the text attached I'm getting worked up about. He's offering his daughter for sale, asking how much he can get for her since she's reached prime breeding age. It appears as if Roxanne was only spared because his purchaser was too slow with his calculations. His offer of fifty thousand dollars was received two minutes after Roxanne's teary exit.

I feel as if our search is going in circles when Smith replies, "It was a burner phone, but its last ping was off a cell tower a few miles out of Ravenshoe."

"Did Ian receive a down payment for Roxanne? A contract? Anything we can seek similarities from?" The fact Ian said 'breeding age' has my interests immensely piqued. It could be a coincidence my wife was taken when she was eight months pregnant, but Roxanne's constant thrust into my life the past two years has me looking at any angle.

Smith slumps low into his chair. "Not a thing. He either had an attack of the conscience or…" His words trail off as aware as me that Roxanne's father would have only pulled out of negotiations if a better offer was placed on the table.

"Where's Roxanne's mother?"

Air hisses between Smith's teeth as he shrugs. "If she's still alive, she's clever at hiding her tracks."

"Or making tracks that don't require a credit card."

Smith jerks up his chin, agreeing with me.

After a beat, I shift the direction of his focus for the third time this week. Although it appears as if I've got him working on the ghosts of Roxanne's past, this will benefit Fien as much as it will Roxanne, so I'm okay with it. "Find Sailor's last movements. As much as we wish it were different, no one just disappears. Everyone leaves tracks. Center your focus around the time of Roxanne's meeting with her father. I don't care how much of a deadbeat she was, no mother would sit on the sidelines when her daughter pops up on the radar for the first time in almost a decade. She was either at that restaurant watching or fighting for the chance."

Smith twists his lips, shocked he hadn't considered that angle. I give his slip-up some leeway. He isn't a parent, so he shouldn't be expected to think like one.

"And him?" He once again nudges his head to Roxanne's father, Ian. "Rocco made him shit his pants. If we don't do something soon, the guests might start complaining. That's the last thing we want. They already have their knickers in a twist from having the location of their 'working holiday' changed last minute."

I take another moment to ponder. It does little to ease the tick of my jaw. "Send Clover down to pay him a visit. Tell him not to kill him. Just drive him to the brink of death. He hurt Roxanne, so, at the end of the day, it's up to her whether she wants him dead or not." I wasn't supposed to articulate my last sentence, but I'm glad I couldn't hold back. It felt good passing the responsible baton to another person even if it was for only a second.

"Before you go," Smith says just before I dart through the door as fast as I barreled through it only minutes ago. Roxanne and Rocco are still in the bathroom. It has me super eager to leave, although not as eager as I am to pummel someone when Smith adds, "I know you want my focus on Roberto, but something in your father's schedule deserves mentioning."

I hadn't meant for my quest to find Roberto to diminish his inquiries on my father. His shadiness deserves more than a once-over.

When I lift my chin encouraging Smith to continue, he hands me a sheet of paper. "A credit card scanned at Slice of Salt the night Audrey was taken was used to buy a ticket to an event your father is hosting. I didn't think much of it until I noticed the recipient's address. She's originally from Ravenshoe."

"She? The purchaser is a female?"

When an agreeing hum vibrates his lips, I scan the name of the person attached to the credit card search. Usually, we immediately discount any women who come up in our searches. However, Roxanne's comment from days ago still rings in my ears. It's right up where her begging moans will now be. *Because your daughter's captor is a woman.*

"Get me tickets to this event."

As his fingers tap on his keyboard, a smile tugs on Smith's lips. The reasoning behind his smirk smacks into me like a wayward missile when he asks, "The event is a couples-only event. Would you like me to put Roxanne's name down as your plus one?"

My eyes dart between the feed from Roxanne's room, the dingy one holding her father captive, and the last still image I have of Fien before I shake my head. "I'll call in a favor with a friend." I can't have Roxanne distracting me like she did tonight, so for that reason, and that reason alone, I have to pull back the reins of our ruse.

It could be my raging heart having me mishear Smith, but I swear he says, "It's your funeral," as I bolt out the door of his wired-up hot box.

My first thought is to race up to Roxanne's room to see what the fuck she and Rocco have been doing in the bathroom the past ten minutes, but my blood is too hot to give that thought proper consideration. I'm seeking answers, and since only one person can give them to me, I take a left at the base of the stairs instead of climbing them.

Smith wasn't lying when he said our guests would soon start complaining about the smell coming from the basement. The man bound to a chair in front of the boiler is in desperate need of a shower. He stinks like shit, piss, and vomit, and once I'm done with him, he'll also smell like death.

I've paid millions of dollars to keep my daughter safe.

He tried to sell his for fifty-thousand.

That means we can't be friends, and I'm more than happy to show him how I treat people I don't class as friends.

Chapter Twenty-Four

Roxanne

The zealous gleam in Rocco's eyes catches the dimmed lights above our heads when he slants his to the side to get a better look at the sketch I'm undertaking. The shy bob of his head would have you convinced his arms aren't double the width of an average man's nor covered with a range of interesting tattoos.

He has everything you could think of when it comes to art. Popeye with a can of spinach. A seahorse. He even has a half-naked gypsy with one of her eyes gouged out. His array of body art has had me scratching pencil to paper nonstop for the past hour. I usually only sketch nudes when I'm drawing the human form, but I've mixed things up tonight. It's nice focusing my attention on something other than the sting on my backside.

While drawing the top half of Rocco's body, I've barely had a minute to think about the bruise my ego got from Dimitri leaving me stranded in the middle of a sex-scented room on the brink of ecstasy. It was almost as painful as the spanking he gave my backside. I've channeled the energy into something more cathartic, purging it from my body in a way that won't get me killed.

Well, I hope it won't.

Dimitri's response to Mitis's stalk didn't end well, so I doubt he'd appreciate his second-in-charge sprawled on the bathroom floor of his room without his shirt on, and I won't mention how authentic the bumps in Rocco's midsection look on paper. Considering I'm using pencils designed to enhance my face, they've done a mighty fine job outlining all his good points. My drawing is so realistic, I'm fighting the urge to fill in the parts I can't see with my vivid imagination.

With my cheeks burning, I peer down at the eyeliners teetering between Rocco and me, seeking a better color to match his unique-colored eyes. When I find one with just the right amount of golden, Rocco's lips tuck in the corner. "What did I tell you? Just like shop-bought ones."

He grabs a green eyeliner from the pile of many before holding it up to my face like I did his. He's also drawing on the paper he stole from a cleaner during our silent journey to my room. He hasn't commented on my punishment, but I'm reasonably sure he witnessed it. His eyes are as telling as mine. I also think it's the reason he chose to host our art lesson in the bathroom. The cool tiles are a godsend to my burning back-side, although the hardness isn't as welcoming.

I float my eyes up to Rocco's when he asks, "How did you get the spinach to sparkle like that?"

He's not happy with the grassy green coloring he's selected for my eyes, but since lime green went out of fashion many moons ago, he doesn't have a better option for my eye coloring. The makeup kit Alice shoved into his chest before our flight four days ago is massive, but it doesn't have the endless color palette artists generally work with.

"It's all about getting the right mix of colors." I pick up a gold eyeliner I wouldn't use in a hundred years before snagging a pair of eyelash curlers off the vanity sink. "A little bit of contrast will pick up the color you want."

With his skills a mix between novice and a first-grader, I shave the slightest bit of the gold pencil onto the circles of green in the middle of his picture, hopeful they're my eyes.

Rocco's laugh is a nice thing to hear in a dark and dreary place. "That was supposed to be your hands, but I guess it'll work."

"Sorry," I say with a grimace. "You have a Jackson Pollock vibe going on."

"Is that your way of saying my drawing is shit?"

His question is laced with humor, but I still shake my head, mortified he thinks I'd pick on him when he's been nothing but kind to me. "One day, people will pay good money for that."

"Of course they will." Because I'm leaning close to him, the faintest smell of toothpaste lingers in my nose when his tongue darts out to replenish his lips with spit. "It's a picture of you. That makes it priceless."

I stagger backward with a squeak when the rough and gravelly voice of Dimitri fills my ears. "Not as priceless as you'll be when I weigh you down with bricks before dumping you in the deepest ocean."

When Rocco's smile switches from a smirk to a full-blown grin, I stare at him like he's mental. Dimitri's voice didn't have an ounce of amusement behind it. He sounds really mad like he's on the verge of killing someone.

I realize that someone is more likely to be me when Rocco stands to his feet. "I guess we'll finish *this* later." His 'this' was much too throaty for my liking. He made it seem as if we've done more than drawing the past hour and a half.

With a wink of a man not in fear for his life, Rocco twists on his feet and stalks away from me. I try to keep my eyes on the mess next to my thigh, but I can't help but gawk when Dimitri halts Rocco's departure partway through the door. His clutch on his Rocco's arm makes his knuckles go white, but it doesn't dampen Rocco's grin in the slightest. Anyone would swear they're playing a game of chess, and Dimitri just fell straight into Rocco's well-thought-out game plan.

My eyes drift past a set of well-splayed thighs, a belt that's more haggard than new, a crisp, recently laundered dress shirt, and a stern set of lips when a pair of polished black shoes enter my peripheral vision a few seconds later.

After dragging his eyes over my semi-nude sketch of Rocco, Dimitri asks, "Have you showered?"

I shake my head, shocked. "No. That would be a little hard to do with Rocco babysitting me, wouldn't it?"

My breathing shortens when he asks, "I don't know, Roxanne, would it? You two seem very comfortable with each other."

When his jaw tightens after taking in Rocco's shirt dumped under the vanity sink, checkmate rings in my ears on repeat. I just unearthed Rocco's game plan, and for once in my life, I feel as if I'm on the winning team.

"I prefer sketching people au naturel. Wet hair doesn't allow that." Still salty about how he left me hanging after my spanking, I snatch up Rocco's drawing as if I can't bear to part with it before making my way into the main part of my room. "It's a pity you arrived back earlier tonight than the previous three. I can't finish my sketch now."

I realize exactly who I'm messing with when Dimitri's hand darts out to seize my wrist. His hold isn't close to nice, and it has my heart rate climbing as high as it did when he spanked me in front of an audience—even more so when I notice the splatters of blood on his hand. They're proof his shirt is new because there's no way he could have got that much blood on his hands and none on his shirt. He's changed since our exchange in the sex chamber, and for some reason, that annoys me more than the aggression of his hold.

"Let. Me. Go," I seethe through clenched teeth.

My show of jealousy doesn't faze him in the slightest. He's too bristling with his own idiosyncrasies to pay mine any attention. "You need to shower before going to bed. I can smell Rocco's aftershave all over you."

"That isn't aftershave. Just like the hairs on his chest, Rocco's smell is au naturel—" My last two words leave my body in a grunt when Dimitri pins me to the main wall of the bathroom with his heaving, he's-going-to-kill-someone form. I went one step too far, and he's more than happy to call me out on it.

He crowds into me so profoundly, I'm blanketed by his big, brooding frame in less than a second. The contrast of our heights is undeniable. He literally towers over me as he did in my dreams many times the past year, except now, I don't just feel his hot breaths on my neck, I also see his sexy, yet angry face.

"Shower. *Now*."

He stops the shake of my head by gripping my face in a determined hold. It's an aggressive clutch that has me wondering if my childhood affected me more than I realized. Instead of being scared by his dominance, I'm turned on by it. His mouth is an inch from mine. I can smell the whiskey he was drinking earlier on his lips and feel the hardness my closeness is inspiring. This could only be better if we were kissing.

"I wasn't asking, Roxanne. Whether I hold you under freezing-cold water until you're drenched through or dump you into a scalding-hot bath, you will shower before you'll ever enter my bed smelling like another man."

He steals my chance to reply by gripping the front of my dress and shredding it off me with the strength of the Hulk. Buttons fly in all directions as an unexpected moan leaves my lips. That was fucked, but it was also exhilarating. It has me truly unsure how to respond.

I'm not wearing a bra, so there's no hiding how hard his aggressiveness made my nipples, but my hands are itching to slap him across the face. I've never felt such a conflicting array of emotions. I want to kiss and hurt him at the same time, and I'm not the only one noticing this.

Dimitri brings his lips so close to mine, I get drunk off the whiskey fumes in his breath as much as I do the knee he wedges between my legs. His closeness makes me dizzy. I'm panting, hot and on the brink of begging for him to kiss me.

I hate how weak he makes me, but it can't be helped. He's as brutally beautiful as I imagined in the alleyway all those months ago, and he has my head void of a single thought that doesn't include him.

Desire pulses through me when he shoves my head to the side so he can drag his nose down the throb in my throat. It has me all types of excited until he growls in my ear, "I should have killed you in the alleyway like I did the guard. Gunned you down like you thought I was going to. Then you wouldn't have me so fucking confused."

When I push him away from me, too angry to let his hurtful comments slide without protest, he crowds me even closer to the wall. "It would have been awfully convenient for me if your boyfriend achieved what he set out to do, then I wouldn't be wasting my time chasing ghosts, years too fucking late! Do you have any idea how much time I've wasted on you this week?

How many hours you've added to my daughter's captivity? Even now, instead of working on pinpointing her location, I'm here, dealing with you… again."

"No one asked you to do that. I was perfectly fine with Rocco."

My shouted response agitates him the most. He doesn't speak a word, but I can see the last four ones I spoke filtering through his head on repeat. He works them over and over and over until the tension crackling between us turns dangerous.

Confusion draws my brows together when Dimitri takes a step back, unpinning me from the cool, tiled wall. For how worked up he is, I hadn't expected him to give in so easily.

I realize I still have a lot to learn about this man when he says, "I wonder how 'perfectly fine' Rocco will be when I remove his scent from your skin with more than water?"

Not giving me time to decipher his cryptic message, he yanks me forward by a rough tug on my wrist, throws an arm around my thighs, then hoists me onto his shoulder.

When he moves me in the opposite direction of the washing facilities, I fight him with everything I have. I slap, kick, and bite at him, aware he has a gun in his bedside table, a big scary gun I have no clue how to use, much less defend myself against.

When I'm dumped onto the bed with the same aggression Clover used only days ago, I spring onto my feet. I make a dash for the door, but Dimitri's grab-sweep-yank routine on my ankle sends me toppling on the mattress.

With one hand pinning me to the mattress, the other works on undoing the buckle on his well-worn belt. Instincts scream for me to protect my face when he drags the battered material out of the loops of his trousers, but its quick clatter to the floor halves my efforts, and I'm not going to mention the lowering of his zipper, or you'll accuse me of being mental.

This sucks to admit, but I'm more petrified I'll miss Dimitri's unexpected strip than worried he's going to beat me like my father did my mother any time her moans seemed too authentic for him. He was happy to humiliate and degrade her, but at no time was she to get pleasure during his quest for happiness.

Twisted emotions spiral through me when Dimitri's painfully erect cock springs free from his trunks he yanks them down his thighs. He's thick and angry, hard to the fact I'm worried he's about to pass out.

How is it possible to direct so much blood to one region of the body and not get dizzy?

I suck in a quick, terrifying breath when the removal of his trousers is closely followed by him fisting my hair in a white-knuckled hold. He uses his leverage on my overbleached locks to drag my head toward his impressive cock he's strangling like he is angry at it.

I won't lie, I've dreamed about this very moment for over a year, but it wasn't like this. It wasn't against my will. In my dreams, I sucked the dangerous and mysterious stranger's dick because I couldn't wait a second longer to discover how delicious he tasted. He didn't force me. I did it willingly.

I realize I have the situation wrong when Dimitri's thick timbre breaks through the panicked breaths shrilling in my ears. "Look at me."

When my eyes immediately jump to the command in his tone, the flare of his nostrils mesmerizes me in under a second. He stares straight at me while frantically working his cock in and out of his clenched fist.

A gleam in his eyes reveals the mammoth restraint he's exuding, but for once, he's not harnessing his desire to kill me. He's fighting not to take what I'm unwilling to give, holding back the urge to finish what he started downstairs.

He's doing everything in his power not to make me his, even with his actions doing precisely that.

My eyes return to the angry, red beast rocking in and out of his fist an inch from my breasts in just enough time to witness the final two pumps needed to bring him to ecstasy.

He grunts when a stream of white cum jets out of his engorged knob.

I moan.

Watching him bring himself to climax is both thrilling and excruciating. Thrilling because it doubled the erotic tingles between my legs that haven't quit since he spanked my ass raw, but excruciating because the cruel curl of his lips tells me this is as far as our exchange will go.

This isn't about getting me off. Even with his hand strangling his still-erect cock to ensure every drop of his cum is expelled onto my breasts, this isn't even about Dimitri. He removed Rocco's smell from my skin by replacing it with his as a reminder that I'm his property. His gimmick. His toy to fuck with time and time again.

I am his, despite the fact he has no plans to fully claim me.

Chapter Twenty-Five

Roxanne

I pull away from my bedroom door with a groan, appreciative of Rocco's concern, but also mortified by it. I'll never play a damsel-in-distress skit well. "He didn't hurt me."

"Other than the occasional spanking, he won't physically hurt you. That isn't D's way. Up here, though." After joining me in my room, he taps on my temple still wet from a recent shower. I'm not usually a fan of showering late in the day, but Dimitri only granted me permission to wash off his cum twenty minutes ago. I thought it was so I could get ready to attend the fancy event he had a tuxedo delivered for late this afternoon. Silly me. He left our room within two minutes of me entering the bathroom, and my door remained locked until Rocco's unexpected arrival thirty seconds ago. "That's an entirely new ball game. You've got to play this game with wit, Roxie, or he'll never let you in from the cold."

Still frustrated about what happened last night, I take my

anger out on the wrong person. "Maybe I don't want him to let me in. Have you ever thought about that?"

With a laugh, Rocco flops onto my bed. It flashes up images of Dimitri doing the same to me last night, and for some crazy reason, it has my knees almost touching instead of my face screwing up.

What did I tell you? I'm certifiably insane.

"If that were true, you wouldn't have invited me into your room." After straying his eyes to the camera perched in the corner of the large space, Rocco asks, "Are you hoping my visit will have him ordering for his car to be turned around? Or are you praying for a re-run of last night?"

My throat grows scratchy. *He knows about last night?*

Upon spotting my shocked expression, Rocco hits me with a frisky wink before he props himself onto his elbows. "I don't know exactly what happened, Smith cut the feed..." I smile at the immature roll of his eyes, "... but I got the gist of it when Dimitri arrived at my room late last night with these."

Mortified heat blazes across my cheeks when he digs a teeny tiny thong out of the pocket of his black trousers. They're the pair I was wearing yesterday, the pair that were soaked through when Dimitri smeared his cum over my breasts, collarbone, neck, and lips with the same hand he used to stroke himself.

Once my torso was coated with the sticky substance, he tugged off my panties before he demanded me not to move until he returned. I thought he was taking a breather to regather his bearings. I had no clue he went to hand my soiled panties to the man responsible for his blood-thirsty rage.

I attempt to snatch my underwear out of Rocco's grasp while asking, "Why do you have them?" I say 'attempt' as my efforts are fruitless. Rocco is too quick for my weary head. I hardly slept a wink last night. Not only was the smell of

Dimitri's cum keeping my heart rate high, once he returned to our room, his eyes burned a hole into the back of my head the entire night.

I give up on my endeavor to free my underwear from the now insanity of my life when Rocco says, "He used them as a deterrent. Said if I don't step back, then next time I see your panties, they'll be smeared with your blood."

As unease treks through my veins, my throat works hard to swallow. "Then why are you here?" After calculating how many steps it will take to barge him out of my room, I triple it, aware his large frame will require additional shoves. "If you leave now, maybe Dimitri will go easy on me. Tell him you were bringing tampons or something. I'm sure you can make something up on the fly."

My eyes snap back to Rocco when I spot him shaking his head in the corner of my eye. "I'm not leaving."

"Why not?" I want to punch myself in the gut for how whiny my voice is. It can't be helped, I like Rocco. Outside of this dark and demented world, I believe we could be friends, but I'm soon learning you can't take notions from outside these walls and use them here. This is a different world. Nothing is as it once was. The fact I almost came twice from two highly demoralizing activities is proof of this. "If you don't go, he will kill me, Rocco. Is that what you want?"

He shoos away my worry as if it's a fly. "He won't kill you."

"You just said he threatened you with panties smeared with my blood!"

I take a step back, horrified when he replies, "Your virginal blood. Not *blood* blood."

"What?" One word shouldn't be so breathy, but when your lungs are void of air, you work with what you have. "Who said I'm a virgin?"

The hits just won't stop coming. "Your daddy. He used it as

a bargaining chip when Dimitri had him brought in. Don't worry. I worked him over so good, he won't use it again any time soon."

"You beat my dad because he used my 'supposed' virginity to bargain for his freedom?" Surprise is the last thing I feel when Rocco nods for the second time. If he has the chance of making money from it, nothing is off-limits for my father. "And Dimitri heard him?"

Rocco's head bob shifts to shake. "Nah, he was getting ready to spank your ass around that time."

The fact he talks so nonchalantly about certain subject matters should shock me, but for some reason, it doesn't. "So how does Dimitri know I'm a virgin?"

He rubs his hands together like a kid in a candy shop. "So, you *are* a virgin?"

"That isn't what I said."

His wink makes me hot even when it shouldn't. "It doesn't matter what you say. We both know it's true." When I fail to deny his accusation, he adds, "And so does, Dimi. He paid your old man a visit last night. Discovered he held off on your sale with the hope he'd fetch top-dollar for your virginity first. There is a heap of dirty old men willing to pay in the six figures to break in a tight cunt for the first time."

He bombards me with so many facts at once, I don't know which one to respond to first. I guess I should start at the most important point, although it doesn't feel like he should have the top rung on my worries. "Is my father alive?"

Rocco halfheartedly shrugs. "Kinda. Might not be if his theories don't stack up."

"Theories?" Although I'm asking a question, I don't wait for him to answer. "You can't believe anything he says, he's a pathological liar. He'll say anything if it helps him."

"Like saying you're a virgin?" I shoot him a wry look. It

doubles the width of his toothy grin. "He had information about a baby-making ring near your hometown." His smile is completely obliterated when he mutters, "He told Dimitri the names of the playmakers he met when he tried to sign you up for their service." I haven't gotten over my first shock when he hits me with another. "His confession hit Dimi hard. That was too close to home for him to ignore." After dragging his eyes over my face, he says, "You remind him of his wife."

I groan before joining him on the bed. "That's the last thing I want to hear."

Dimitri spared my life on the belief I could help locate his daughter, but what has his focus been on the past four days? My fucked-up past.

The pain in my chest eases when Rocco barges me with his shoulder. "Not who she was, what she was missing. The spark. The feistiness. The desire so strong, even when you hate him, you'll still take his dick between your lips." He laughs when I scoff during the last half of his comment. "Deny it all your like, Princess P, you've been walking around the past four days with a doe-eyed look I haven't seen since a rainy afternoon in an alleyway many months ago."

After falling backward onto the mattress, I throw an arm over my eyes. "You saw the footage from the alleyway?"

Rocco drags my arm to my side while answering, "Nah. I saw Dimitri's face when he re-entered the limo." He boinks my nose. "He had the same doe-eyed look you have now. You fascinate him." He laughs like I'm an idiot when I roll my eyes about his highly inaccurate statement. "Why do you think he reacted the way he did last night?"

I make a 'duh' face. "Because he didn't want your aftershave embedded in his pillow?"

I slant my head, so I can peer at him beneath lowered lashes when he chuckles out, "Dimi isn't worried about me.

You're not fucked-up enough for me. He's just struggling to understand why he wants you when he shouldn't."

"He isn't the only one struggling," I say before I can stop myself. "He killed my boyfriend, murdered men directly in front of me, and had my father brought in to be tortured—"

"To be tried for crimes we both know he committed," Rocco corrects.

I continue talking as if he never interrupted me, "Yet, I forget everything happening when he's standing across from me." My horrified expression grows. "My brain must have seeped out of my head when it cracked open."

Rocco laughs like I'm joking. I wish I were. Something drastically changed for me in that alleyway all those months ago. Unfortunately, I don't mean the night Eddie used his car as a weapon. My life hasn't been the same since my eyes locked on a dark, shadowy figure in the pouring rain. I was so convinced he'd award me the adventure I was seeking, it made everything since seem mundane.

After a prolonged stretch of silence, I roll onto my hip until I'm facing Rocco front-on. He's stretched out lazily, at ease with our friendship as me. "Can I see my father?"

Any humor left on his face evaporates before he shakes his head. When he sees the disappointment on my face, he says, "Dimitri won't kill him until you give him the go-ahead, but seeing him like that won't do you any favors."

He appears as shocked as me when I ask, "What if I don't want him to die? What if I want him to live?"

"Is that what you want?"

I shrug, truly unsure. My father isn't a kind man, but does the occasional whack of a belt across the back of my thighs warrant the loss of his life? I say no, but I also don't know the full extent of my so-called 'sale.'

"Will keeping him alive help get Dimitri's daughter back?"

Rocco waits a beat before halfheartedly jerking up his chin. "Possibly."

"Then I guess we have to keep him alive." I roll off the bed, straighten out my clothes, then walk to the door to open it for Rocco. "That's why I'm here, isn't it? To help Dimitri find his daughter?" It sounds as if I'm asking questions, but I am more summarizing my position in Dimitri's life than seeking answers from Rocco. "Forcing him to interact with me won't do that. It will only make matters worse."

As the creak of my bedroom door being opened sounds though my ears, Rocco slips off my bed. "There's no shame giving a man a reason to live, Roxie."

"That's what his daughter is for."

While shaking his head, he *tsks* me. "Some things you can't get from your blood." He tucks a strand of blonde hair behind my ear before trekking his finger down the throb in my throat. "You should know that better than anyone."

Chapter Twenty-Six

Dimitri

I clutch my phone in a death-tight grip when Rocco trails his index finger down the vein working overtime in Roxanne's neck. She's giving him no indication whatsoever she's interested in anything he's selling, but he still can't help but touch her.

I'd order for the valet to bring my car around immediately if I hadn't noticed Roxanne's panties in the middle of our bed. If Rocco truly wanted her, he wouldn't give up her panties for anything. He would have kept them as a trophy, paraded them in a way I tried to act unaffected by when I handed them to him. You only ever give something away like that when you're not interested, or you want people to believe you have no interest in them.

I'm in the latter field.

Do you have any idea the immense amount of control it took for me to end things where I did last night? My cum was smeared from Roxanne's collarbone to the rim of her teeny

"

tiny panties, yet, it still wasn't enough. I wanted every inch of her smelling like me—her tits, her ass, that delectable pussy that appears more ravishing the more times I see it. I just don't want my insatiable appetite to negatively impact my daughter as it has in the past.

Claiming Roxanne's virginity would do that. Her purity gives me a way into the world I'm petrified is holding my daughter captive. It's the key I've been seeking the past twenty months, and the very reason my gut is twisted up in knots.

A virgin—fuck. I still can't believe it. Roxanne has the spunk of five women, and the gall of a hundred, but she hasn't even unleashed her full potential yet. Imagine the power she'll yield when she realizes how some men can be controlled by their cocks? They move mountains for the right woman, break the rules.

They even feel sick at the thought of selling her purity to the highest bidder.

I don't want to do this, however I don't have a choice. If I want any chance of raising my daughter, I have to sell my soul to the devil, or at the very least, Roxanne's.

Fighting the urge not to demand Smith to send someone to Roxanne's room to forcefully remove Rocco, I shut down the live stream of her room, slip my phone into my pocket, then slide into the booth one of my father's most respected comrades just vacated.

My father's eyes reveal his shock at my arrival, but he plays it cool like he always does. "Son, what brings you to New York? I didn't think this was your scene."

While silently mocking me about my dislike of the wife-swapping caucuses that net the Petretti entity a tidy profit every year, he strays his eyes over the two-hundred plus attendees at the annual event. I understand most of the men's objectives in this room, fucking the same woman for the rest of your life could get tedious, but why shell out thousands of dollars to have another man's leftovers for the night? And don't get me started on the fact they're happy to loan their wives out. That isn't something I could ever do. If you touch what is mine, expect to pay dearly for it.

Rocco is about to learn that the hard way.

"I have a business proposal I'd like your opinion on before moving forward with plans. I heard whispering that you're in favor of this type of industry. Although I could have waited until you returned home, this is a time-sensitive matter."

After signaling for the topless waitress responsible for keeping my father's glass well-stocked to bring me a double shot of whiskey, I dig out the photo I had Smith print earlier today before sliding it to my father's side of the table. It's a still image of Roxanne after I left her in the sex chamber. Her eyes are wide and terrified, her cheeks are flushed, and the undeniable gleam of lust makes her pasty white skin look almost translucent. She puts forth the image of a woman in desperate need of a hard and rough fuck, but her innocence is undeniable.

I'm not surprised when my father tosses Roxanne's photo down without the slightest smidge of recognition forming in his eyes. When you've been in this industry as long as him, you don't recognize one blonde over another. It's why I had a member of my staff peroxide Roxanne's hair before booking an emergency dermatologist appointment to lighten her scar. Two simple changes immediately removed her from my father's radar.

I was hoping it would be the same for me. Alas, even knowing how much grief she's brought into my life hasn't altered my opinion of her. I'm as captivated by her as I was when she tried to hide her beauty with chunky boots and punk meal attire. I just can't react to my impulses this time around. Until Fien is safe, business must come first.

My dreary thoughts snap back to the present when my father says, "She'll fetch a few thousand a night. Call Mario, he'll put her straight to work."

He arches a bushy brow when I reply, "I want more than a few thousand for her. She's untouched. Pure. The wholly fucking grail of womanhood." My father tries to act disinterested, but I can smell the excitement slicking his skin. "She can cook. She had above-average grades in school and is obedient to a fault. I doubt it would take much to train her to her master's specifications, but I'm also curious to discover if there's a way I could profit off her more than once." My words aren't mine. I stole them from Roxanne's father.

My father stares at me for several heart-thrashing seconds before he lowers his hooded gaze to Roxanne's photo. "Has her purity been verified?"

"Yes," I lie. "I attended her appointment in person. Moses could barely slip his index finger inside of her."

When the waitress sets down my glass of whiskey, I raise it to my mouth, needing something to hide the clench of my jaw when the recognition I was seeking earlier darts through my father's eyes. I've never met Moses. I merely used a name Roxanne's father blurted out when I crucified his insolence one nail at a time.

He isn't bound to a chair with rope anymore.

He's nailed there.

My smirk slips when my father asks, "What were the results of her scan?"

I almost stumble, but the quickest memory of Ian blubbering about him not being able to afford a scan of Roxanne's ovaries and uterus for the delay in her sale keeps my ruse authentic. "They were clear. She's ready to breed."

"Hmm…" He slouches low into his chair before twisting his lips. He hates the idea of trusting me, but since I've never given him any reason not to, he does. *Thank fuck.* "She'd make a decent profit by selling her virginity then putting her in the trade, but I think you're right, the margin will be larger in another market." Not willing to give away his trade secrets in front of people he considers lesser than him, he props his elbows onto the table wedged between us before leaning over to my half. "There are several ways you could do this. Where do your interests lie?"

"On whatever makes the most money."

He huffs out a proud chuckle. That's all my father cares about—money. "It does make the world go around." After another laugh that's more creepy than exciting, he asks, "Is she your only asset?"

"For now," I lie again. "I have others in the works, but I figured I'd tip my toes into the water with her first, get a sense of the market. I've grown bored of the prostitution conglomerate. I need something fresh and exciting." Don't ask why my mind strayed to Roxanne during my last sentence. It just did. "But I'm out of my league here, Pops. I need a big gun to show me the way." That fucking hurt to say. Every word was the equivalent of dragging a razor blade up my throat. It stung like a thousand bees, but it was extremely effective. I've never seen my father look as pompous as he does now.

"Let's talk somewhere private. We can't be sure our competition isn't listening in."

I down my whiskey in one hit before following his slide out of the booth. Its burn gives me an excuse for the heat on my cheeks when a ghost of my past flies back into my life on her witch's broom.

Theresa Veneto was once in charge of the narcotics division at Ravenshoe PD. She's also one of the female officers I mentioned who are willing to disregard drug distribution tips when she's flat on her back being fed my dick. We played nice when we needed to. When we didn't, things turned ugly.

I lost thirty thousand dollars in un-cut coke when she walked in on her deputy giving me head. That's a street value of over two hundred thousand dollars. I didn't take the hit in revenue well. If it weren't for Audrey calling to tell me she was pregnant with Fien, Theresa wouldn't have left Ravenshoe PD breathing.

Strands of long blonde hair fall onto Theresa's shoulder when she leans in to place a kiss on the edge of my father's mouth. "I thought we were dining alone tonight?"

A well brought up person would acknowledge her quiet tone as a wish to keep her conversation between my father and herself. I'm not close to normal. "Plans changed. You can see yourself out."

When I click my fingers two times, demanding for one of my father's goons to show Theresa the door, she locks her eyes with my father's. "Col?" Shock filters across her attractive face when he doesn't immediately jump to her defense. "We have business to discuss."

"Yes, yes, I'm aware of why you're here and what your nagging will entail." My father's snapped tone reveals he's less than impressed with her whine. "But this can't wait. Megan can."

After dismissing Theresa with a wave of his hand, he commences walking toward the exit. I shadow his stalk, albeit a little slower. I've heard the name Megan before. It's a common name, so that isn't surprising, but it isn't every day it's mentioned in front of a cop who put a man away for life for the murder of a woman with the same name.

My father agreed to spare Justine's life on the agreement Maddox would take the wrap for the murder of a local woman. Her name was Megan Shroud.

"Smith—"

"Cross-referencing all Megans who've had contact with your father and Theresa Veneto now. I'll come back to you as soon as I have anything significant," he says down the bead-size listening device in my ear.

Even though he can't see me, I jerk up my chin before increasing the length of my strides. I reach my father just as he breaks through a group of people milling on the sidewalk. Worry that he overheard my brief conversation with Smith smacks into me when he grumbles under his breath, "I should have known he'd be around. He's always meddling in business that has nothing to do with him."

I'm about to defend Smith but lose the chance when my father tears away from my side. I curse into the cold night air when I spot who he's making a beeline for. Isaac Holt is making his way out of a nightclub a few spots down from the venue my father's function was held at. He's clutching the hand of a pretty brunette with flushed cheeks and a wobbly stride.

I don't know what my father says to Isaac when he reaches him, but it changes the expression on Isaac's face in an instant. He's wearing the same haunted look he had the night Ophelia and I organized for him to fight at our father's underground fight circuit.

We rigged the fight schedule, knowing our father would never value Ophelia's life enough not to use it as a bargaining chip. We were right. He offered her up as if she was worthless. We just had no clue CJ was fighting that night until it was too late.

Isaac won their match as anticipated, but his victory came at a cost I never anticipated. Ophelia didn't handle his win well. She was so distraught seeing CJ lying bloody and lifeless on the boxing ring floor, she took her anger out on Isaac instead of our stupid ruse.

Her anguish was nothing on what I felt when Tobias arrived at our family compound only hours later. Ophelia and CJ were in a car accident. CJ was wearing a seat belt. Ophelia wasn't. She didn't survive her sail through the windshield, and our family has been in tatters ever since.

After signaling for my father's goon to follow me, I join my father on the curb in front of Club 57, a famous nightclub in the heart of New York, where he's undertaking a pissing contest with a man undeserving of his wrath.

I should have accepted Isaac's answer when I attempted to recruit him to my family's fighting circuit when he was still in college. If I had, perhaps my life would be starkly contradictory to what it is. Karma has a way of biting back, and she's been gnawing my ass nonstop the past seven years.

"What has it been?" my father asks, acting oblivious to the fury radiating out of Isaac's gray eyes. "Six years and I don't even get a greeting from you." He snarls like Isaac should be bowing at his feet, unaware the millions of dollars he lost after Ophelia's death wasn't solely Isaac's doing. I had a hand in his demise as well.

How do you think I funded CJ's retirement to a wood cabin in the middle of whoop whoop?

When my father's attention shifts to the brunette plastered to Isaac's side, Isaac pulls her behind him in a protective stance. It doubles the arrogance slicking my father's skin with sweat, whereas it triples my inquisitiveness. Isaac cared for Ophelia, he may have even loved her, but I never saw him act as possessive with her as he is with this unnamed brunette.

Before I can work through half my curiosity, several voices bark down my earpiece in one go. They're so loud, I almost want to rip the device out of my ear. The only reason I don't is because one voice is instantly recognizable. It too angelic to be wrangling two angry mobsters.

"She's not FBI, Smith. She's part of the Russian Mafia."

Although Roxie's voice is crystal clear, it's obvious she isn't talking to me. I don't even think she's aware I can hear her.

"She was featured in a crime documentary last year."

I slant my head to the side, inconspicuously cupping my ear with my shoulder to ensure I don't miss Smith's reply. "That documentary was filmed three decades ago. It isn't possible for her to be the same person."

I'm drawn from their debate when my father's beady eyes burn a hole in my temple. I raise my head immediately, lost as to what the fuck I missed. My father is glaring at me, Isaac looks smug, and Murph, my father's goon, looks relieved all the focus is on me.

"Go!"

My father's roar startles several partygoers mingling in the distance to watch a battle of mafia kingpins. I'm just as shocked, but instead of freezing to watch the charade unfold, my hand itches to slide into the back of my trousers to retrieve my gun.

I've been embarrassed by my father many times—chewed up, spat out, and used more times than I can count—but this is the first time he's disrespected me in front of an enemy.

His disregard will open a floodgate for many more incidences. If you're not respected by those in your realm, you're not respected by anyone. I can't explain it any simpler than that.

He broke the ultimate rule, and it's taking everything in me not to retaliate with the same amount of inanity. I wouldn't hold back if it weren't for Fien. As much as this pains me to admit, her survival rate is hinged on my father's immortality.

Roxanne's virginity is the key to unlocking my daughter's freedom.

My father owns the lock.

I can't do this without them.

With that in mind, I pivot on my heels and walk away as per my father's request. My anger is so stubborn, I grip my date's arm with more force than needed to guide her to my car I requested for the valet to keep close by. Leah doesn't seem to mind. She's as worked up as I am after witnessing my father's conversation with Isaac.

"He won't let bygones be bygones, will he?" Her guilt is as palpable as mine. If she hadn't encouraged Ophelia to consider my ruse, her college roommate/best friend would still be here.

After sliding into the back seat of a rented SUV on Leah's heel, I rip the earpiece out of my ear, yank my cell phone out of my pocket, then dial Smith's number.

He answers two rings later. "I'm still cross-referencing—"

"What was that?"

The noise of his chair clicking into place sounds down the line before his confused hum. "What was what?"

"The argument between you and Roxanne."

A brief stretch of silence teems between us.

It agitates me to no end.

"Smith—"

"She must have accidentally hit the mic button."

Leah's pretty hazel eyes float from the scenery whizzing by her window to me when I snarl, "Why was she there to begin with? She should have been in her room." She's fine with women being traded as long as it's of their own free will. Only when you hold them captive, as I have Roxanne the past four days, does she have an issue.

I don't know if it's anger skating through my veins or worry when Smith replies, "She found my hub when looking for her father."

"You didn't think to lock the door?"

His laugh has me itching for a blood bath. "She didn't

exactly sneak up on me, Dimi. I knew she was coming before she entered."

"Then you should have escorted her back to her room."

He scoffs like I'm being irrational. It's barely heard over Leah's disappointed sigh when I say, "I put a price on her virginity tonight. If she's wandering around unsupervised, someone might be tempted to claim it without paying for the privilege."

"Fuckin' hell, Dimitri." Smith's relapse to my full name exposes his annoyance. "You were supposed to use Ian's information to get *your* foot into the industry, not dump Roxanne knee-deep in it."

"I couldn't get my foot in the door without using Roxanne's virginity." When he remains quiet, I stack some reassurance onto my ploy. "She won't be touched under my watch. I won't let anyone hurt her."

"You wanna fucking hope so, D." This gravelly tone doesn't belong to Smith. It's the voice of an undeniably pissed Rocco. "Because if she gets hurt, you'll have to load your own bullets into the gun you want to kill your father with because I'll be done."

It takes everything I have not to smash my phone when Rocco ends our call by doing precisely that to Smith's cell. The only reason I don't is because Smith's face on the screen of my phone is quickly gobbled up by the symbol I use for my father —a reversed pentagram.

Col: *Meet me at Chasity's at midnight. Come alone. It's time to expand the family franchise.*

Chapter Twenty-Seven

Roxanne

My eyes lift to the door when the creak of overworked hinges sounds through my ears. Relief engulfs my senses when Dimitri enters my room. I haven't laid my eyes on him in over twenty-four hours. He didn't return to our room after he snuck out yesterday afternoon, and none of his staff knew of his whereabouts when they brought in my meals. It was as if he vanished into thin air.

Even though I shouldn't have worn a hole in the rug fretting about him, I did. The last time we were together, he was a raging, neurotic caveman, but I still get a weird sense of comfort from sharing a bed with him. Seeing his bad points firsthand awards me the knowledge that he is able to protect me if needed. It arrives with a heap of possessive idiocies, but I'd rather those than to have him sit back and watch the carnage unfold like my father would.

The more my conversation with Rocco yesterday afternoon

filtered through my head, the sturdier my disdain for my father became. He tried to sell my virginity—more than once. That burns. I've known for a very long time that possessions are more valuable to him than anything, but still, I'm his daughter, his flesh and blood. He isn't supposed to profit off me.

My thoughts snap back to the present when Dimitri crosses the room. When I drink in his features, the knot in my stomach tightens. He looks exhausted—that isn't unusual, he always looks exhausted, but it's more prominent this morning. Dark rings circle his eyes, a crinkle is burrowed between his brows, and he's wearing the same tuxedo he snuck out of the room with last night—but he also looks as sexy as hell. His scruffy beard has been replaced with an almost clean-shaven chin, and his dark hair has been slicked back off his face. With a teasing number of tattoos peeking out of his impressive-looking tuxedo, he's showcasing the ultimate bad-boy persona— brooding mood and all.

"Hey," I greet him when he stops at the end of my bed. I'm not a fan of his quietness. I'd rather he pin me to the bed and scream in my face than tackle the bad aura suffocating his usually vivacious personality. "Are you just getting in?"

I loathe the jealousy my question was asked with, but it can't be helped. I know he didn't attend his function alone. I spotted a pretty redhead hovering in the wings of the surveillance footage Smith wasn't quick enough to shut down before I saw it last night. Before Dimitri left her alone to speak with his father, she was fawning all over him.

"Yeah. It was a long one." Eager to skip the awkwardness of a martial-like conversation when we're not close to being in a relationship, Dimitri lowers his eyes to the stacks of drawings on the mattress. "What are these?"

His inquisitiveness is understandable. I usually only sketch erotic nudes or cute animals. The twenty-plus works of art I slaved over for hours last night are life-like portraits.

"These are the faces of the people I remember seeing at Joops the night your wife was kidnapped. I drew the ones I couldn't cross off from Smith's database." I copy the scan of his eyes. "Most are entire faces, but a handful are a mix of side profiles or the angle I saw them at. It isn't much, but something as simple as an odd-shaped nose or a risqué haircut could add a name to your list of suspects." I lean over to snap up a drawing of a woman's hand I finished just before he arrived. "Like this one. Her ring is a custom piece. Perhaps Smith could locate the designer who made it? Or this one…" I snatch up the picture of a man with a military squadron tattoo on his arm. "His tattoo is only for current or previous servicemen and women. An everyday civilian can't get it."

My eyes float up to Dimitri's face when he asks, "Why are they separated into two piles?"

"This pile…" I point to my left, "… are the people who left before you arrived with your wife. These ones…" I shift my hand to the stack on my right, "… were still at the restaurant after I left."

I grow worried I've overstepped my mark when a brief stint of silence stretches between us. I'm confident Dimitri is appreciative of my help, but I doubt he's ever been given it without a heap of stipulations attached.

The hammer hits the nail on the head when Dimitri asks a few seconds later, "Why are you doing this, Roxanne? Why now?"

I lick my dry lips, hoping a little bit of wetness will help ease out my next set of words. "This is why I'm here, isn't it? To help get your daughter back?" Although my presence doesn't eliminate the reason Dimitri had Rocco follow me for the nine months after my accident, my offer of assistance was the only chip I had during our negotiation. "You don't want my help in the way Rocco suggested, so I'm trying to find another way to be helpful."

"It isn't that I don't want your help. I just…"

When his words trail off to silence, I help him out. "Blame me for what happened?"

He shakes his head, but his eyes say differently.

When he realizes I've spotted the truth in his eyes, he rakes his fingers through his dark locks. "She was right there, Roxanne, right fucking there, but I stopped to find you, and I couldn't take back the time I'd lost."

Unease twists in my stomach. "You stopped for me?"

He doesn't need to nod, I can see the truth in his eyes, but he does, nonetheless. "You made it two miles from where you were run down." A *pfft* vibrates his lips. I don't know if it's a good or bad *pfft*. "Your effort that night should have been applauded, but all it did was create months of misery. I lost contact with my daughter for *nine* months. There were no demands for ransom. No proofs of life. She was gone, and I was convinced I'd never see her again." Although this hurts to hear, I'm loving his brutal honesty. "Then you showed up again… and so did Fien."

Reading between the lines, I say, "I didn't have anything to do with her disappearance or reappearance, Dimitri. You have to believe me."

Our conversation ends as quickly as it begins when he mutters, "Belief takes trust. I don't give that to anyone." His eyes bounce between mine for several heart-thrashing seconds before he adds, "And neither should you." He dumps the drawing of a petite blonde with big blue eyes onto the stack on my right before he heads for the bathroom. "I'm going to wash up before having a drink downstairs." I'm anticipating for him to announce he'll have his staff bring a nightcap to my room, so you can imagine my shock when he says, "You can join me if you'd like."

Chapter Twenty-Eight

Dimitri

While exiting the bathroom I've shared with Roxanne the past five days, I dry my hair with more aggression than needed. Roxanne is stretched across the mattress, picking shards of pencil shavings out of the bedding. One of my shirts she's wearing as sleepwear is riding up high on her thighs. Since she isn't wearing any panties, inches upon inches of her delectable ass are on display. The exposed regions of her body reveal where her spanking marred her skin, however my handprints don't deter her sexiness.

A woman's virginity is supposed to automatically cloak them in innocence. They're usually seen as pure and unadulterated, the unsullied angels of a dark and twisted world.

Roxanne blows those theories out of the water.

She's ridiculously sexy, so much so, I'll have to tame down her looks for tonight's ruse to be effective. Important guests are arriving for festivities this evening. They're not the Arabian tycoons I usually cater for. They're just as rich, arrogant, and self-proclaimed, but instead of paying out the eye for a hooker for a night or three, they purchase wives specifically trained to their specifications.

I've had suspicions for months that my family was dabbling in this industry, but only last night did I receive official confirmation. For longer than I've been born, the Petrettis have been distributing mail-order brides, trained sex slaves, and the absolute kicker, babies.

Don't let your mind wander too far just yet. I almost killed my father where he stood when he disclosed how many children our family had sold over the past four decades. My mind instantly went to the gutter, aware if it brought in an income, it was to be explored—the pedophilia market included. It was only after inconspicuously passing on a handful of names to Smith did I learn otherwise. The purchasers of the newborn babies appear to be average, everyday Americans, although in the highly-craved two percent of the population. They had money—enough they could buy their way into parenthood.

Did the information lessen my agitation? Hardly. I'm still pissed, and it has me taking my anger out on the wrong person.

"Did you wear panties while lying on *our* bed with Rocco last night?" Think of the most possessive, disturbed prick you've ever met, then you'll have an indication on how bluntly I asked my question.

My foul mood can't be helped. Being an asshole sucks the life right out of me, so you can imagine how hard the fight becomes when the faintest whiff of the woman I should hate stirs my cock in a way no other woman has. Although Roxanne didn't hold the knife to Audrey's throat when she was marched out of Slice of Salt, nor to her stomach when she was forced through a dangerous caesarian, I can't help but still blame her.

It's ten times easier than shunting all the blame onto myself.

As Roxanne spins around to face me, she pulls down on the hem of her shirt. "I was wearing panties then. I took them off when I showered."

The honesty in her eyes does little to ease my annoyance. "Then why didn't you replace them when you got dressed?" Eighty percent of my staff are men, meaning the odds her meals today were delivered by a male is highly probable. The thought of them seeing her as I am now pisses me off. They were eager before her virginity was unannounced. Now they'll be blood-thirsty.

Roxanne's throat works hard to swallow. The liquor I guzzled down to keep my expression neutral while my father revealed his bag of tricks has me picturing her swallowing my cum while staring up at me with her pretty eyes out in full force. "The idea of drawing the people I saw smacked into me in the shower. I was so eager to start, I borrowed one of your shirts so I could get straight to work."

"Did you borrow my shirt or steal it?" I ask, looking for any excuse to punish her. Punishing her may be the only way I'll make it through tonight without killing everyone in attendance. That's how worked up I am.

Roxanne's reddish-blonde brows join as confusion crosses her features. "I didn't steal it, Dimitri. I'd never steal from you..."

Her words shift to a gasp when I interrupt, "Take it off."

"W-w-what?"

She heard what I said. She's just testing me as much as her big green eyes are testing the durability in the thread of the towel wrapped around my waist.

After jutting out my left leg to hide the crease my cock is causing to my towel, I growl out in a menacing tone, "Take. It. Off."

My switch-up in footing doesn't do me any favors. There

could be a truck parked between us, and Roxanne would still spot my raging boner. I'm so fucking hard, my cock is seconds from uncinching the knot holding my towel to my waist. My thickness has nothing to do with Roxanne's hand inching toward the hem of my shirt, and everything to do with the little wildcat rising in her eyes. She's noticed my body's reaction to my request for her to get undressed, and she's milking it for all its worth.

Do you blame her?

I could tell her until I'm blue in the face that I don't want her, but my cock will always say otherwise.

Roxanne's breasts lift high on her chest when she pulls my shirt over her head. Alice was right, the symmetry of her breasts and hips are perfect. They're meaty enough to be appealing but small enough they won't be weighed down by gravity any time soon. Her nipples are more a reddish-brown than the bright pink natural redheads usually have, but there's no denying her heritage. The slightest slither of hair hidden by the shadows between her legs leaves no doubt the vibrancy of her hair days ago didn't come from a bottle.

"Leave it," I demand when the whoosh of my shirt to the floor is closely chased by her bobbing down to gather up the hideous dressing gown she uses to hide more than to keep warm. "You need to shower. You smell…" I almost say like Rocco, but I can't force the lie out of my mouth. She smells like I was balls deep inside of her when I released my load onto her chest instead of in her delicious-smelling cunt like I really wanted to.

Mistaking my delay as an insult, Roxanne rolls her eyes before she sidesteps me to head to the shower. I try to let her go, to act unaffected by both her closeness and her disappointment, but before I can stop myself, my hand darts out to seize her wrist.

She freezes in an instant, her chest falling and rising in rhythm to mine when the alcohol steeped through my veins speaks on my behalf, "You smell like me."

Goosebumps break across her skin when I drag my nose down the throb in her throat. A growl rumbles in my chest when our intermingled scents linger in my nostrils. She smells so fucking intoxicating, it's taking everything I have not to double her scent.

Roxanne strains her eyes to look at me without moving her head when I say, "No one will ever believe you're a virgin if you smell like me. I'm tainted. Dirty. I smell of pure evil." I shift on my feet to face her front on. "If I want any chance of getting my daughter back, I need you to smell nothing like me."

Confusion is the first emotion to register in her eyes. It's quickly followed by determination. She doesn't know my plan, but she's willing to follow it.

Her silent pledge of assistance has me deviating my ruse in an instant.

As my cock flexes, I scrub my thumb over her ruddy lips. She wasn't lying when she said the tension between us is so blistering, no one could ever deny it. It crackles in the air, thickening my cock to the point it's painful.

Her needy breaths fan my lips with minty freshness when my hand lowers to the budded peaks on her chest. Her nipples are as erect as my cock, painfully strained with undeniable desire.

Unable to fight a battle I'm never going to win for a second longer, I brush the back of my hand down her budded nipple. When its tightness firms from my briefest touch, a growl rumbles in my chest. She's so responsive to my touch, even more than I've wondered too many times to count the past year.

When I brush my hand down her nipple for the second

time, her thighs shudder like she's on the brink of ecstasy. One flick on her clit, and I'm certain she will be done.

As the heady scent of a hungry cunt clutches my senses, I return my eyes to Roxanne's face. She stares straight at me, soundlessly begging for me to loosen the restraints I've lived with the past almost two years.

After the shit twenty-four hours I've had, I'd give anything to forget my life for an hour. To push Roxanne onto the mattress and test the authenticity of her virginity. To taste her. To smell my skin against hers. To claim her like my fucked-up head tried to last night.

I want her in a way I've never wanted a woman, but in a way I can't have her.

At least not until Fien is home. Not until she's safe.

Roxanne's needy breaths switch to a groan when I glue my hands to my side. If she thinks this is easy for me, she has no fucking clue how I operate. Excluding my search for Fien, I've never fought so hard in my life.

Something so simple shouldn't cause such a catalyst of emotions, but the thought of never touching her feels worse than death. I've been drowning since the moment I studied Fien's lifeless, upside-down face, now I'm being strangled as well.

Upon hearing my unvoiced rejection, Roxanne scuttles into the shower as fast as her quivering legs can carry her. She has barely left my side for a second when the itch to kill skates through my veins. I'm angrier now than I was when I agreed for a handful of my father's clients to visit my compound unvetted. His request means I'm walking into tonight's festivities blind. I have a list of aliases and their favorite kinks, but no indication of how they fit into the industry I've been trying to get my foot in the door of. All I know is that they prefer them young and unbloodied—just like Roxanne.

While working my jaw side to side to weaken its strain, I head to the closet to get dressed. Tonight's festivities will run similarly to my previous event, but the women were hand-selected by my father. Roxanne was his first choice. The rest are a random variety of women. He didn't do that for no reason. He's testing the authenticity of my ruse, aware not every man will set aside lifelong dislikes for money. We're not all like him. Sometimes we value people more than possessions.

Partway to the walk-in closet, a stack of papers on my desk draws my focus. They're the sketches Roxanne showed me earlier. They are still separated into two piles. One stack is much higher than the other. They're the group of people still in attendance after Roxanne left with a flood of tears rolling down her cheeks.

Too curious to discount, I head to my desk instead of the closet. My mind was spiraling too much earlier to give Roxanne's drawings the consideration they deserved.

My cock hardens when I lift the first sketch off my desk. Roxanne's attention to detail is phenomenal. Just like her nudes, only the grain of the cheap pencils she used gives away the fact they're drawings. You could almost accuse her of tracing the images from photographs. I know she didn't, though, because none of these faces register as familiar, and I've scanned the images from that night over a dozen times the past twenty months.

"Smith, how long will it take to do a facial recognition scan for around two dozen people?"

"Photographs or sketches?" The fact he asks that tells me he's watching me. He better have logged into the feed after Roxanne entered the bathroom, or we'll have more than words.

I try to keep my annoyance on the down-low, but it still echoes in my tone when I say, "I need to know who these people are." I twist the sketch of a man with long-ass sideburns and a chipped front tooth around to face the camera in the corner of the room.

Even with the screen of my phone being as black as night, Smith's reply comes through the speakers with precise clearness. "Have someone bring them down. I'll get a start on them while waiting for the rest of Megan's info to come through."

Fuck! With everything going on, I completely forgot I sent him down that rabbit warren several hours ago.

While heading to the closet to get dressed in a pair of black trousers and a pinstriped dress shirt, I ask, "What have you unearthed so far?"

Smith's disappointed groan tightens my jaw. "Her case is a fucking mess. There's no body—"

"That's not unusual. There's *never* a body."

A smirk tugs at my lips when he replies, "You're preaching to the choir, but tell me one time a murder investigation is open and closed on the same day with no DNA, no witness, and no missing person report from a relative or friend?" He doesn't wait for me to reply. "Something is off with this case. Megan rarely used a credit card before her death." The way he spits out 'death' means he's as disbelieving of her homicide as I am. "But there were sprinklings of her in other electronic means… bus tickets, online music purchases, an annual subscription for *Rock Punk* magazine."

"Did she cancel her subscription?"

I can't see Smith, but I picture him shaking his head when a whoosh sounds down the line. "That's the thing. Her subscription was renewed last month."

"Last month?" I double-check, certain the blood rushing to my lower extremities has affected my hearing. "Megan has been dead for over a year."

"Mm-hmm. Don't you know all dead people keep their rock obsession current?"

After a beat, I say, "Keep me updated on anything that comes in, however I don't see us getting the answers we need from a computer. For now, shift your focus to the men arriving tonight and Roxanne's sketches."

"All right." His chair clicking into place sounds down the line. "I've got everything ready to go, but I must warn you, Dimi, this won't be as easy as you're hoping. Facial recognition isn't like it is in the movies. It takes time."

"I can be patient." When Smith's snicker rolls down the line, my hands ball into tight fists. "I can." His chuckles reveal he has no clue how much restraint I just exuded. It keeps him off my hit list—for the night. "I've waited this long for answers, so what are a couple more days?"

Before he can remind me that every second I'm away from my daughter feels like a year in hell, I toss my cell phone onto a stack of drawers next to the walk-in closet before slamming the door shut, blocking out anything he has to say.

Chapter Twenty-Nine

Dimitri

"Fuck me."

For the first time tonight, Rocco isn't swearing at me. His focus isn't even on me. He's staring at someone across the room with an unhinged jaw and bulging eyes.

My jaw doesn't know which way to swing when I discover who has caught his attention. If it wants to tighten with fury, I'll need to collect it from the floor first.

Like Cinderella arriving at a mafia ball, Roxanne floats into the parlor at exactly eight. The modest hem of a pale blue dress swishes against her thighs when she twists to face the group of thirty or so men watching her every move. Although her bangs remain fanned across her forehead, the rest of her hair has been pulled back into a high ponytail. Her makeup is basically non-existent. Only the slightest sheen of lip gloss glistens on her mouth. She looks nothing like the sex-pot I left hungry and impish forty minutes ago, and everything like the naïve virgin my guests highly crave.

With my suspicion high, I drift my narrowed eyes to Rocco. "What did you tell her?"

When Rocco returns my watch, my blood pressure goes through the roof. His eyes are massively dilated, ensuring there's only one jaw about to swing—to the left when my fist lands on it with a crack. "I didn't tell her shit."

"Then why is she dressed like that? Why does she look like every dirty man's wet dream?" My interrogation ends when my exchange with Roxanne before she entered the bathroom rolls through my head. I told her to smell the opposite to me, to smell pure. If that wasn't a flashing red beacon warning her to the shitstorm I was about to thrust her in, I don't know how much more obvious I could have been.

If she knows my ruse, why is she here? Shouldn't she be responding to my attempt to sell her with the fury I instilled on her father when he tried to do the same? Or at the very least, be as mad as hell?

I take a staggering step back when the truth smacks me hard in the gut. She isn't parading her virginity for me or her. She's pimping herself out for a child she's never met—my child. She's doing it for Fien.

Before I can get over my shock that the lady responsible for my daughter's captivity is doing everything in her power to free her, Roxanne stops to stand next to me. Although she seems put together, her nerves are noticeable. The furious shake of her hands is indicative enough, much less the rattle of her vocal cords when she asks Rocco if the drink he's nursing has alcohol in it.

Rocco lifts his chin. "Vodka. Do you want—"

Roxanne cuts off his offer to fetch her a drink by stealing

the one in his hand. She downs it as if getting smashed is something she does every weekend before requesting another.

When she throws down a second double nip like it's water, I remove the glass from her hand before placing it on the mantlepiece behind us. I understand she needs some liquid courage, but her life will never be the same if she ends up with one of these men in a room while she's drunk. They won't spank her and walk away. They take everything she has on offer—even the stuff she isn't willing to give.

The fact she's putting her life on the line for my daughter ensures I'd never let that happen. I'd massacre every man in this room before I'd let her be hurt under my watch. When you are on my side, you're on my side for life. Roxanne's efforts tonight expose whose team she's on.

"Point me in the right direction." It dawns on me that Roxanne isn't talking to me when her eyes float across the men gawking at her like she's a movie star. It isn't just the occasional nod she does that gives it away. It's overhearing Smith advising her which guests he's got hooks into that makes it obvious.

Once she has a rundown of the room, Roxanne locks her wide eyes with mine. "Anything identifiable, right?"

It takes everything I have to jerk up my chin, and even then, it's a soft, weaselly lift. Throwing her to the wolves and standing back to watch the show feels fucking wrong, but when you're desperate, you must take desperate measures.

"All right. Wish me luck." Not waiting for further instructions, she glides across the room with slow, wary strides. Her chin isn't held high like the women paid to keep the guests entertained. She tucks it into her chest while fiddling with the material of her dress.

Her shy act awards her even more attention than her beautiful face. Men are drawn to her like moths to a flame, their interest so notable, my father's underhanded comment that she'd fetch a record-breaking price seems logical. Her ruse is the ultimate display of how easily men can be manipulated. They're practically fighting to secure her attention, completely oblivious to the fact she's hoping to take them all down. Not even I feel safe from slaughter.

"Follow them," I say to Rocco when a man with slicked-back hair and a heavy set of wrinkles guides Roxanne toward the library at the side of the parlor for a one-on-one compatibility chat. From the whispers of the group tonight, he needs a new wife after his was strangled during a sex act. He thought she was holding back on how much she could take. He was proven wrong when his multiple attempts to resuscitate her were fruitless.

My pulse thuds in my chin when Rocco asks, "If he gets out of line?"

Deliberating the consequences of my actions usually takes longer than half a nanosecond. This time around, it doesn't. "Take him out."

I'll be out on my ass if I kill any of my father's wealthiest associates, but just the slimebag's hand on the small of Roxanne's back has me thirsty for a bloodbath. This isn't an itch I can scratch without someone dying. If that someone ends up being me, at least my daughter will have a reason to be proud.

Up until now, I haven't given her much to work with.

Although Rocco is still pissed I forced Roxanne's involvement in this industry, his annoyance isn't as noticeable when he enters the library on Roxanne's heel. He had no clue my ruse would pan out the way it did. In all honesty, neither did I. I wouldn't have hidden my plans from Roxanne if I had any inkling she'd go along with them.

I wait for Roxanne and Rocco to disappear from view before shifting on my feet to face a camera in the corner of the room. I don't say anything. I don't need to. Smith's squawks reveal he can feel my wrath. "She didn't want to go in blind. I should have told you she came to me——"

"Yes, you should have."

He continues talking as if I didn't interrupt him. "But she asked me not to."

"Who do you work for, Smith?" When a stretch of silence teems between, I ask my question again, with more fury this time around. "Who *the fuck* do you work for, Smith?"

He says the last name I expected to hear. "Fien. I'm here for Fien." He wets his lips before adding, "And so is Rocco, Clover, and Roxanne, so how about you appreciate the help instead of seeking reasons for it. I know you were raised to believe different, Dimi, but not everyone is out to play you." The heavy drone of him giving his keyboard a thrashing sounds down the line before he says, "Don't mind me, I've got sicko pedophile identities to unearth."

Stealing my chance to reply, not that I have anything to say, he disconnects our connection.

Even though I deserved Smith's anger hours ago, it cut deeper than I care to admit. It's been fucking with my psyche as much as seeing Roxanne work the crowd. She's been in and out of rooms all night, her suiters so eager to get her alone, some offered cash incentives just for five minutes of her time, others offered to pay her college tuition in full on top of their prospective bids.

Although I am as edgy as fuck, her one-on-one meetings have given Smith crystal clear images of the men's faces to run through the nationwide database. It's been a long, drawn-out process, and I'm feeling every second of it. Most of the men have been respectful of the rules they agreed to abide by when they arrived, however a handful have been testing the boundaries.

Take the man Roxanne is talking to now. If it were anyone but me watching Roxanne's every move, they wouldn't notice his sneaky touches of her elbow or his gentle strokes down her inner arm. He doesn't go for the obvious areas Rocco and Smith deem unacceptable. He's touching her like he intimately knows her, caressing her as no one ever has. He's being tender to the point of being a gentleman, and it's pissing me off to no end.

Even a novice in this industry knows there are rules you can't break. Touching something that doesn't belong to you is at the top of the list. As much as this dweeb wishes it weren't true, Roxanne isn't his, and I'm more than happy to remind him of that.

"Shutdown surveillance before requesting Rocco to take Roxanne to my downstairs' office." Smith isn't just shocked at my request, he's pleased with it. The profiles of tonight's guests would even make non-parents' stomachs swirl. We have every combination you can think of. Millionaire tech giants, school-teachers, politicians, doctors, and the absolute kicker, an OBGYN who was so eager to place a bid on Roxanne, he didn't attempt to woo her with the coin he was willing to spend a night with her. He went straight to the hierarchies with an offer, the amount staggering.

My father would have accepted his offer in an instant. It was three times the amount the other bids received, and there were no added stipulations such as proof of her purity or that shipping costs be included in the sale of her virginity.

Dr. Bates' eagerness won't go over as easily with me. Nothing against Roxanne, she has the looks to set any man's pulse racing and a body of pure dynamite, but in this industry, you only pay over the asking price for one reason—you're not planning to follow the rules. Roxanne's sale was touted as a virginity-only trade. There were no long-term commitments or talks of marriage. This was a one-night-only deal. So why the fuck is Dr. Bates offering a little over five hundred thousand dollars for the privilege?

His bid set alarms off in my head, but for once, instead of them ringing in warning, they're sounding in victory. For months, I've constantly felt one step behind my enemies, but tonight is the first time I feel like we've raced ahead. Although we've been working toward this for months, I truly don't believe it would have been achieved tonight without Roxanne's help. She has the bidders eating out of her palm so readily, they divulged information to her the sternest torture wouldn't have unearthed. She was handed business cards, blank checks, and keycards for permanently-booked suites in Manhattan. That's a treasure trove of information that makes our guests tonight easy to trace, and it was handed to Roxanne quicker than Smith could run their faces through the database.

The shocked excitement on Smith's face grows when I say, "Once I've shown our guests out, I don't want to be interrupted for the rest of the night unless it's urgent." I should have said morning considering it's well after two, alas, I am too tired to consider how stupid I'm acting.

I didn't sleep a wink last night, so I'm not just tired, the whiskey I've been guzzling to dampen the fire in my gut is hitting me harder than usual. I'm half fucking tanked, but alcohol isn't giving me the buzz I need. I need something more potent, more addictive. Something you can't get artificially.

I need blood and warfare, and perhaps the heat of a woman's cunt around my cock.

Aware Smith will follow my orders no matter how imprudent, I exit his computerized hub. While pacing through the party-like atmosphere which died remarkably quick since all the guests were chasing the same woman, I scan my eyes over the ones who barely got a once-over. My gaze usually sharpens on the redheads in the room, my favorable choice, but tonight, they seek a sultry blonde with a tiny waist and grassy green eyes that are more sinful than saintly.

When my eyes collide with a woman matching my requirements, she stumbles like she chugged down the fifth of whiskey warming my veins. Even with her focus seemingly on a man with ginger-red hair and a knockoff Tom Ford suit, she watches me cross the room. The heat of her watch is as stifling as it was before I joined Smith to assist with surveillance, and the exact reason I kept my distance the past six hours.

If I hadn't stepped back, our ruse would have never had the effect it did. Not even men who pay are willing to look past undeniable chemistry. They would have mourned the missed opportunity for a few seconds before moving onto their next target.

I owe it to Fien not to let that happen.

That's done and dusted now, though. Preferring to go home alone than with a woman not close to Roxanne's league, the high-priority guests lodged their bids and left. Although they'll still be scrutinized with the same fine-tooth comb as the more well-to-do guests, I don't believe the stragglers have the gall to pull off the scam Rimi has been running the past two years. Kingpins don't let their prospective playthings be wooed in front of them without incident. He'd control everything she does from the moment she registered on his radar, and perhaps mark her with his scent so every other man would get the hint to back the fuck up. He might even go as far as removing the fingers that touched her skin without his permission.

Roxanne's virginity may have been on offer tonight, but her sale came with a heap of rules, the main one, she wasn't to be touched. I don't appreciate my directive being ignored, and will have no trouble relaying my annoyance in both physical and non-physical manners.

I don't know which side of the coin Roxanne's punishment will be on yet. With my cock as tight as my jaw, it may end up being a combination of both.

Don't misconstrue. I'm not saying Roxanne should be punished because she was touched against her wishes. It's the way she leans into her prospective purchasers' side to keep her legs upright I'm frustrated about. Instead of letting her knees buckle out in response to the tension bristling between us, she accepts comfort from another man.

That is unacceptable.

Women like Roxanne don't want to be nurtured like children. They want to be claimed like we're still in the Stone Age, protected with the infamy of a madman, and fucked like possessiveness is the highest form of flattery.

They also want to be owned, and I'm about ready to stake my claim.

Chapter Thirty

Roxanne

Nerves tap dance in my stomach when the handle of a door that was locked earlier tonight slowly lowers. A man with so many distinguishable features, Smith unearthed his true identity faster than I could snap my fingers and attempted to guide me into this room earlier tonight. Timothy Jamison—a primary-school teacher if you can believe it—was so desperate to talk to me in private, he acted as if he could sidestep Rocco's shadow as easily as Dimitri avoided my heated watch from across the room.

It was unfortunate for Timothy that Rocco didn't cave as easily as Dimitri. I was only onto suitor number three when Dimitri made a beeline for the exit with clenched fists and a firm jaw. He raced out the room like his ass was on fire, and if you exclude him offering to show my final suitor the way out an hour ago, I hadn't seen hide nor hair of him since.

I won't lie. When the full extent of Dimitri's ruse smacked into me while I was showering, I was fuming mad. I couldn't believe he was undervaluing me as my father always had. Then I thought about it a little longer. For years, I wanted what every little girl wants—the love of her father. I did everything and anything to get it. I was the good girl who didn't speak when told to be quiet, spoke politely when given a chance, and I always remembered my manners.

When common courtesies didn't work, I gave the opposite a shot. I lashed out and got angry. I screamed at the top of my lungs. I became an exact replica of my father. And do you know what? It still didn't work. No matter what I did, he didn't give me the love I was seeking.

Even with the crazy world still being new to me, I'm confident in saying Dimitri's daughter will never face the same issue. He hasn't seen her in the flesh, yet he loves her so much, he constantly sets aside his needs for her. I doubt one thing he's done the past two years has been for him. Every decision he makes is based on how it will affect Fien. He wouldn't even breathe if it had a chance of negatively impacting her. That's how much he loves her.

My decision to forgo tonight's event was already teetering, but when I exited the bathroom, they fully imploded. The sketches I had worked on for hours on end weren't where I left them. They were gone, replaced with an art lover's vault of pencils, paints, sketchpads, and charcoals. The items covering every inch of the desk in Dimitri's room couldn't have been gathered on the fly. Some of them can't be picked up at any store. Whoever purchased them for me went out of their way to do so.

My gut wanted to believe Rocco is as generous as he is stirring, but my heart refused to consider it for even a moment. It knew my gifts were from Dimitri, just like he knew I was going to participate in his ruse even if it came with a risk I wouldn't come out of it unscathed. Fien deserves the chance to experience a father's love as I never have. If I help her achieve that, perhaps my own failure won't feel so horrific.

I jump up from the couch like an obedient lapdog when Dimitri enters the large office in the lower half of his compound. Although the well-decorated space is shrouded in blackness, I know who he is. Not only have my eyes adjusted to the dark, his scent is highly distinguishable as is his suffocating aura.

It chokes the air of oxygen even more when he barks out, "You did good tonight, Roxanne. The bidders' eagerness to woo you had them spilling secrets left, right, and center." Air whizzes out of his nose. "But you also did bad. What was the first rule Smith told you tonight?"

The nerves twisting in my stomach are heard in my reply, "That I wasn't to touch anyone." I'm not worried I broke the rules. Just remembering the men were here to buy my virginity assured my hands wouldn't get close to them. I'm petrified I haven't given Dimitri a reason to punish me. His punishment would have been far more pleasurable than painful.

When Dimitri slants his head, the light outside the hall unshadows half his ridiculously handsome face. "And what did you do?" I'm about to answer, *kept my hands to myself*, but he continues talking, foiling my chance. "You touched."

I almost shake my head until I realize it isn't anger pumping out of Dimitri. It's jealousy.

A one-way ticket to hell drops into my inbox when I mumble, "I didn't mean to. I find it hard to communicate without my hands."

I anticipate for him to call me out as the liar I am, so you can imagine my shock when he commences pacing to a big wooden desk in the corner of the room. His arrogant walk wasn't dissuaded from the seediness of tonight's undertakings. It's as cocky as ever, and it has my pulse racing.

Once Dimitri has the starchy material of his dress shirt rolled up to his elbows, he strays his eyes to mine. They are as brutally beautiful as ever. "Remove your dress and bra. You can keep your panties…" His lips curve to his infamous half-smirk before he adds, "… for now."

I almost double back, stunned he's gone straight for my jugular. I'm not comfortable being naked, but the collision of our eyes alters the direction of my course in an instant. Just like when he commanded me to remove his shirt earlier tonight, his steely blue eyes expose this is another test.

Although I hate that he's forever testing me, only days ago, I decided that failure will no longer be associated with my name. So, with that in mind, I raise my shaky hands to the neckline of my dress to undo the first button.

The first four buttons come away without too much drama. The same can't be said for the final few. The heat teeming out of Dimitri is too much. It has me torn between wanting to fall to my knees and beg forgiveness for my lie and marching across the room to soak up every blister of his scold. I'd rather he not be angry, but I also prefer his jealous fury over no emotional response whatsoever.

Once my bra is sitting on top of my dress, I raise my eyes to Dimitri's. Not even the dark can take away from their allure. They're icy pools of seduction.

My already brisk heart rate breaks into a canter when he jerks his chin up. "Come here."

I pace across the room, my strides so shaky, you'd swear I was wearing heels instead of flats. Alice's choice of wardrobe nearly made it impossible to validate my father's claims I'm a virgin. If it weren't for Smith suggesting that I ask Dimitri's housemaids for help, I may have still been in my room, sewing together four skimpy outfits with the hope of making one modest one.

Smith's unexpected assistance scared the crap out of me, however it also assured me I wasn't going into tonight blind. I had eyes on me—many of them—including the pair gawking at me now.

After sitting in his fat leather chair, Dimitri pushes it away from his desk. "Sit."

I want to crawl into a ball and die when my attempt to straddle his lap has the faintest of chuckles ringing in my ears. This is more horrifying than I could ever explain and has me suddenly knowledgeable about why I've only ever dated men who thought they could milk my loins of their nectar.

"Ass on my desk." When Dimitri lifts and locks his eyes with mine, the lust in them reveals my embarrassment is unwarranted. He isn't chuckling because he thinks I'm an idiot. He's pleased I am as naïve as his guests tonight hoped. "Legs opened wide."

Through quaking, breathless lungs, I do as requested, confident Dimitri is too possessive to let anyone see me in a vulnerable state. I like when he watched me climax in the alleyway many months ago, but that doesn't mean I'm open to a free for all.

After planting my backside on the edge of his desk, I part my thighs in an unladylike manner.

"More."

My thighs are stretched to the width of Dimitri's large frame when he scoots his chair back in close to his desk.

"Keep them there."

It's virtually impossible to follow his clipped command when he runs the back of his hand down my lace panties. Since I couldn't morally borrow underwear, I had no choice but to don one of the many risqué thongs Alice added to my collection. They leave nothing to the imagination, which means I feel every delicious callous on Dimitri's newly-battered hand.

"How much?" Dimitri strains his words through the jealousy clutching his throat. I know this as his voice has the same gravelly deliverance mine had when several women approached him at the start of tonight's event. They didn't have the eyes of any of the men wanting to get to know me. They didn't care. They had their target locked, and they weren't going to stop until they had him. "How much was the highest bid you received tonight?"

Even aware he knows the answer since Smith recited each offer to him as they were received, I say, "One hundred and eighty-three thousand dollars."

My thighs press together when his low growl races lust through my womb like a wildfire. It has my knees curving inward even faster than it has his face sitting within an inch of my aching pussy. "Then why aren't your panties soaked through with the scent I can smell building in your clenching cunt? Weren't you turned on knowing how much men we're willing to pay to spend one night with you?"

While fighting my hips not to gyrate toward his mouth, I shake my head. They could have offered me ten times as much, and I wouldn't have been flattered. Money shouldn't enter the equation in exchanges like this. Hell, right now, I'm not even sure love should. It's all about lust and chemistry so blistering, even if it fizzles out as quickly as it ignites, it deserves to be explored. Ignoring something this sweltering should be criminal.

When I say that to Dimitri, he runs his hand down my panties for the second time. His fingers don't make it through the carnage unscathed this time around. The wetness glistening on them is as noticeable as the fiery glint darting through his eyes. I'm soaked in an instant, and it has Dimitri paying more attention to me than he did my final suitor when he kissed my cheek goodnight. He looked seconds from killing him, although it has nothing on the urge masking his face now.

"Some of the bids tonight were the highest I've ever seen." I lose the ability to breathe when he mutters, "Yet here you are, sitting on my desk, getting wet over my briefest touch."

After switching on the lamp on his desk, he scoots in so close, nothing but his next breath is on my mind. They batter my aching pussy with so much heat, my delirious head has me confusing them as excited breaths instead of angry ones. I've never been more turned on and terrified in my life.

I'm not scared of him. I'm terrified he'll never touch me like I'm silently begging him to. The amounts thrown around tonight were impressive. If my esteem was as low as my father aimed for it to be, I may have considered their offers to fund my studies. Alas, even with him wrongly believing I'm to blame for his daughter's captivity, my body yearns for only one man.

I begin to wonder if Dimitri has mindreading capabilities when he says, "You could have your choice of any man, but that isn't what you want, is it, Roxanne? You don't want a man. You want a monster, a bastard, a man who'd rather destroy you than ever have you believe you deserve more than him."

His usually icy eyes switch to the color of a bottomless ocean when I shake my head. "You're not a monster, Dimitri. You're angry and confused, and oh-so-fucking tired, but you're not a monster."

The air that whizzes out of his nose sends my senses into overdrive. "I allowed men to bid on your virginity *after* beating a man for doing the same thing."

His underhanded confession about hurting my father should dampen the intensity brewing between us. it doesn't. Not in the slightest. If anything, it doubles it. "You may have let them bid for me, but you never had any intention to let them cash in their bids." He's too possessive for that, too neurotic, but since that confession could possibly knock our exchange back a few spots, I keep my mouth shut.

It's for the best. I can barely breathe when he slips my panties to the side. When my pussy is awarded the heat of his breaths without hindrance, the dampness his fingers briefly felt moments ago jumps to saturated. His thorough inspection of my private parts should make me feel vulnerable, whereas all I'm feeling is wanted. My prospective buyers peered at me with the same hungry, wanton eyes, but not once did their gawks have the edge Dimitri's does now. He stares at me as he did in the alleyway a year ago, his watch so needy, if he can't get past his neurosis that he shouldn't touch me, I'm willing to pick up the slack on his behalf.

"Please," I beg when the tension tethering us together as if we're one becomes too much to bear. His mouth is an inch from my pussy, my orgasm is just as close to the finish line. This is the cruelest form of torture.

Panicked sexual deprivation is only the beginning of his punishment. I skate my hand toward my pussy. One flick of my aching clit will have me free-falling off the cliff. That's how crazy the tension is between us.

My hand makes it halfway to my pussy before Dimitri snatches it away. "When you touch what isn't yours, you lose fingers." The heat trekking through my veins becomes dangerous when he growls out, "If you don't believe me, ask the guest I just showed out."

The trickle of desire surging through me turns catastrophic. I hate he felt the need to intervene when his guests get overly friendly, but I also love it. I'll never make anyone feel guilty about protecting me. I've been seeking this level of protective-ness since I was three. Furthermore, his comments imply that he classes me as his. That excites me more than how danger-ously close his thumb is hovering near my clit.

When nothing but needy breaths fill my ears for the next twenty seconds, I get desperate. "Please, Dimi."

My rare use of his nickname sees his eyes locking with mine. They're not the same withdrawn pair I'm used to seeing. They're still full of danger, darkness, and recklessness, but there's a yearning gleam to them that makes them unique. "Please, what?"

Desperate, I blurt out without thinking, "Touch me. Please. I'm begging you. I won't intrude on your time or seek more attention than you're willing to give. I just can't take it anymore. The tension is too much. I feel like I'm about to explode—"

My shameful beg is cut off by Dimitri sucking my clit into his mouth. When he tugs at the bundle of nerves with his teeth, I call out in an erotic scream. He gives head better than the many daydreams I've had about him doing precisely that the past five days.

While his tongue snakes out to toy with my clit, I weave my fingers through his dark locks. My frantic tugs on his hair has him eating me more expertly. He pokes his tongue inside of me, drags it up my slit, then tangles it around my clit until I chant his name on repeat. Then he does it all again just for fun.

My prediction months ago was one hundred percent accurate. His skills at giving head are out of this world. Every lick, nip, and suck doubles the fiery warmth spreading across my midsection. It burns me up as much as the tension that's raged between us the past five days.

"I fucking knew you'd taste delicious," Dimitri moans into my throbbing pussy when he takes a breather to survey the damage he caused. "As did every man here tonight. They wanted to taste you, fuck you, and smear their cum over every inch of you." His dangerous aura that mesmerized me since day one beams out of him when he says, "Then there were the ones who wanted you for so much more than your virginity."

His confession has him eating me faster, more aggressively. It's a painstaking blur of bites, licks, and nips that have me riding his face like our exchange won't cost me a thing. It's silly of me to believe, but right here, right now, I don't care. He can have my soul for all I care. I'd give it to him willingly if he promised not to end our exchange until the bomb in the lower half of my stomach detonates.

"Oh, God," I pant when he drags his tongue up my slicked slit before circling it around my clit. The flicks he hits my clit with are delicious as is his tight grip on my ass. They have me freefalling so quickly, it should be embarrassing.

While shuddering and shaking in the cool evening air, Dimitri's name rips from my throat in a husky moan. The blistering sensation blasting through me lasts for several long minutes. I've never experienced anything close to this in all my life. It's better than I predicted and has me craving a second hit even with the first one still occurring.

When my orgasm finally relents its firm clutch of my senses, I'm emotionally and physically wiped. It wasn't building for days, weeks, or months. It's been gaining intensity for years. Its body-limping strength is a sure-fire proof of this.

"Fuck…" Dimitri growls in a low, shallow tone as he soaks up evidence of my arousal with two hearty licks. "You taste better than predicted, but you hit the target for speed."

The shame burning my cheeks shifts to desire when he stands from his seat so he can work his trousers down his thighs. Even with his trunks hiding the mouth-watering visual I'm dying to see, I'm confident in saying he's harder than he was when he blew his load on my chest. The sheer girth of his cock has me hopeful my taste was addictive enough to have him craving me time and time again.

The primitive part of my brain takes hold when Dimitri frees his cock from his trunks. Pre-cum is already wetting the head of his perfect manhood, and it has my mind blank on how much pain a cock that size will cause. His penis is large, angry, and arrowing toward an area of my body that won't stop clenching in anticipation.

"Are you sure you want this, Roxanne?" Dimitri asks as he fists his cock to give it a hearty squeeze, "Because it'll hurt. Your tight little cunt is going to feel me for days once I'm finished with it."

I nod, a better response above me. I thought my earlier orgasm was as powerful as they'd get, but the image of him working his cock in and out of his fist while staring down at my drenched vagina reveals I starkly underestimated their abilities. The one cresting in my womb now feels like a tsunami, growing more devastating when he loses the ability to harness his desires for the second time.

He doesn't plunge his thick cock into me like my devious mind was hoping. He falls to his knees, spread my thighs wide, then burrows his head back between my legs. "You taste too fucking good for only one sample."

After notching a single finger inside of me, he delves his tongue around his frozen digit, easing the burn his fat finger caused. He eats me for the next several minutes before adding a second finger to the mix.

I don't realize how noisy I'm being until my moans bounce off the walls of Dimitri's office. I grunt and moan on repeat while fighting the urge to tell him to stop. I don't want him to stop, but if I don't say something, I'll explode into a blubbering mess of wetness and sin even quicker than I did the first time. I hadn't considered the thought of him fingering me and giving me head at the same time. None of my college boyfriends could multitask. I either got one or the other, there was no option for both.

Seemingly linked to my inner workings, Dimitri grips my ass, thrusts my pussy off his desk, then eats the living hell out of me. I'm brought to climax by his tongue within seconds.

"Yes," he hisses into my pussy when my nails grip the top of his shoulders. As scream after scream rips through me, I ride the intensity of my second climax like its more vital than my lungs needing air to function.

I've barely merged from hysteria when he attempts to squash a third finger inside of me. Unlike his earlier penetration, this one can't enter without protest. I'm drenched from front to back, but no amount of wetness will simplify this process. It's not meant to be easy.

"You're close to taking a third finger," Dimitri mutters under his breath as he swivels the two inside of me, "But it won't be done without pain." His bedroom skills are undeniable when he continues finger-fucking me without pause while standing to his feet. "I want to hurt you, but I don't want to hurt you so much, you're out of action for days on end."

Any worries on me drying up fly out the window when he fists his cock in his other hand for the second time. He doesn't choke it to calm it down. He strokes it to bring himself to climax like he did when his jealousy got the better of him. His pumps are fast and fluid despite the fact his eyes never once leave my face. He watches me watching him come undone, his stroke quickening the more my eyes dart between his face and his impressive cock.

I moan when the heat of his cum mingles with the fiery warmth between my legs a few seconds later. Instead of coming on my chest to intermingle our scents, he ejaculates on my pussy, so his climax slicks with mine.

As his nostrils flare to cool his dangerous body temperature, he rubs his climax around the opening of my pussy before he pushes it inside of me. Once he's confident I'm the wettest I've ever been, his cock's head overtakes the helm of our scorching exchange. He coats himself in my juices before lining up, gripping my hips, then driving home.

I won't lie. It fucking hurts—a lot.

While kicking out, I scream like I'm being murdered. This is worse than I could have comprehended. It makes me convinced I should have joined a nunnery. There was no way I would ever take a man the size of Dimitri without pain, but this goes beyond that. He's doesn't have impressive length, he's got eyewatering girth too. I'm full to the brim and doing everything I can not to cry.

As shards of pain claw through me, Dimitri drops his thumb to my clit. His dedicated attention to my achy bud lessens my pussy's vicious clutch on his cock. He circles the bundle of nerves on repeat, bringing me back from death one delightful swivel at a time. Within seconds, I've withdrawn my application to sainthood and resubmitted one to the fiery depths all orgasms come from.

It's amazing how responsive my body is to his touch. He could beat me to the point of death, however, and I bet my body would still respond positively to him. It's fucked up to consider, but the most honest I've ever been.

Only seconds later, I'm more frustrated with Dimitri's calm than terrified about additional pain. Excluding his initial thrust that pushed me to the brink of hell, his cock hasn't budged an inch. He's inside of me—very *very* deeply rooted—but he isn't rocking his hips how his delicious 'V' muscle is designed to move. He's completely still, frozen like a statue.

The worry blistering through me nosedives toward the negative when I lock my eyes with his face. He is inside me like no man has ever been, but he isn't in the room with me. He's far *far* away from here.

"Dimitri?" I gabble out on a groan when he withdraws his cock as quickly as he jabbed it inside of me.

I thought the blood smeared on his rapidly deflating cock would have his chest swelling with pride—it was clear tonight the men in his realm view virginities as a gift. They're willing to pay over a hundred thousand dollars just to secure a night with a virgin, however Dimitri's chest is filling more with anger than smugness. He once again looks set to kill, and once again, all of his fury is directed at me.

After tugging up his trousers with enough aggression the thread around his zipper pops, he says, "Get dressed and go straight to your room."

My hands instinctively move to cover my chest, suddenly vulnerable about the angsty in his tone. "Is everything okay—"

"Get dressed and go straight to your room!"

Tears almost spill down my face when his roar makes me jump out of my skin. When he spots their sudden arrival, the mask over his face is the sternest I've ever seen him. He appears as if he wants to strangle me until the light he lit in my eyes has been extinguished, or better yet, until I'm dead.

Confident I won't defy him for the second time tonight, he pivots on his heels and stalks to the door. "I'll be back to deal with you later." The way he says 'deal' confirms my earlier worry. Dimitri Petretti no longer wants to claim my virginity. He wants my life.

Chapter Thirty-One

Roxanne

Ibrush away stupid blobs of wetness sitting high on my cheeks when the creak of a door breaks through my quiet sniffles. I'm so angry, so fucking mad, but more than anything, I'm hurt. I gave myself to Dimitri in a way I can never repeat, and what did I get for it? Another cold, hard rejection.

He made me come undone twice, marked me with his cum, then spat me out as if I was worthless the instant I fell for his tricks. God, I thought I was smart! I didn't have the best upbringing, and my parents loved drugs more than me, but I've always had a good head on my shoulders.

Well, I did. Perhaps I lost more than my integrity in the alleyway all those months ago. Maybe this is punishment for my wicked sins.

I continue my deliberation on my opposite hip when the shadow from the door moves to my side of the bed. I know its Dimitri because I can smell myself on his skin like his sudden departure from his office was too important to wash off the desecration my desperateness shrouded him in.

"Roxanne."

When he tugs on my shoulder, I stay perfectly still, my body ignoring his touch as skillfully as my mind does his snapped delivery of my name. I'm not scared of him anymore. How can I be scared when all I'm feeling is embarrassed?

"Roxanne." Dimitri's voice is louder this time—as is his shove. "I know you're not asleep."

I almost bark out that he doesn't know me well enough to know when I'm fake sleeping, but hold back the urge. I'm done playing his game as much as I'm done playing nice.

"Do you want to know how I know you're awake?"

More silence—lots and lots of silence.

"Your nipples always bud when I touch you, but when you're asleep, you instinctively roll onto your back, begging for more."

I don't know what to respond to first. His confession that he touches me when I'm sleeping or his lower, more controlled tone. I can feel how worked up he is, smell it roasting on his skin, but he's fighting to keep his anger under wraps. For why? I have no clue.

The stranglehold of emotions clutching my throat flies out the window when Dimitri tries a different tactic. "We got a solid lead from one of your contacts tonight."

I roll over, too inquisitive for my own good. "Who?"

Dimitri's smile when he calls me for being a sucker shouldn't make me hot, but it does. "Dr. Bates."

"The OBGYN?" I sound shocked. Justly so. Dr. Bates was the least creepy of the bunch. He was half the age of my other suiters and wasn't shy about his intentions. He didn't just want a virgin for the night. He wanted something more long term.

When Dimitri nods, I scoot up in the bed. "What type of lead?"

He fiddles with the cuffs on his shirt, a sign he's stressed. "His practice ordered more prescriptions, fertility drugs, and pregnancy supplements than what was needed for the number of patients he's had the past three years."

His confession appears to be a solid lead, but I'm a little lost. Smith went light on details when he explained what happened to Dimitri's wife, but he let it drop that she wasn't given any type of anesthetics, so what does a prescription scandal have to do with any of this?

When I advise Dimitri of my confusion in a way that won't drudge up bad memories for him, he shunts my horror into terrifying blackness. "Tonight's guests weren't here solely to bid for your virginity. Some are involved in the baby-farming market."

"Farming? As in, they produce babies—"

"For well-to-do clients who can't have their own," Dimitri fills in as if I'm talking slow for any other reason than confusion.

Although his see-sawing personality has me all types of baffled, I can't hold my curiosity back. "But that isn't what happened to Fien, right? You paid to keep her safe."

An unfamiliar expression hardens his features when I say his daughter's name, but he's quick to shut it down. "The incident with Fien is different than what we're investigating, but like most things in life, there are a handful of common links I can't ignore." When I remain quiet, too confused to speak, he keeps talking. "Over the past couple of days, I've been led to believe that the people who took Audrey didn't realize who she was to begin with. They didn't know she was my wife."

I twist my lips. "That kind of makes sense. They'd have to be nuts to go against a man as powerful as you."

I thought my comment would lift a thousand bricks off his shoulders. Regretfully, it seems to have had the opposite effect. "A baby farm nets a tidy profit every year, but its overhead is high. You have to feed the women, cloth and house them—"

"Let alone a woman can only give birth on average once a year. You might get a rare one who can pop out two kids in eleven months, but that's generally not recommended."

A spark darts through Dimitri's eyes before remorse strangles it. "That's why they changed tactics. The upkeep of a baby is nowhere near as expensive, especially when you have a father willing to pay any amount requested."

"About that, something has been bugging me." It's obvious Dimitri isn't familiar with two-way conversations. He doesn't know whether to be amused or annoyed by my interruption. "Why are Fien's ransoms so minute? The figures tossed around by your guests tonight were ridiculous, and then there was the money being laid down for gambling last week. You'd have to be making a killing, so why are her captives only asking for a little over a million dollars every year. If I had an endless money pit at the ready, I'd milk it for all I could."

My throat grows scratchy when Dimitri's eyes narrow into tiny slits. "Perhaps if you're still around tomorrow, you can give me your opinion on a fairer amount."

Still around? Am I going somewhere?

A rock-hard mask slips over Dimitri's face when he spots my unvoiced questions in my eyes. After standing from the bed, he rolls up the sleeves of his dress shirt like his night isn't close to ending before he nudges his head to the door. "Come with me."

A part of me wants to tell him to go to hell. After what he did, I don't owe him a thing, but the stonewalled expression on his face keeps my lips locked tight.

The desire to bend in two bombards me when Dimitri

hands me my dressing gown. He hates it as much as Estelle. I've heard him threaten to burn it under his breath multiple times the past five days. "It's cold where we're going. I wouldn't want your lips turning blue."

Ignoring the dread in the lower half of my stomach, I slip into my dressing gown and cinch it around my waist before following Dimitri's stalk out of our room. My pace is a little slower than his. Although our tryst didn't end as I was hoping, pain is still being felt.

The atmosphere in the lower half of the compound is starkly contradicting to the party-like one I faced only hours ago. All the guests have gone—even the scantily clad ones who were hoping to occupy Dimitri's bed for the night.

A worry that Dimitri no longer needs me skitters through my veins when our descend down the stairwell is quickly chased by another decline. We're heading toward the basement—the dark and dingy basement Dimitri had Rocco order for me to stay away three times earlier tonight. He was adamant I wasn't to go anywhere near it. Now he's walking me right into the underbelly of it. It has me sick with worry.

I didn't think my life could get any worse until Dimitri swings open a door at the end of the corridor. My father isn't bound to a chair by rope, chains, or any humanitarian way to keep a captive hostage without carnage. He's nailed to the wood. If that isn't bad enough, almost every inch of his skin is covered with a range of bruises, nicks, and cuts. However, they aren't the cause for the sob racking through me. It's the low hang of his head. The purple mottling of his skin. The evidence he's dead even without seeing the bullet pierced through his skull.

When I take a stumbling step back, Dimitri grips the tops of my arms, forcing me to stay in my nightmare longer than necessary for him to get across his point. I said he wasn't a monster, that he was just tired and angry. I realize my error now. He's a cruel, vindictive man who'd rather cut out someone's heart than have it handed to him willingly.

As I'm forced to scan an image too horrifying to share, I choke through the ragged breath I scarfed down to swallow the vomit racing up my throat. I can't believe I gave myself to him, that I thought he was misunderstood. He killed my father, my flesh and blood, all because he tried to sell me just like he did.

"I hate you." I'm sobbing now, full-on crying. Tears stream down my face as my body uncontrollably shakes. "Rocco said you wouldn't kill him. He promised it would be my choice."

"Is that why you helped, Roxanne, because you thought it would see your father's life spared? Is that why you almost gave yourself to me?"

"*Almost?*" His words make me sick. "I didn't *almost* give myself to you. I *gave* myself to you. There was no almost. I was yours! I would have always been yours!"

I push him off me, hating that I ever felt an ounce of anything for him. Remorse, lust, I'm disappointed by them all.

He's a murderer.

A cheat.

He doesn't deserve to get his daughter back.

When I say that to Dimitri, he gets up in my face in an instant. He pins me to a blood-splattered wall, towering over me like he's seconds from crushing my windpipes with his bare hands. "I should kill you where you stand."

"Then do it," I snarl in his face, my fear non-existent. "Kill me like you've threatened time and time again. Drain the blood from my veins and parade my dead carcass like you are my father's so your enemies will see you as a real man." The way I spit out the last half of my sentence reveals I think he's anything but a man. "But remember, no matter what you do, and no matter what you say, one thing will never change. I'm someone's daughter. I'm someone's Fien, so when Karma responds to what you've done, you better pray she doesn't gnaw the wrong ass."

Dimitri leans into me deeper, fully stilling me. His large, teaming-with-anger body isn't solely responsible for my frozen state, though. It's the words he screams into my face, "He cut my daughter out of my wife's stomach! He held her like she was a fucking animal. He deserved to die!"

When he shoves a freshly printed piece of paper into my face, my stomach heaves. I feel like I'm drowning like my worst nightmare is coming true. The image of my father sitting lifeless in a pool of blood is horrific, but this is ten times worse.

Not only does Dimitri have undeniable proof my father was a part of the backyard operation to remove his daughter from his wife's stomach, he has evidence I was there too.

Dimitri and Roxanne's story continues in the next explosive episode of* The Italian Cartel *Series. It is titled Roxanne - you can find it here:
Roxanne

If you want to hear updates on the next books in this crazy world I've created, be sure to join my social media pages.

Facebook: facebook.com/authorshandi

Instagram: instagram.com/authorshandi

Email: authorshandi@gmail.com

Reader's Group: bit.ly/ShandiBookBabes

Website: authorshandi.com

Newsletter: https://www.subscribepage.com/AuthorShandi

Isaac, Nikolai, Trey, and Enrique stories have already been released, but Rocco, Maddox, and all the other great characters of Ravenshoe/Hopeton will be getting their own stories at some point during 2020/2021.

Subscribe to my newsletter to remain informed:
www.subscribepage.com/AuthorShandi

If you enjoyed this book please leave a review.

Acknowledgments

This book was a hard one for me to write. We were in the middle of a pandemic, I found out my mother has cancer, and the entire world went to shit. Yet, here we are, at another acknowledgement page. It wouldn't have happened without the support of my readers and those who continuously prop me up every day. My husband is my number one supporter and my mother slots right in next to him. Even with the unknown keeping her thoughts occupied, she read Dimitri's first draft like she has every one of my books. She helped fix my many stuff ups (I'm infamous for them) and discussed what she thinks will happen in the next book.

Her strength the past month has been phenomenal. I hate that it takes something like cancer to truly understand how strong someone is, but it does make it undeniable. There's no one stronger than her.

I hope you enjoyed Dimitri's story, even with that cliffhanger ending. The second instalment will follow shortly.

Take care, and hug your loved ones.

Shandi xx

PS: A special shout out to my editing crew, Nicky and Kaylene at Swish Design and Editing. I can't thank my cover designer, as that is me, but I can thank Jonny James for having such a sexy face. He adds to Dimitri's dark and dangerous aura with an edge of sexiness I hope you can appreciate.

Facebook: facebook.com/authorshandi

Instagram: instagram.com/authorshandi

Email: authorshandi@gmail.com

Reader's Group: bit.ly/ShandiBookBabes

Website: authorshandi.com

Newsletter: https://www.subscribepage.com/AuthorShandi

Also by Shandi Boyes

Denotes Standalone Books

Perception Series

Saving Noah *

Fighting Jacob *

Taming Nick *

Redeeming Slater *

Saving Emily

Wrapped Up with Rise Up

Protecting Nicole *

Enigma

Enigma

Unraveling an Enigma

Enigma The Mystery Unmasked

Enigma: The Final Chapter

Beneath The Secrets

Beneath The Sheets

Spy Thy Neighbor *

The Opposite Effect *

I Married a Mob Boss *

Second Shot *

The Way We Are

The Way We Were

Sugar and Spice *

Lady In Waiting

Man in Queue

Couple on Hold

Enigma: The Wedding

Silent Vigilante

Hushed Guardian

Quiet Protector

Enigma: An Isaac Retelling

Twisted Lies *

Bound Series

Chains

Links

Bound

Restrain

The Misfits *

Nanny Dispute *

Russian Mob Chronicles

Nikolai: A Mafia Prince Romance

Nikolai: Taking Back What's Mine

Nikolai: What's Left of Me

Nikolai: Mine to Protect

<u>One Night Only Series</u>

Hotshot Boss *

Hotshot Neighbor *

<u>The Bobrov Bratva Series</u>

Wicked Intentions *

Sinful Intentions *

Devious Intentions *

Deadly Intentions *

<u>Coming Soon</u>

Nanny Dispute *

Protecting Nicole (December 26) *